CRACKING THE R.I.C.H.™ CODE

Mehul Darooka is a multi-talented professional with strong academic roots. He holds degrees in commerce and management and was a top student in marketing at Pune University. He started **MDEEC**, a company that offers corporate training, makes films for businesses, runs ads, and helps entrepreneurs grow.

He has started two successful businesses and helped set up a well-known management institute. Over the years, Mehul has trained more than 100,000 people across the world, giving him wide experience in different industries and cultures.

Mehul has written six books—four on entrepreneurship (one now in its third edition) and two on special topics. One of his books was launched in Silicon Valley in front of leading business minds.

He's also a creative storyteller, having written and produced many corporate and short films. His work has won recognition from national film organizations in India. While working in California, he hosted a radio show called *Saturday Swag*, which talked about entrepreneurship and reached over half a million listeners.

Mehul mentors young businesses and students through respected groups like JITO and Symbiosis. His advice and ideas are often shared in top newspapers and media, inspiring people around the world.

MEHUL DAROOKA

CRACKING THE

Why Being Resourceful,

R.I.C.H.™

Influential, Commanding &

CODE

Habit-Driven Is the New Flex

Om Books International

First published in 2025 by

Om Books International

Corporate & Editorial Office
A-12, Sector 64, Noida 201 301
Uttar Pradesh, India
Phone: +91 120 477 4100
Email: editorial@ombooks.com
Website: www.ombooksinternational.com

Sales Office
107, Ansari Road, Darya Ganj,
New Delhi 110 002, India
Phone: +91 11 4000 9000
Email: sales@ombooks.com
Website: www.ombooks.com

ISBN: 978-93-5376-740-2

Printed in India

10 9 8 7 6 5 4 3 2 1

I want to dedicate this book to all those who dream and aspire to create something meaningful out of their lives.

And those who dare to create their own journey, who believe in themselves, who smile at challenges and face them head-on—this book is for you.

And one last, but the most special, dedication—to my late parents, the most sorted, kind-hearted, and generous souls I have ever known.

Contents

Prologue

Cracking the R.I.C.H.™ Code is a means for you to reach your goals and not a destination.

Now, you may ask me what the difference between a goal and a destination is. Let us break it down.

What is a destination in one's life? It is evolving constantly and changing. So, reaching a destination is a mirage in the desert. The more you move towards it, the more it moves away.

Most people do not consciously set a destination. Even many successful people do not have explicitly stated destinations. What people have is 'aspiration' or 'desire'. To me, a destination implies a blueprint of a targeted place to reach within a time frame.

Let me illustrate a few examples. As children, we believed in academic achievements. When we grew up, we set finding a good job as a target. Having found a job, earning good money became the next desire. In later years, professional excellence and the position we hold in the organization (and society) became an important yardstick. At the time of retirement, future safety, health, and children's welfare become the concern. At no point did we arrive at the destination. Each stage is not a destination but a landing, as explained below.

When you are climbing stairs to reach a top floor, you find intermediary landings between any two consecutive floors, where the stairs turn in a different direction. Don't confuse a landing with a destination. A landing is a temporary halting place to catch your breath before you continue your journey to the top floor. The same is true in life—stages like academics, a new job, profession, monetary growth, achievements, and excellence are all 'landings' in your journey of life. The only end destination is… you know what I mean. I don't want to sound pessimistic.

That's why learned people call life a continuous journey till the final destination. So, R.I.C.H.™ should enable you to enjoy this eternal journey, rather than get confused thinking that a series of 'landings' are destinations.

This brings me to my next question: what next after reaching the earmarked destination? No one has answered it satisfactorily till date. Hinduism describes each landing as 'Purushartha', saying there are four stages in every individual's life with superordinate goals—Dharma, Artha, Kama, and Moksha—with only Moksha (salvation) considered the final destination. This, to some extent, gels with the Western behavioral science model propounded by Abraham Maslow's Need Hierarchy, with self-actualization as the goal.

So, life is an eternal journey. Enjoy the journey. Use landings to catch your breath.

Another example is that of a cricketer. As a boy, I was interested in playing for my school. What next? Maybe I wanted to play for the Under-19 team. What next? Maybe I now wanted to play for my state. Ok, what next? Maybe I now wanted to be a Ranji player. What next? Maybe now I wanted to be part of the national team. So far, so good! But now what next? Retire? Nobody likes this destination.

So, they behave as though they are now at a *landing* of a staircase, about to take a turn in a different direction. The result: become a coach, commentator, businessperson, or even a politician. These are not destinations, as they were not originally envisaged, but just landings in your journey. Bill Gates, Dhirubhai, Jack Welch, Steve

Jobs, Laxmanrao Kirloskar, all of them *landed* without worrying about the destination.

My next question for your fertile minds is: why should anyone set a destination and try to reach there? Christopher Columbus missed his destination (India) and mistakenly reached America. Had he reached the destination he had originally set, he would be unknown today. Missing the destination brought him accolades. Robert Boyle accidentally dropped a few pieces of iron nails into a jar containing dilute hydrochloric acid and got recognized as the father of hydrogen, as hydrogen was previously unknown. Newton did not go in search of a destination where falling apples could be witnessed before enunciating gravitational laws! Falling apples were a *landing* on which he built an edifice.

In fact, people who went in search of a destination often found themselves in *landings*. The ancient Egyptians were chasing a non-existent substance called the Philosopher's Stone, which, when rubbed on base metals, was believed to turn them into gold. The result? This mad activity led to the creation of modern chemistry. In the Egyptian language, *chem* means black—the entire Egypt has black soil (hence, cotton growing), and *mystery* joined to form *chemistry*.

So, in essence, what I am saying is that life is a journey with only one end destination. The rest are landings or intermediate stations en route. Any landing can, perhaps, have the potential to change the course of one's life, unwittingly or otherwise. Mohandas Gandhi being thrown out of a train in South Africa (a landing—and surely not a destination) heralded the new avatar of Mahatma Gandhi.

This book will therefore help you recognize your en-routes and define your journey better to reach your goals. Happy reading, and enjoy your journey here.

Mr. T Pradeep Kumar
CEO/ Group CTO of a Global Renewable Energy company

Foreword

The great Deepak Chopra once said, "By becoming self-aware, you gain ownership of reality; in becoming real, you become the master of both inner and outer life." I wholeheartedly believe this statement, as it resonates with me deeply. When I embarked on my journey of building Quick Heal, my first step was to understand myself—my limitations as well as my strengths. I am grateful for this introspection because it allowed me to explore my true potential.

Now, many of you may wonder why it's necessary to know oneself. The simple answer is: "Know yourself to understand the world better." Julia Child, the beloved chef, author, and television personality, remains a familiar name in the homes and hearts of Americans to this day. She gained popularity and fame later in life. When Julia reached the pinnacle of her self-awareness journey, she realized her desire to break barriers and attain the legendary status she is widely known for today. Once she discovered herself, she understood the world and how it works. She adapted accordingly and achieved immense success thereafter.

Similarly, there are numerous legendary tales of individuals who found their true calling after gaining self-awareness. Once we understand who we are, we can determine what we need to work on and how to improve our lives. I was never one to blindly follow conventional rules; instead, I defied the norm of attending rigorous classroom sessions and redirected my curiosity and hard work toward starting my own business. Today, I am grateful that my vision and self-awareness have transformed Quick Heal into a brand to be reckoned with. We are leading from the forefront and establishing ourselves as a global player in our industry.

When most of us embark on a new journey, our initial thoughts revolve around how and where to begin. There are numerous questions, yet too few answers. Therefore, it is crucial to develop and fortify our thoughts so we can lead ourselves and achieve the goals we envision.

This leads me to another significant milestone: understanding your goals and strategizing to achieve them. However, that's only half the battle. The other half—and perhaps the more challenging part—is executing your plan to attain those goals. You must ask yourself: Am I prepared for it? Am I willing to pay any price to make it happen? Am I determined enough? Am I proactive or reactive?

While these questions may arise, the key is whether we truly grasp their depth and are prepared to adapt accordingly. I firmly believe in the value of hard work, and there are no shortcuts to success. When Mehul approached me with his concept of R.I.C.H.™, it immediately resonated with me because what he proposes makes sense.

He has eloquently presented the concept of R.I.C.H.™, which is an acronym for:

R - Resourceful

I - Influencing

C - Commanding

H - Habit

His concept of R.I.C.H.™ derives from the observation that we often make excuses when faced with failure or a lack of support

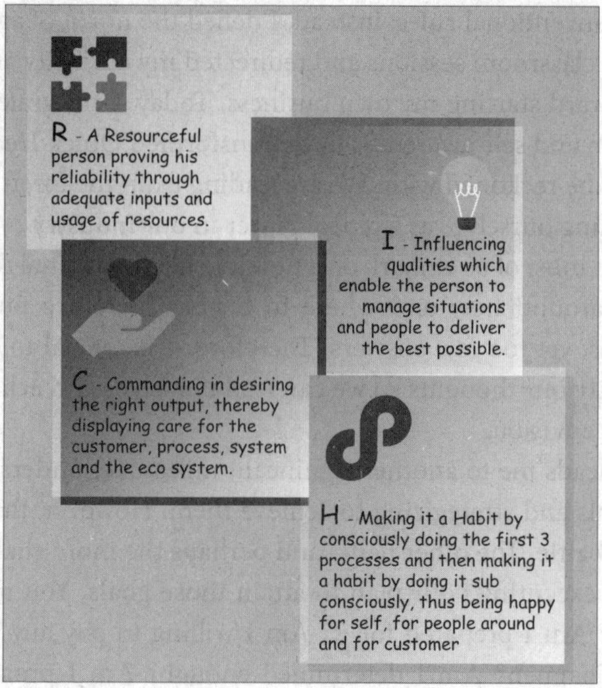

from others. The crucial question is: what lies within us to overcome these obstacles?

I previously mentioned a key aspect: whether we are reactive or proactive. Reactive behaviour occurs when we respond only after something has happened, whereas proactive behaviour involves anticipating outcomes and taking timely action to influence or control the situation, thereby improving our circumstances.

In Mehul's theory of R.I.C.H.™, he proposes that "R" stands for Resourcefulness, which is indeed the fundamental and most crucial element of being proactive. Resourcefulness entails managing requirements by being prepared, reaching out to people, and organizing things effectively. While some may refer to this as being "Jugadu," it's important to note that such improvisations are not always permanent solutions and thus cannot be relied upon. Resourcefulness also encompasses being trustworthy, compassionate, understanding, and mature in one's actions.

The "I" in the R.I.C.H.™ model represents the art of influencing. An influential individual is someone who can sway people and situations in their favour. Author and consultant Ron Flavin recently emphasized the importance of communication skills for leaders in reaching their full potential, highlighting influencing as a crucial aspect. I have personally experienced instances where I successfully influenced situations and individuals to achieve my desired goals.

Another challenge we encounter is the loss of control over situations or dynamics. While not everything can be controlled, possessing the aptitude to exert control can lead to positive outcomes. Many times, external factors or individuals may try to sway us from our path. However, it is essential to remain steadfast in our goals, which brings us to the "C" in the model, signifying commanding or controlling the situation. A commanding individual identifies:

- The right thing to do
- The right way to do it
- The right person to involve
- The goal to be focused on
- Not to compromise and lead the front with full vigor

Such a person ensures completion of a project without being dismayed or going off track.

Being commanding does not equate to being arrogant. Rather, being in command entails holding onto the situation and maintaining control over it.

Last but not least is "H," representing your inherent habit to perform and make actions second nature to you. This ingrained habit enables you to achieve goals effortlessly, as your subconscious mind is programmed accordingly. The elements of R, I, and C must be aligned to facilitate the proper functioning of your H, working in harmony with your chain of thoughts.

I firmly believe that despite the challenges and obstacles we face, we must exhibit qualities such as strength, courage, and determination to overcome them and emerge victorious. The rationale behind this is that problems exist, and by adopting certain tools, we can ensure success, which will be explored in this book. Mehul has adeptly combined renowned theories such as Ikigai, Blue Ocean, and others with R.I.C.H.™, offering a fresh perspective. This will be the focal point of the book.

Therefore, I urge you to pick up this copy, discover yourself, and align your actions with your preferred ways of working. While it's easy to remain passive observers, true passion, ambition, and forthrightness drive us to take charge. It all comes down to the direction and perception we carry. As I firmly believe, 'Talent' and 'Competency' are two distinct concepts. While someone may possess talent, it doesn't guarantee competency. Let me illustrate with an example: Sachin Tendulkar, hailed as the 'God of Cricket,' undoubtedly possesses extraordinary talent. However, when he assumed the role of captain, he struggled. Why? Despite his prowess on the field, he lacked the competency required for leadership. He needed qualities such as proactiveness, diplomacy, and leadership skills to lead his team effectively. Therefore, having talent alone is insufficient. One must cultivate their mind, aptitude, attitude, and more to achieve success consistently.

This book will precisely do that—guiding you towards remarkable feats and igniting thoughts that propel you towards success.

Through this medium, I extend my best wishes to every entrepreneur, student, businessperson, or individual holding this book. May you and your loved ones experience happiness and good health, and may you achieve love, peace, and success at every stage of your life. All the best!

Dr. Kailash Katkar

MD and CEO, Quick Heal Technologies Ltd.

India's leading IT security Solutions Company

To My Readers

Thank you for choosing this book. I am confident you will find it enjoyable and gain valuable insights from it.

I have a single request: please note that interspersed among the chapters are exercises intended for the characters in my book to solve. These exercises are designed for you as well, and I encourage you to engage with them actively as you read.

At the book's conclusion, you will find a competency framework to assist in developing your R.I.C.H.™ competency. This self-assessment tool is designed to help you identify and focus on key areas to enhance your R.I.C.H.™

Following this, the book provides a detailed explanation of the R.I.C.H.™ model, which I have adopted. This model has been crucial in preventing my failures from reaching a critical point. It enabled me to rise from adversity and contributed significantly to the vast and varied portfolio I am honoured to possess today.

The subsequent chapters illustrate how this model has equipped me to navigate various challenges and circumstances in life. It became a subconscious part of my existence, fostering the development of my cognitive abilities. I am confident it will similarly enhance your skills, better preparing you for life's complexities. Life is an amalgamation of joys and sorrows, and it is up to you to make the most of each. I hope this book guides you in achieving that balance.

I wish you all the best and hope you and your families enjoy a happy, healthy life.

Mehul Darooka

The Model R.I.C.H.™

R - Resourceful becomes Reliable.

I - Influential becomes Inspiring.

C - Commanding becomes Caring.

H - Habits become Happiness.

A. Resourceful becoming Reliable

According to a study published on the Harvard Business Review's website, resourcefulness fundamentally means making the most of what you have at your disposal. Innovation isn't limited to creating entirely new things; it also includes enhancing the functionality of existing ones. For instance, a skilled mechanic can perform miracles in car repairs using a blend of aftermarket parts and sheer ingenuity. As the pandemic continues to affect us in cycles, it becomes imperative for all of us to cultivate the virtue of resourcefulness.

To further illustrate this point, I recall a cherished incident from my childhood involving my mother. On one occasion, as she was about to prepare tea, we realized we were out of sugar. Initially hesitant and almost giving up on the idea of making tea, her ingenuity swiftly came into play. She adeptly substituted sugar with jaggery, thereby not only saving the day but also exemplifying her capacity to seize opportunities through resourcefulness. At first glance, the substitution may appear trivial since jaggery is a well-known alternative to sugar. However, the real takeaway lies in the quick-wittedness and presence of mind this act demonstrated, prompting reflection on our own alertness and ability to think on our feet in everyday scenarios.

Resourcefulness fundamentally embodies the ability to swiftly address and overcome challenges. It characterizes an individual who adeptly navigates situations to achieve desired outcomes without relying on extensive resources. Such a person doesn't make excuses or get trapped in the mindset that insists, "This is the only way," showing resistance to adaptability and change. Instead, they exhibit flexibility and creativity, finding alternative paths and solutions to obstacles, demonstrating that progress and innovation often stem from the ability to rethink and repurpose the resources at hand.

- A resourceful individual stands out through their inclination to question established norms and assumptions. They do not take things, people, prevailing conditions, or circumstances at face value without thorough scrutiny and validation. Such individuals are driven by a proactive desire to effect change and bring ideas to life.
- This proactive nature is supported by a commitment to staying informed and well-versed in global market trends, pivotal economic developments, and advancements within their fields of interest. They amass a wealth of resources, including networks of individuals, comprehensive knowledge, and access to a variety of services. While they may not claim expertise in all areas, their broad understanding enables them to grasp the core concepts necessary for informed decision-making.
- Resourceful people are distinguished by their availability and reliability, regardless of the situation's complexity. They

navigate challenges with keen timing and an aptitude for employing the most effective strategies and resources for the task at hand. Their skill in judiciously utilizing available resources allows them to resolve situations effectively, showcasing their versatility and adaptability in both favorable and adverse conditions.

Consequently, a resourceful individual prioritizes developing their people management skills and expanding their knowledge base, actively challenges prevailing assumptions, and, through these actions, becomes a dependable figure. This approach not only enhances their ability to navigate complex situations but also solidifies their reputation as a versatile and reliable problem-solver. By continuously broadening their understanding and network, they position themselves as invaluable assets in any context—capable of leading and innovating with foresight and adaptability.

Write down a situation when *you observed someone being resourceful:*

____

____

____

____

____

____

As per a popular article by Mr Brian based out of Washington D.C, USA, 'Mastering the Art of being Resourceful' dated March 2011:

If you look at our history, there are tales after tales of how humans have progressed exactly because of our resourcefulness. Consider the people who lived in caves tens of thousands of years ago. They hunted animals and used everything, from the meat and offal to the bones and skin. We used meat for food; used dried skin, turned into leather, and used for clothing, while the bones were used to make tools. We used even the fat for lighting. It was both a sign of respect to the animal for providing for them and it was also natural to use up everything because they couldn't just pop down to the corner shop to buy a parka if the weather suddenly turned cold or another kilo of meat if they ran out.

Another great leader Bob Lutz, the legendary auto executive who worked for all of the Detroit Three said:

That when he was at Chrysler one reason, his people wanted to buy American Motors (aside from its ownership of Jeep) was because it could teach Chrysler how to develop more vehicles with fewer resources. Everyone — as the joke went then — half- expected American Motors to make something out of nothing. That is being resourceful. So how can you nurture resourcefulness? Well, the first thing you do is you adopt a mantra of possibility that John Wooden popularized: "Don't let what you cannot interfere with what you can do." Too often we stymie the creative instincts of employees because we focus first on constraints rather than possibilities. We think too much of what our boss's boss might think, or what our annual budget is, prior to thinking about what we might do.

A case scenario: Arun is a sales lead in his organization. He faces a special customer demand that requires exceptional financial concessions from the company. In this challenging situation, Arun's resourcefulness will be key to navigating bureaucratic hurdles and securing the necessary approval from the CFO—without alienating the customer or compromising the deal. Here's how Arun demonstrated his resourcefulness:

Suppose you were in this situation how would you have been resourceful?

____

____

____

The scenario with Arun and Ms. Malini illustrates a classic example of resourcefulness in action. Arun's approach diverges from passive acceptance of the challenges at hand; instead, he engages actively and creatively with the situation. His refusal to be deterred by Ms. Malini's reputation and warnings from others is the first step in showcasing his resourcefulness. Rather than seeing the situation as a barrier, Arun views it as an opportunity to navigate a challenging environment with creativity.

Here's how Arun's actions embody resourcefulness:

- **Personal initiative**: By choosing to personally meet Ms. Malini or call her, Arun takes direct control of the situation. This demonstrates his willingness to engage directly with challenges rather than avoiding them or delegating to others.
- **Strategic communication**: Arun's decision to seek Ms. Malini's assistance without initially disclosing the matter, making her feel important and valued, is a strategic move. It shows his ability to navigate interpersonal relationships effectively—using tact and diplomacy to his advantage.
- **Acknowledging contributions**: By planning to express gratitude and acknowledge her cooperation, Arun ensures that Ms. Malini is recognized for her role. This not only paves the way for smoother interactions but also fosters a positive environment for future engagements.
- **Emphasizing urgency**: Arun's emphasis on the urgency of the meeting with the CFO demonstrates his understanding of the stakes involved. It shows his ability to convey the importance of his request clearly and persuasively.

- **Turning information into advantage**: The critical aspect of Arun's resourcefulness lies in how he leverages the information about Ms. Malini's nature. Instead of seeing her demeanor as a roadblock, he uses it as a key resource in strategizing his approach—demonstrating his ability to transform potential negatives into positives.
- **Active problem solving**: Arun's refusal to adhere to a passive "this is the only way" mindset illustrates his proactive problem-solving skills. He actively seeks solutions and alternatives, showing a flexible and adaptive approach to obstacles.

In essence, Arun's handling of the situation showcases his resourcefulness by demonstrating that challenges can be navigated through thoughtful strategy, personal initiative, and effective communication. His ability to transform information and perceived obstacles into resources highlights the essence of being resourceful—finding creative and effective ways to achieve goals, even in the face of adversity.

B. Influential becomes inspiring

The incident involving the Peoples Temple, led by Reverend Jim Jones, stands as a stark and tragic example of influence taken to an extreme. Founded in Indianapolis, Indiana, in 1954 and later relocated to California, the Peoples Temple was an American new religious movement that intertwined elements of Christianity with communist and socialist ideologies, placing a strong emphasis on racial equality.

However, the influence wielded by Jim Jones over his followers culminated in a horrifying event: on one fateful evening, he ordered his congregation to consume a cyanide-laced, grape-flavored beverage—leading to the deaths of 918 individuals, including 276 children. This incident underscores the profound and sometimes dangerous power of influence, particularly when exercised without ethical boundaries or considerations.

The influence Jones had over his followers exemplifies how the trust and loyalty built within a community can be manipulated. It illustrates an extreme case of leadership, where the charisma and authority of a single individual led to a tragic outcome. The Peoples Temple tragedy serves as a reminder of the potential consequences when influence is used to exploit trust and loyalty, highlighting the importance of ethical leadership and the critical need for individuals within a community to retain autonomy and critical thinking.

This case also brings to light an underlying principle of influence: people are more likely to comply with requests or directives from those they know and trust than from strangers. In the context of the Peoples Temple, this principle was exploited to a devastating end. It emphasizes the importance of critically evaluating the sources of influence in our lives and the necessity of fostering environments where questioning and dissent are not only allowed but encouraged—to prevent such tragedies from occurring again.

Can you share an incident where you actually wanted to say 'No' but the other person's influencing skills made you go ahead and be a part of what they were expecting from you? If yes, why did you agree to do the job?

____

____

____

____

____

____

- An influential individual possesses the remarkable capacity to shape people and circumstances within their sphere. This capability stems from a profound power of persuasion, heavily reliant on concrete facts and data, which serve as the bedrock of their convincing authority. Such a person wields their influence with finesse, affecting those around them both directly and indirectly, inspiring action, change, and thought through their presence and engagement.

- Central to their influence is the mastery of communication skills. They refine their ability to articulate ideas clearly and persuasively, enhancing the impact of their words. Moreover, effective listening is integral to their approach, allowing them to understand deeply and respond to the concerns and aspirations of others, thereby fostering a connection that goes beyond mere transactional interactions.
- This influential figure prioritizes the cultivation of a keen understanding of the individuals they interact with, dedicating time to discover their strengths and weaknesses. Such insight enables them to tailor their influence, addressing specific needs and motivations, and leveraging these insights to guide, support, and inspire others toward collective goals and personal growth. Through these strategies, an influential person not only leads but also empowers, making a lasting impact on the lives they touch and the situations they navigate.

Author and consultant Ron Flavin recently wrote a blog for LinkedIn Pulse that posited: '*Many leaders might not be reaching their full potential as professionals because they are lacking in the communication skills department and are not even aware of the problem. After providing a brief synopsis of why leadership-level employees need strong communication skills, he dove into some of the more common signs that there is an issue in need of correction.*'

For example, Flavin stated that some of the indicators are a bit more subversive and difficult to pin down, such as poor clarity when delegating tasks or delivering information to employees. If staff members do not speak up about this problem, it will often go unnoticed for long periods, while operational productivity and employee engagement may suffer in the meantime.

He went on to assert that deception, bullying, arrogance, and even being too reserved are all signs that a leader is not striking the right chord with respect to communication skills and is certainly in need of further training. As it is always more difficult for a manager to objectively assess themselves and understand what needs improvement, superiors at the executive level should enable performance improvement in these areas.

Where to begin: Decision-makers can begin by evaluating the influence skills of managers and supervisors through assessments and surveys of lower-ranking employees. This should quickly reveal where problems are originating and what steps are needed to correct them. It is generally considered best practice to conduct these types of evaluations at least a few times a year, as allowing such issues to fester will only hold the firm back from achieving success.

Literate Terry R Bacon has rolled out the TOPS formula for influential skills.

> *To second my thoughts, he says that when you try to influence people, you are applying power in order to accomplish a goal. Your success depends on several factors, some of which you can control and others which you cannot. The ones you can control are shown in this formula:*
>
> *TOPS = influence effectiveness where T = your choice of influence technique*

Influence: The Psychology of Persuasion by Robert B. Cialdini is a seminal work in the field of psychology and marketing, offering deep insights into the mechanisms of persuasion that can lead people to change their attitudes or behaviours. The book outlines several key principles that effective influencers use, whether consciously or subconsciously, to persuade others. Here's a brief overview of the approaches Cialdini discusses:

- **Reciprocation**: This principle is based on the idea that people feel obligated to return favors or gestures. If someone does something for us, we naturally want to reciprocate.
- **Commitment and consistency**: Once people commit to something, verbally or in writing, they are more likely to honor that commitment, as it aligns with their self-image.
- **Social proof**: People often look to others to determine their own actions, especially in situations where they are uncertain. We're more likely to do something if we see others doing it.
- **Liking**: We're more easily influenced by people we like. Factors that enhance liking include similarity in interests, compliments, and cooperative efforts toward mutual goals.
- **Authority**: People tend to respect and follow the lead of credible, knowledgeable experts. Demonstrating authority or expertise in a subject can increase the persuasiveness of your message.
- **Scarcity**: Opportunities seem more valuable when they are less available. Highlighting the uniqueness or limited availability of something can make it more desirable.

Cialdini's principles of influence explain why people say "yes" and how to apply these understandings ethically in various aspects of life. These insights are particularly useful in marketing, negotiations, and leadership—helping navigate and influence social interactions and decision-making processes effectively.

The Harvard Business Review describes the essence of influence in leadership as the capability to shape the character, development, or behavior of individuals or entities. This requires cultivating a deep emotional bond with oneself and others. Individuals who excel in wielding influence are adept at engaging with the emotions that motivate others to act. This highlights the parallel between influence and leadership. Behind every distinguished leader lies a dedicated group of followers, committed to advancing their vision or cause. Indeed, when Time magazine enumerates the 100 most influential figures worldwide, the most substantial category isn't sports personalities, music stars, or philanthropists, but leaders such as Michelle Obama, Xi Jinping, Jacinda Ardern, and Bob Iger.

For example, in the case study involving Arun, Ms. Malini's significant role as the CFO's secretary was a double-edged sword. Her authoritative position, which she often exercised with a degree of arrogance, ultimately became a detriment, earning her the reputation of being 'difficult.' However, Arun, demonstrating remarkable adaptability, reframed this perceived weakness into an opportunity by focusing on the objectives at hand.

The crux of persuading Ms. Malini to schedule the appointment hinged on the how. Arun's strategy not only gained Ms. Malini's approval but also secured the crucial meeting. He skillfully enhanced her sense of self-importance and prestige, using these traits to his benefit and effectively navigating the dynamics of the situation. Through this approach, he showcased his influential capabilities—underpinned by strong communication and interpersonal skills—to accomplish his goal. This achievement stood as a testament to the power of employing effective tactics, clear communication, and assertiveness, among other competencies.

C. Commanding becomes Caring

Often, external circumstances or interactions with others may lead us to drift away from our goals or intentions. Unless this detachment aligns with our desires, we must resist being influenced off our path. A person with a commanding presence distinguishes themselves by:

- Identifying the correct course of action.
- Determining the most effective method to execute it.
- Choosing the right individuals to engage.
- Keeping focus on the intended objective.
- Refusing to compromise and leading with unwavering determination.
- Overcoming distractions, obstacles, or challenges without losing focus.

Donald Clark, a proponent of effective leadership, challenges the simplistic view of command as merely directing others. He posits that true command goes beyond issuing orders; it involves inspiring an organization or individuals toward a common goal through a clearly articulated vision. This process requires the development of a coherent and compelling vision, followed by its effective communication to all stakeholders. Command, in Clark's view, underscores the importance of success and reward. It's not just about ensuring the organization's survival; it's about fostering a culture of achievement that rewards members both intrinsically and extrinsically. Thus, command becomes a holistic approach to leadership, focused on motivation, direction, and the well-being of everyone involved—aiming for collective success that benefits the whole organization.

For example, in the interaction between Arun and Ms. Malini, Arun maintained a commanding position through subtle influence, guiding Ms. Malini to meet his objectives without her realizing it. This approach didn't require any concessions from him, yet he successfully achieved his goals. Being commanding is anchored in deep commitment and a laser-focused pursuit of objectives, supported by a sincere dedication to achieving results.

Arun's ability to command the situation stemmed from his dedication to:

- The purpose of his role
- The methodology he employed
- The system he operated within
- The people he worked with

His commitment to these elements not only kept him focused but also ensured his continued command over the situation. Arun's case exemplifies that commanding leadership is not about overt dominance, but about steering outcomes through a combination of clear objectives, strategic influence, and a commitment to the process and the people involved.

D. Habit becomes Happiness

- Every individual possesses both a conscious and a subconscious mind, each playing a distinct role in daily life. The conscious mind is our immediate awareness of the present moment, including both our external environment and internal mental processes. It allows us to be aware of our surroundings, physical sensations, and current thoughts.
- The subconscious, or preconscious mind, stores information that can be readily brought to conscious awareness when needed, such as recalling a memory. This part of the mind operates without active, conscious input, enabling us to perform tasks like walking home or having a conversation on the phone without thinking about every action. It also stores habits and frequently uses information like phone numbers—allowing automatic retrieval and action without conscious effort.
- Habits, whether physical actions like leg shaking or mental ones like using specific phrases, form in the subconscious

mind through repetition and become automatic responses or behaviors.

- Stephen Covey's renowned concept, the 7 Habits of Highly Effective People, emphasizes the power of daily habits in achieving success. Being proactive—the first of these habits—highlights the need to be prepared and resourceful. This idea suggests that to be effective, the development of skills and habits must be ongoing and ingrained.
- In the example of Arun and Ms. Malini, Arun's habitual use of Resourcefulness, Influence, and Command (R.I.C.)—along with his addition of Habit (H) to form R.I.C.H.™—illustrates how making certain behaviors habitual can lead to successful interactions and outcomes. By integrating these practices into his subconscious, Arun managed situations and relationships effectively, leading to mutual satisfaction and happiness.
- The R.I.C.H.™ framework suggests a method for personal and professional growth, emphasizing the importance of developing habits that enable individuals to navigate competitive environments, engage constructively with others, and achieve ambitious goals. It proposes that embodying Resourcefulness, Influence, Command, and Habit can transform how individuals approach challenges and interact with the world.
- This approach is not just a strategy but a lifestyle embraced by many successful leaders. Being R.I.C.H.™ in qualities and habits signifies a deeper, subconscious alignment with behaviors that foster success and fulfillment. It shows that success and leadership are as much about the subconscious cultivation of effective habits as conscious decision-making and actions.

Let us see how

Bill Gates: Once the world's richest man and a Harvard dropout, Gates rose to become an unparalleled innovator. His resourcefulness, leveraging both knowledge and capability, enabled him to profoundly influence those around him, marked by a blend of dominance and charisma. His mastery of his work and habitual drive to realize his visions exemplify the essence of the R.I.C.H.™ principles—Resourcefulness, Influence, Command, and Habit. These principles were not just practices but the foundation of his approach to challenges and opportunities.

Dhirubhai Ambani: The story of Dhirubhai Ambani, the celebrated industrialist and one of India's wealthiest figures featured regularly in Forbes rankings, is a testament to vision, risk-taking, and entrepreneurial spirit. This humble man from Gujarat repeatedly demonstrated exceptional ability to foresee and seize opportunities until his untimely death. The modest beginnings of Reliance Commercial Corporation—in a 350-square-foot room on Narsinatha Street, Masjid Bunder, equipped with just a telephone, one table, three chairs, and supported by two assistants—marked the start of what became a conglomerate.

During these early days, Ambani and his family resided in a modest two-bedroom apartment in the Jai Hind Estate in Bhuleshwar, Mumbai. A significant turning point came in 1965 when the partnership between Champaklal Damani and Dhirubhai Ambani dissolved. The divergence in their business philosophies—Damani's cautious approach contrasting with Ambani's propensity for risk-taking—highlighted their different temperaments and visions for conducting business.

Ambani's willingness to take calculated risks (Command) by building inventories, coupled with his anticipation of market trends (Resourcefulness), showcased his strategic foresight. He didn't just see inventory as stock; he viewed it as an opportunity to capitalize on potential market fluctuations to generate profits. This approach wasn't merely about taking risks but about commanding the situation to ensure the risks worked in his favor, demonstrating a blend of courage and strategic thinking that underpinned his later success. Ambani's story is not just about wealth accumulation but a lesson in leveraging command and resourcefulness to reshape an industry.

Shah Rukh Khan: The acclaimed Bollywood superstar, renowned for his exceptional acting skills and ventures beyond the silver screen, epitomizes the essence of success in multiple arenas. His interests span film and TV production, visual effects through VFX, interactive centers like KidZania, and sports franchises including the Kolkata Knight Riders (KKR) cricket team and a football team. With an estimated net worth exceeding 5000 Crores INR, he stands as one of the wealthiest actors globally. His journey reflects not just innate qualities aligning with the R.I.C.H.™ framework but also a concerted effort to cultivate and apply these attributes effectively.

His R.I.C.H.™ factor encompasses:

- **Resourcefulness**: Armed with extensive knowledge, a clear intention, and the ability to turn visions into reality, he has navigated the complexities of both the entertainment industry and various business ventures with remarkable acumen.
- **Influence**: His unwavering determination has allowed him to shape situations and sway individuals, utilizing his exceptional people skills and influence to maintain engagement and control, always working to his advantage.
- **Command**: Facing media scrutiny, accusations, or negativity, his commanding presence has enabled him to

manage and mitigate challenges, demonstrating resilience and leadership that keeps situations firmly within his grasp.

- **Habit**: The consistent application of these principles, through deliberate practice and dedication, has been pivotal in realizing his ambitions and achieving sustained success.

Shah Rukh Khan's story is a testament to the power of the R.I.C.H.™ framework as a foundation for achieving and maintaining high levels of success. It underscores the importance of being resourceful, influential, commanding, and habitual in one's approach to both personal and professional life. Embracing and nurturing these qualities can indeed propel individuals to reach new heights, overcome challenges, and emerge victorious in their endeavors.

Sr. No.	Resource	Influence	Command	Habit
1	Be knowledgeable about current affairs and your own domain.	Get people and situations to change when the situation demands.	Don't let crises or others' mean agendas sway you from your goal	The effort of investing time and energy should minimize as; after practicing repeatedly, it should become a habit.
2	Do not assume things. Break the assumption-making process.	Learn the knack of impressing upon people's thoughts and understanding them. Be passionate.	Have your objectives clear and well-laid out so that the situation remains in your control	Learn to adapt the theory and make it your habit
3	Your advanced knowledge and ability to manage resources at the 11th hour will distinguish you from others.	The right communication and interpersonal skills will help people understand you and your intention better.	By managing situations and people with the right commanding techniques, you can slay any opposition with ease	Improvising yourself to suit the scenario and consistently maintaining your performance will enable you to accomplish your goals.

CHAPTER 1

Introduction

After dedicating nearly three years to rigorous work in the USA, I decided to take a well-deserved break and return to India for personal reasons. Little did I anticipate that India would once again become my home. While I'm content, this turn of events was unexpected at the time. Initially, coming to India felt like a transitional phase, filled with both anticipation and relief. I was eager to reconnect with my roots and take a brief respite from the demanding pace of my professional life overseas.

I remember feeling a profound sense of gratitude when Riya and Aditya showed up to welcome me at the airport. Their presence marked the beginning of what would become a journey of learning and mentorship—not just for them, but for me as well. It was an opportunity to put into practice my R.I.C.H.™ model—a framework I had developed and refined over the years, built around the principles of Resourcefulness, Influencing, Commanding, and Habit.

Riya and Aditya, both brimming with curiosity and eagerness to learn, proved to be ideal protégés. They weren't just learners in the traditional sense, but active participants in a shared journey of discovery. As we embarked on this path together, it became clear that the lessons ahead would extend far beyond the theoretical confines of the R.I.C.H.™ model.

The time I had spent in the USA, coupled with my return to India, provided a unique backdrop for our interactions. It highlighted the universality of the principles I hoped to impart—how they could be applied across different cultures and contexts, and how they could serve as a compass in both personal and professional spheres.

Reflecting on this experience, I'm reminded of the transformative power of mentorship and the importance of staying open to learning from every situation and every individual we encounter. The journey with Riya and Aditya was as much a learning experience for me as it was for them, reinforcing my belief that growth is a continuous, collaborative process. It was a reminder that no matter where we are in the world or what we're doing, the principles of R.I.C.H.™ can guide us toward our goals and help us live a life of purpose and fulfilment.

Riya, a vibrant 20-year-old Arts student with dreams of music and artistry, embodies the spirit of Resourcefulness and Habit. Her aspirations to own a music studio and compose albums in serene solitude resonate deeply with my beliefs. Watching her determination to make these dreams a reality reminds me of the power of nurturing one's passion with dedicated effort. She's the daughter of my friends, Mr. and Mrs. Roy. Though they're older than me, they've always felt more like friends than mere acquaintances.

Aditya, on the other hand—a friend of Riya—thrives in the world of computer engineering, aiming for the pinnacle of his profession while balancing his unique hobby of ventriloquism. His ambitions and the way he navigates life's challenges demonstrate the qualities of Commanding and Influencing. The drive along the 90-km expressway in his sleek 2016 Volkswagen sports edition—a moment he had long awaited—offered a tangible representation of seizing the moment while keeping an eye on future goals.

Our spontaneous decision to celebrate with chocolate ice cream—a simple yet profoundly joyful moment—underscored the Habit component of the R.I.C.H.™ theory. It's these small celebrations, these moments of gratitude for what we have, that build the foundation for lasting success and happiness.

As I shared my experiences and the principles of my R.I.C.H.™ theory with Riya and Aditya, I aimed to foster a practical, experiential learning process. This wasn't just about imparting knowledge; it was about guiding them to apply these principles in their lives, to see how Resourcefulness, Influencing, Commanding, and Habit could propel them toward their aspirations.

The promise of a surprise for their outstanding engagement with the R.I.C.H.™ principles added an element of excitement and motivation. I wanted this learning journey to be engaging and transformative, encouraging them to integrate these principles into their daily lives and witness their profound impact.

As we continued our drive home from the airport, I realized this journey was more than just a physical transition. It was a metaphor for the journey of personal and professional growth. Through my mentorship, I hoped to instill in Riya and Aditya a deep understanding of how being resourceful, influential, commanding, and habitual could not only guide them toward their goals but also make the pursuit of these goals an enriching and fulfilling experience.

Since you've already learned about the R.I.C.H.™ model, I began explaining its principles to Aditya and Riya. By sharing this model with them, I aimed to inspire them to embark on their own journeys of self-improvement and discover the profound impact these values could have on their lives and the world around them.

CHAPTER 2

Challenging times to overcome

"If I am a believer of good work, there is certainly no bad end either here or in the world to come."

—Lord Krishna

I could see the curiosity in Aditya's eyes as he absorbed the model I had laid out for him. "Thank you, Mehul sir. The model makes a lot of sense. However, I'm not entirely sure how to apply it," he said, his voice tinged with a genuine thirst for understanding. I looked at him, seeing so much of myself at that age—on the cusp of life's great journey.

"You will learn, my friend. The game of life has just begun for you, and gradually, you will gain wisdom from your own experiences," I assured him, hoping to instill patience and the promise of personal growth that comes with time.

As I spoke, I noticed a shift in Aditya's focus; his hands tightened on the wheel as the car began to veer to one side. At first, he seemed to dismiss it, perhaps thinking it was just a quirk of the road. But as the car continued to pull left, concern grew in his eyes. Without hesitation, he decided to pull over.

Watching this, I couldn't help but draw a parallel between the car's unexpected behavior and the life lessons I was imparting. Just as the car required attention and action, so does life. It demands that we stay alert to the subtle pulls and tugs of our conscience and circumstances, ready to stop and steer our course carefully whenever necessary.

In that moment, as he stood there, the weight of responsibility hit him. He had been at the helm of our journey, unknowingly driving on a deflated tire. This oversight, small as it seemed, spoke to a larger lesson I had been trying to impart—the importance of awareness and attention to detail, not just on the road but in the grander scheme of life. It was a practical demonstration of the principles we had discussed earlier—an unplanned yet invaluable life lesson presented in real time.

The concern in Aditya's voice was evident as he turned to us, a tinge of regret lacing his words, "Oh gosh, I guess we need to replace the tire." His apology hung in the air—not for the situation itself, but for the inconvenience it might have caused us. Riya and I exchanged a glance before stepping out of the car to join him.

It was one of those moments that bring to light the unforeseen events life throws at us. There we were—three figures by the roadside, united by a small misadventure. As we gathered around the deflated tire, I couldn't help but see the metaphor in our situation. Just like the tire, we sometimes find ourselves deflated—not quite ready for the journey ahead.

Without hesitation, we sprang into action. This was more than just replacing a tire; it was about facing challenges head-on, together. It was a lesson I hoped Aditya would carry with him—the importance of tackling setbacks with resolve and the understanding that it's okay to rely on others when the road gets tough.

As Riya examined the tire closely, her question broke the silence, "But isn't this a tubeless tire?" Her tone held mild confusion, perhaps wondering if a simple repair was possible instead of a full replacement.

Aditya responded, a hint of self-reproach in his voice, "Well, yes, but I guess I failed to notice the tire and its dwindling air pressure. I kept driving, and now this tire is a complete write-off and needs to be replaced." He was apologetic, acknowledging his oversight with a sincerity that underscored his earlier failure to maintain the car properly.

Seeing his discomfort, I stepped in. "Let me quickly call a tire mechanic to fix this," Aditya suggested, but a moment later, he paused, phone in hand, realizing he didn't have the number of a mechanic.

The situation underscored a lesson I often shared with younger friends—the need to be prepared. As Aditya stood there, phone in hand, the gravity of being unprepared was clear. It was a reflection of life itself, where sometimes, despite our best efforts, we lack the necessary resources to fix our problems. It was a teachable moment I hoped would resonate with him long after the tire was replaced and our journey resumed.

Amid the hassle, Aditya's fingers danced over his phone as he searched for a solution. With a stroke of luck, he found a number for a nearby service station. Dialing with a mix of hope and urgency, his relief was palpable when the operator promised a technician would arrive within 20 minutes.

I stood by as a silent observer to the unfolding events. Aditya's handling of the situation had been prompt, yet there were nuances that left room for improvement. Seeking to turn this into a constructive lesson, I posed a question to him, "Aditya, you did two things that were fine but could have been improved. Can you guess which two I'm referring to?"

The question seemed to catch him off guard. He glanced at Riya, then back at me, a furrow of concentration forming on his brow. In that silence, filled with his contemplation, I hoped he would grasp the deeper lessons we often overlook in the heat of the moment: foresight and preparedness. This was not just about a flat tire or a delayed response; it was about anticipating life's bumps and having the wisdom to navigate them with grace and knowledge.

Aditya's response was tinged with newfound understanding: "Perhaps I should have checked the tires this morning before we left," he said, his voice carrying the weight of hindsight. It was a start, but not quite the introspection I was hoping for.

With a light smirk acknowledging his partial insight, I gently steered him back to the present. "Indeed, you could have done that, but I'm referring to the actions you took in this current situation. We can't change the past, so let's focus on what we could have done better right now."

The essence of my teaching was not to dwell on oversights but to recognize them and learn how to act more wisely in the moment of crisis. My aim was to guide him toward a deeper understanding of how to approach problems—an understanding that would serve him well beyond the immediate predicament of a flat tire.

Seeing Aditya struggle to pinpoint his missteps, it was clear he was stumped. Resignation flickered across his face as he surrendered to the puzzle I had laid before him. It was time for a lesson, one that might stick with him far longer than any lecture.

I decided it was time to clarify: "Well, the two things are this: first, you could have saved your emergency contacts' numbers in your phone, so in situations like this, you wouldn't waste time searching for them. Second, you could have learned how to change a car's tire. Because you didn't, we now have to wait 20 minutes for the mechanic to arrive, plus another 15 minutes for the tire replacement."

The words weren't meant to chastise but to enlighten. I hoped Aditya would see them as stepping stones to self-sufficiency and foresight. These lessons were about more than mere convenience; they were about being prepared for life's inevitable hiccups, about not leaving to chance what one could control with a little preparation. In the stillness that followed, with the distant hum of traffic as our backdrop, I believed this roadside impromptu class would impart lasting wisdom.

The lesson continued to unfold as I explained that in total, it would be at least 35 to 40 minutes before we were back on the road. And that's the minimum time we'd spend here. Now, let's assume Aditya knew how to change the tire; he probably could have done it in about 20 minutes, saving us 20 to 25 minutes.

The point was clear: self-reliance is invaluable. It wasn't just about the time we'd save; it was about the empowerment of knowing how to handle situations ourselves. By being prepared, by having the knowledge and resources at our fingertips, we could turn a problem into a mere pitstop, a delay into a brief interlude.

This wait by the roadside wasn't just downtime; it was a classroom without walls, where the curriculum was life itself and the lesson was independence. I hoped that this moment of pause would not only teach Aditya the practical skill of tire changing but also the broader skill of anticipating life's challenges and meeting them head-on.

"Oh yes, you're right," Aditya conceded after a moment, his acknowledgment reflecting a mix of realization and resignation. Riya nodded in agreement, her expression mirroring the logic of my argument.

Yet, as I observed Aditya, his mind seemed to churn with deeper contemplations. Was he questioning the practicality of knowing everything? I decided to address his unspoken thoughts directly, to clear the fog of doubt clouding his understanding.

"Are you wondering how anyone can possibly know everything?" I asked, my tone inviting deeper dialogue. "Following the logic I presented, one might think that to avoid such situations, one should know everything in life."

It was a legitimate question—one that often arises in the journey of learning. My goal wasn't to encourage the impossible task of knowing it all, but to instill the wisdom of preparedness in areas that directly impact our lives. The intent was to foster a mindset of proactive learning and adaptive thinking, so that while one may not know everything, they are equipped with the resourcefulness to handle life's many turns.

In a moment of clarity, I affirmed Aditya's concern. "Absolutely, you're right," I said, aiming to soothe his shaken sense of capability. "But isn't it worth a try? Striving to continually develop your skills leads to greater self-reliance."

The lesson I intended to impart wasn't merely about the mechanics of changing a tire. It was a metaphor for life's unpredictable challenges. "The point I'm making goes beyond the actual task," I explained. "It's about cultivating awareness and preparedness for emergencies. It's about having a backup plan."

To drive home the concept, I offered a relatable analogy. "Imagine you have a routine of waking up at 7 a.m. every day. But if an opportunity arises for an early morning hike that requires you to wake up at 5 a.m., what would you do?" This wasn't just about altering a wake-up time—it represented the adaptability we need in life, the importance of planning, and the foresight to be ready for change. It was about the resilience to adjust our habits in the face of new adventures, ensuring that we're not caught off guard by life's twists and turns.

After a brief pause to gather his thoughts, Aditya found an answer. "Maybe I could set two or three alarms to ensure I wake up on time for the hike, even if it's not my usual wake-up time." His solution was simple but effective—a perfect example of the practical application of resourcefulness.

"Exactly," I affirmed with a nod. "And by the time the third alarm goes off, you're quite likely to be out of bed. This is how we handle potential problems—by anticipating them. The ability to think ahead like this is a hallmark of a resourceful mind—the 'R' in the acronym R.I.C.H.™ Another way to apply this resourcefulness is to set an alarm on someone else's phone, or to ask for help waking up if you don't manage on your own. Does that make sense?" I asked, looking into Aditya's eyes, seeking confirmation of understanding.

His nod was all I needed to know the lesson had landed. This conversation was not merely about overcoming the inconvenience of a flat tire or changing a routine. It was a reflection on living a R.I.C.H.™ life—a life shaped by Resourcefulness, Influence, Commanding, and Habit. Through this roadside incident and our discussion, I wanted to plant the seeds of a mindset that would flourish into a life skillfully lived, with the agility to adapt and the foresight to prepare—not just for hikes, but for the journey of life itself.

Riya, glued to the conversation, broke through the comfortable camaraderie with a question that demanded depth. She asked me to explain all this in the context of my model.

I was happy to explain. My voice took on a reflective tone as I considered the weight of the model that had not just been a mental framework, but a lifesaver in a tumultuous time.

"The R.I.C.H.™ model is more than just an acronym—it's a lifeline that pulled me from the grips of chaos. It came to my rescue when I was ensnared in life's complexities, and I'm profoundly grateful for its wisdom."

I took a breath, letting the words settle. Then I continued, "R.I.C.H.™ teaches you to be resourceful. In my "As for the situation at hand," I gestured toward the tire, now a symbol of our broader conversation, "if you had been prepared with your resources in place, you could have quickly addressed the issue, rather than losing precious time searching for a solution. Thus, the 'R' in R.I.C.H.™ emphasizes the importance of always being equipped with your resources—be it supplies, contacts, relationships, or readiness to act. It's about having that skill set, or whatever else you may need, at the ready. The crux is preparedness."

My eyes met Riya's and then Aditya's, hoping to impart the crucial nature of the R.I.C.H.™ model—not just as a concept but as a practical tool for living. "The key is to be ready," I reiterated, hoping this idea would resonate with them as much as it did with me.

In my book, I want to share how, during tough times, we face a choice: we can either give in, allowing the waves of hardship to drown us, or we can stand firm, fighting with all our might to conquer obstacles and emerge victorious.

I've seen many approaches to hardship; some are sound and effective, while others falter. It's vital to draw on validated strategies and proven methods to navigate tough times successfully. Yet, the path one takes is often as unique as their fingerprint, varying with personal inclination and context.

Let me take you back to when I shared with Riya and Aditya the importance of being equipped with the right resources. Just as having a well-prepared and resourceful plan was crucial for them, it is equally critical for anyone striving to surmount life's challenges. Having a considered and resourceful strategy can indeed make a world of difference.

In the pages of this book, I recount how life teaches us the value of resourcefulness and problem-solving, often in the toughest of classrooms. I've come to understand it's a privilege that the younger generation, like Riya and Aditya, has guidance—a compass of sorts to help them chart life's challenges with more grace.

Mentorship, the kind I was fortunate to provide to these bright minds, is an invaluable asset. It can drastically alter the course of the learning curve, equipping individuals with necessary skills well before they venture too far down their paths. It's my hope that as you turn each page, you'll find mentorship woven through my words, offering you the same advantage on your journey.

Let us consider a real-life case study.

By far, my favorite example of resourcefulness is the ingenious device that saved the Apollo 13 crew during their emergency return to Earth, as photographed with one of their Hasselblad cameras. After Mission Control canceled Apollo 13's moon landing following an oxygen tank explosion in the Service Module, the astronauts moved to the Lunar Module to save power needed later for re-entry. The problem was that the Lunar Module was designed for two people for 36 hours, not three astronauts for 96 hours. They quickly discovered carbon dioxide was building up fast, putting their lives in extreme danger.

They had to replace the circular CO2 scrubbers in the Lunar Module with clean ones, but only had spare square scrubbers from the Command Module. In record time, the Crew Systems Division put together an improvised adapter using all sorts of odd parts—like a flight manual cover, suit pants, and socks. CAPCOM transmitted instructions to the astronauts to assemble this "mailbox" rig—as they worked against the clock, trying to survive the poisonous gas as it threatened their brains. Talk about being under pressure! Wow!

I emphasized this anecdote to show how their ability helped them handle the situation. "Take a moment to consider how they cleverly used unique resources like the manual cover, socks, and suit pants. Who would have thought of those? Remember, it's not about the specific items we use as 'resources.' It's about our cognitive agility, our approach, that enables us to recognize something as a resource. In the framework I'm building, it's critical to understand that 'R' represents a mindset, an approach, and a way of living—not just a physical object."

Aditya, ever the analytical thinker, posed a question reflecting a common concern among those with technical minds: "But I am an engineer, and engineers are known for their methodical and logical thinking. How does this model apply in that context?"

I explained to Aditya that the impulse to act within a person often transcends logic or reasoning. It exists as a fundamental component, as innate as other cognitive functions like logical deduction and analytical processing. In our lives, we frequently find ourselves heeding two pivotal voices in any situation: the voice of our intellect and the voice of our emotions. My model embraces both the rational and the emotional, catering to both mind and heart.

Seizing the teaching moment that had just unfolded, I continued explaining that what happened today is a striking example. Aditya is an engineer, equipped with logical thinking and skills, but what use were those skills in today's scenario? None. And why? Perhaps because he lacked the motivation to deal with this unexpected event, or maybe because it was something he never anticipated. The R.I.C.H.™ model isn't just a theory; it's a living philosophy. It ensures that one remains consistently motivated, enhancing their readiness for situations like today's—a seemingly simple flat tire that took us by surprise. It's about staying vigilant and prepared, so when life catches you off guard, you're not just reacting; you're ready.

Riya's understanding dawned like the first light of day, illuminating her thoughts and dispelling the shadows of doubt. Her realization brought warmth to my heart—the same warmth that comes with witnessing the sunrise after a long, dark night. Her admission that this perspective was new to her underscored the value of our exchange. The dialogue between us had not just conveyed knowledge, it had sparked a transformation in understanding—a true testament to the power of meaningful conversation.

Riya's inquiry was like a key unlocking the doors to my past, prompting me to revisit the genesis of my model's application. She was curious, eager to unearth the roots of my philosophy. "When was the first instance you applied your model?" she asked, her eyes reflecting a blend of curiosity and desire to understand the practical application of abstract concepts.

Gathering my thoughts, I prepared to share a pivotal moment from my past with Riya. I wanted to pinpoint the first time the R.I.C.H.™ model transformed from idea into action. "The inaugural moment I consciously applied the R.I.C.H.™ model was during a time that stretched me to my very limits," I began, the memory vivid in my mind's eye. Confronted with a challenge that appeared overwhelming, I had to delve into my well of knowledge and trust my instincts. It was through this experience that I truly understood 'Resourcefulness'—the 'R' in my model. It was more than a concept; it was a practical tool that guided me through the intricacies of real-life challenges. This wasn't just theory; it was during this challenging period that I discovered the real power of being prepared and the strength found in adaptability.

I leaned in to share my story with Riya—a story of my first real encounter with adversity and the genesis of my model in action. After my post-graduation, I found myself tasked with winding up two of our family's factory units. At that time, my father had taken a leap of faith and moved out of India, leaving me, at the tender age of 22, to helm the family business with little to no external support.

The country was in the throes of an economic downturn, and our business was not immune. The bank loan that once seemed a gateway to growth had become a chain around our necks, with interest piling up and business conditions worsening by the day. I stood at the crossroads, burdened by the looming financial crisis, feeling the heavy yoke of debts that threatened to drag us under.

With the walls closing in, I made a difficult but necessary decision. It seemed the most pragmatic course to close the units, liquidate assets, settle debts, and start afresh. It was a daunting task, and in that crucible, I forged the R.I.C.H.™ model—not just as a concept but as my survival strategy, my way of making sense of the chaos and finding a path forward.

I continued explaining that I had no idea that shutting down the business would be fraught with challenges as well. The process of selling the units consumed most of my thoughts and time. It was a demanding period because I had to pay off loans, sell off plant and machinery, and settle statutory and labor dues.

The experience was a trial by fire, a relentless test of my resolve and capabilities. It required me to be more than just the heir to a business; it demanded I become a negotiator, a strategist, and, most importantly, a problem-solver. Every step in the process was a lesson in resourcefulness, each decision a stroke in the bigger picture of what would become the R.I.C.H.™ model. This wasn't just about business; it was about life—and the resilience and adaptability needed to navigate its complex terrain.

Aditya's response echoed with concern and empathy. "Oh, that's terrible! For a 22-year-old, that was a bit too much. How did you manage it then?" he inquired, his voice filled with a mixture of awe and sympathy for the younger version of myself that he was imagining.

I nodded, acknowledging the gravity of what I had faced. I explained that I realized I had to take control and ensure that things were balanced, pausing for a moment to let the memories surface. At that point, I wasn't consciously aware that I was using my model, but I stumbled upon a crucial concept – the 'C' in the R.I.C.H.™ model, which stands for 'Commanding.' It became clear that taking command of my situation was essential. I needed to start asserting control over my circumstances instead of allowing them to dictate my actions. Achieving balance became a priority.

I reflected on those days—a young man burdened with decisions that would shape not only my future but also the future of my family. It was a period that taught me the importance of steering the ship myself, of not just reacting to the waves but learning to navigate them. This was where the 'C' in my model was born—from the necessity of taking charge and finding equilibrium amid chaos.

"Consider this," I continued, drawing a parallel to bring my point home, "when there's a conflict between two nations at a border, a certain level of command is non-negotiable. Subtlety or passivity doesn't have a place there. Why? Because the consequences of inaction are too great—you can't risk the adversary breaching your defenses and causing harm."

Riya and Aditya nodded, their understanding deepening with the analogy. I seized their engagement, eager to cement the concept. I further explained that, similarly, when you face situations in life where you feel powerless, it's imperative to seize command. If you don't, the tide of events may turn against you, leading to greater challenges. It's about weighing your options, and wisdom lies in making those choices with a strategic mindset.

As I wrapped up that part of my story, the abrupt screech of tires on the pavement interrupted us. Two men stepped out of the vehicle that had just pulled up—they were our mechanics, arriving to fix the puncture that had brought our journey to a halt.

With the tire swiftly replaced by their adept hands, we were back on the road in no time. As we merged back into traffic, Riya turned to me, her expression a mix of contemplation and gratitude. "That anecdote was truly amazing," she said, her words reflecting a sense of discovery and realization.

Looking out the window, a flicker of hunger crossed her face. She suggested we make a brief stop—a pause in our journey to satisfy her growing appetite with some refreshments. It was a welcome break, a chance not only to fill our stomachs but also to digest the rich conversation we'd been having.

Aditya, ever the gracious host, didn't hesitate. "Of course," he assured, and with that, we took the next available exit, ready for a well-deserved refreshment break.

Soon, Aditya asked an insightful question, probing deeper into the mechanics of my R.I.C.H.™ model. "Mehul, sir," he said, bringing our focus back to the pivotal moment of my story, "the 'C' that you applied to command the situation—how did you really implement it? And did the 'R' and the 'I' play any roles in this process?"

I took a deep breath, ready to explain how the model applied during those trying times. I answered that to truly command a situation, Aditya, means to take decisive action. It was about not just facing the reality of our declining business but steering it toward a resolution. The 'R' for Resourcefulness was crucial; I had to identify and utilize every available asset, including negotiation skills and legal knowledge, to address our debts and labor issues. Meanwhile, the 'I' for Innovation meant finding new ways to handle these problems—approaches that weren't standard in the industry but tailored to our unique situation.

Commanding didn't mean just giving orders; it meant taking ownership of the problem and directing all efforts toward a solution. Resourcefulness and Innovation were the allies that supported me in that command, helping me navigate the complex web of challenges we faced.

Each decision I made during that challenging period felt like a delicate balancing act—commanding the situation with authority, drawing upon every ounce of resourcefulness, and innovating at every turn. The 'R' in my R.I.C.H.™ model was about harnessing every resource at my disposal—be it human, financial, or intellectual—while the 'I' represented the innovation in our approach to tackling liquidation and managing debt repayment. These weren't abstract concepts I was toying with; they were the very principles that became my lifeline, helping me navigate through one of the most stormy and unpredictable times of my life.

Leveraging the R.I.C.H.™ model, I steered the daunting task of closing the sale of our plant and machinery toward success. The subsequent challenge was to masterfully manage my time and mindset to ensure a delicate balance between resourcefulness and command. I meticulously crafted a plan, dedicating 25% of my time specifically to identifying resources that would pave the way for future endeavors, ensuring a smooth transition into the next chapter of my professional journey.

I reached out to influential contacts within my network, and with persistence, I found the chance to set up a 'guiding center' in Pune for budding engineers and doctors filled with ambition and hope. This endeavor was to keep me moving forward while I handled the closure of our family's business, and this very motivation propelled me onward.

Riya, intrigued, leaned forward and inquired what this guiding center was.

I was more than ready to share the vision behind it. The guiding center we started was primarily a beacon for aspiring engineers and doctors to navigate the complex admission processes of various colleges. Pune, a hub of education, presented a labyrinth of opportunities and challenges, especially before the internet simplified access to information. Students either had to rely on word-of-mouth or bravely chart their own course. Partnering with an expert in education, we crafted a place that offered clarity and direction on the steps to take, ensuring they could maximize their potential during the admissions process, I recounted, hoping to convey the center's impact on young dreams.

Riya's question struck deep, taking me back to those times when the burden of my decisions weighed heavily on me. She was curious to know if the process of selling the industrial units ever left me feeling disheartened or demotivated.

Reflecting on those moments, I shared my inner turmoil with her. I said that it certainly did, as there were times when despondency crept in. To dismantle what had taken years to build, to part with a legacy, was indeed heart-wrenching. And yes, the prolonged duration—over two years—to resolve everything only compounded the sense of fatigue. But within that struggle lay my growth. It was during those very times that I learned invaluable lessons of resilience and hope, which eventually became integral to the R.I.C.H.™ model I advocate today.

COMMANDING = CARE

Manifest it into reworking your environment and find solutions

Continuing with my story, I emphasized the importance of taking charge. One must take command of the situation, I said. Rather than yielding to the pressures of a crisis, it's crucial to devise a strategy and work towards asserting control. I explained that gaining control in such a context means reevaluating your commitment to the task at hand. It's about caring enough about the work you do, which, in turn, equips you to organize yourself and prepare to face the crisis head-on.

Reflecting on that tumultuous time, I shared a glimpse of hope. The silver lining in that dark cloud was the emergence of a new path. Armed with the determination to be an integral part of a fresh journey, equipped with the necessary resources and the ability to take command, I seized the opportunity before me. This decision set the stage for what would soon blossom into a brilliant new chapter.

Seeing their faces light up with curiosity, I seized the moment to introduce a practical tool from my teachings. I said, "Let us now explore this concept through a small exercise known as the 'Personal Development Plan.'"

Hearing my proposition, Riya and Aditya's enthusiasm was palpable. They were primed and eager to dive into the exercise I had presented.

I elaborated on the purpose of the development plan, highlighting its introspective nature. It's a tool designed to provoke thought about the choices we make and the paths we follow in life. I laid out the ground rules clearly: three questions, fifteen minutes for discussion, with a strict five-minute reflection period for each one. "Ready to engage? Do you both understand the task at hand?" I asked, looking for confirmation that they were on board.

Their nods were all the confirmation I needed. They were ready—mentally prepared to begin this journey of self-exploration and personal growth.

Tool to embrace learning:

Q. Please mention three things you think you will do to ensure things are on track. *(Being on track means achieving or doing what is necessary or expected, and is a part of your small or big goal—your vision.)*

____

____

____

____

____

Q. Please write 3 blessings you are grateful for.

____

____

____

____

____

Q. Please mention of how commanding a situation would affect your life? Will it be a positive outcome? If yes how?

____

____

____

____

____

Riya found the exercise to be incredibly timely. She shared that it sparked a deep reflection on how she intended to carve out her future path. It was the kind of contemplation she needed—a push to think proactively about her life's direction.

I agreed with Riya's sentiment, finding common ground in her realization. "I agree with what you're saying," I told her, and added that we often find ourselves facing setbacks simply because we haven't given enough thought to our actions and their long-term impact. That lack of foresight is precisely what I aim to address with exercises like these. They're meant not only to provoke thought but also to reveal the reasoning behind the choices I've made. Understanding the 'why' can be a powerful tool in shaping the 'what' and 'how' of our future decisions.

Aditya and Riya were engrossed in the task at hand, their focus palpable in the café. They had transcribed the questions onto paper and were deep in discussion. The quiet intensity was punctuated by moments of thought and the occasional head-scratch as they worked through the introspective exercise.

After the time had passed, I broke the thoughtful silence that had settled over us. "What do we have here?" I asked, eager to hear their insights.

Riya looked up, her eyes alight with a sense of achievement. She proudly mentioned that she had finished answering the questions in 13 minutes and used the remaining two to review her answers, making sure they were as thoughtful and complete as possible.

Aditya, ever the playful competitor, grinned and chimed in, saying he had also finished in good time. His tone suggested friendly rivalry, but also a shared feeling of accomplishment between the two.

Their light banter brought a sense of camaraderie to the session, but I gently steered the conversation back to the task. It was time to explore their responses.

Aditya took the lead, addressing the first question on maintaining one's trajectory towards goals. He recognized the myriad distractions and obstacles that could potentially throw him off course—both from within and external influences. He concluded that the essence of success lay in the ability to persist and stay aligned with his objectives, regardless of these challenges. This realization of perseverance, for Aditya, defined true success.

Aditya's answer offered an insightful perspective, and I was eager to hear Riya's thoughts as well.

She began, revealing a personal realization she had during the exercise. "I never realized how easily things could take me off track," she admitted. Music, her true passion, had always been sidelined. She explained how societal expectations had nudged her toward a more conventional path of formal education, steering her away from her musical aspirations. But as she reflected on the question, a new understanding emerged. "Music itself can be an education," she said, a newfound conviction in her voice. "It's possible to focus on music and still achieve great things in life." This epiphany struck her as she engaged with the question, shedding light on the possibilities that lay within her passion.

Listening to their answers, I was genuinely impressed by the depth of their introspection and the clarity of their thoughts. It was evident they had delved deeply into their own experiences and perspectives. I expressed my appreciation for their efforts, commending how thoughtfully they had engaged with the exercise and the insights they had shared.

Aditya's feedback was heartening, affirming the value of the exercise. He expressed his gratitude for the mental workout, noting that it had helped them begin to grasp the essence of my R.I.C.H.™ model—particularly the 'C' for Commanding one's path. His voice carried a note of thanks, underscoring the impact of our discussion. It was clear this session had sparked a deeper appreciation for the importance of maintaining focus and taking charge of one's journey.

I affirmed their understanding, connecting the dots between the introspective questions and a broader realization. "When you interrelate these questions, you begin to see that each of us has something we're aiming for. It may not yet be defined in SMART terms—specific, measurable, achievable, relevant, and time-bound—but it's a flame within us, something we're drawn to, something that fuels our actions."

We might call it an aspiration or a dream, I explained.

For me, the goal was to find solid ground again and engage in work that was meaningful. Initially, it wasn't a SMART goal; it was about movement—taking steps to get back on track. Once I found that track, I could then shape my aspirations into SMART goals. This approach served me well, guiding me toward substantial success and fulfillment.

(Image source-clicdata.com)

Everyone was fully engaged in the conversation, absorbed in the discussion about goals and life paths, when the gentle clinking of cutlery signaled the arrival of our order. The scent of coffee filled the air, and the sight of sandwiches reminded us of the world outside our deep dialogue. It was a welcome interruption—a moment to nourish not just our minds but our bodies as well.

Aditya seemed a bit perplexed, and I noticed his unease as he took sips of his steaming coffee. Sensing something was on his mind, I encouraged him to share his thoughts. "What's on your mind, Aditya? You seem a bit distant," I prompted, hoping to understand what was troubling him. He was concerned about the concept of SMART goals and probably needed me to explain.

I took the opportunity to clarify the concept of SMART goals for Aditya. "SMART is indeed an acronym," I began, "and it stands for Specific, Measurable, Achievable, Relevant, and Time-bound. The idea is to set your goals with a clear structure, so they're not just wishes but actionable targets."

"Let's break it down," I continued. "A goal should be Specific enough that you know exactly what you're aiming for. It should be Measurable so you can track your progress. It must be Achievable—it should stretch your abilities but remain possible. It should be Relevant to your larger life plans, and finally, Time-bound, meaning it has a deadline. This framework ensures your goals are concrete and that there's a clear pathway to achieving them." I hoped this detailed explanation would demystify the concept for Aditya and help him apply it when setting his own goals. Let us now look in detail at what each letter in the acronym means.

S: Specific

Specificity in goal setting means having a clear, unambiguous objective. It's about being exact—defining the who, what, where, and why of your goal—leaving no room for misunderstanding. For example, instead of saying "I want to be healthier," a specific goal would be "I want to lose 10 pounds in three months by exercising four times a week and eating three servings of vegetables a day." This level of detail sets a clear direction and makes it easier to focus your efforts and measure progress.

M: Measurable

I illustrated measurability with a tangible example. "For instance," I told Aditya, "consider the goal 'I want to build my own home.'

While it's a valid goal, it doesn't meet the SMART criteria yet because it's too vague.

To turn it into a SMART goal, you'd need to add specifics and ways to measure progress. For example, 'I want to build a 3,000 sq.ft house by 2023 in Mumbai.' This now becomes a SMART goal. It's Specific with a clear target, Measurable by square footage, Achievable if you have the means, Relevant to your homeownership aspiration, and Time-bound with a 2023 deadline."

This helped clarify how an abstract goal can become a concrete plan.

A: Achievable

A SMART goal should be achievable. It should stretch you but still be within reach. For example, building a 3,000 sq.ft house in Mumbai is ambitious yet attainable with the right resources and planning. However, setting a goal to build the same house in space would be unrealistic due to current technological and practical limits. A goal must consider available resources, knowledge, and constraints. This ensures it's challenging but possible, allowing satisfaction and motivation from achieving real results.

R: Realistic

Realism is key in SMART goals. It means aligning your goals with what's possible now. While we can dream of grand ambitions—like building a house in space—goals must be grounded in current reality and practicality. Today, extraterrestrial construction is science fiction. But who knows? Advances may make it feasible someday. That's the beauty of progress. For now, goals should fit what's achievable with today's resources, technology, and knowledge.

T: Time-bound

A key aspect of a SMART goal is that it must be time-bound. This means setting a specific timeline for when you plan to accomplish your goal. For example, stating "by 2023" gives a clear deadline to work toward, helping plan and execute the necessary steps to achieve the goal. Without a set timeframe, goals can lack urgency and may not prompt action, leaving them open-ended and less likely to be achieved. A timeline acts as a motivator, a checkpoint to assess progress, and a driver that keeps the goal immediate.

After breaking down the components of SMART goals, I sought confirmation from Riya and Aditya to ensure my explanation had resonated with them. Their affirmative nods were a clear sign they understood the concept. It was gratifying to see they were not just following along but were genuinely pleased to have gained this new understanding. It's always rewarding when knowledge is shared and even more so when it is well received and appreciated.

Aditya soon expressed that he had a follow-up question. I was glad they had questions because that meant they were thinking and trying to absorb the concept.

Aditya's question showed a need for clarity on how 'Influence' played a role in my past experiences. I paused to give him a thorough response.

Aditya's persistent curiosity was clear, and I welcomed it as a sign of his engagement and desire to understand fully. It's these kinds of questions that lead to deeper knowledge and personal growth. I explained that influence is about the impact you have on your own life through your actions and decisions, as well as the effect you have on others around you. I further said that in my story, influence was subtle but significant. By taking command of the situation and using my resources, I indirectly influenced the outcome of my goals. Moreover, by starting the guidance center, I directly influenced the lives of students seeking help. Influence isn't just about leading others; it's also about self-leadership—steering your life in the direction you want it to go through the choices you make and the actions you take.

I hoped this would clear up any confusion and help Aditya see the integral role 'influence' played in the narrative of my past, as well as in the broader context of achieving one's goals.

I further explained to Aditya the vital role influence played in my journey. I said influence is also about networking and relationship-building. It's about who you surround yourself with and the opportunities that arise from these connections. By being an influencer in my circle, I was able to find new opportunities and seize them effectively.

This influence was instrumental in my ability to successfully navigate the sale of my industrial units, clear my debts, and tackle the problems that arose. It was this same capacity to influence that enabled me to work on a new dream project while resolving past challenges. Influence, therefore, is not just about leading others; it's also about leading your life in the direction you choose and inspiring action that aligns with your goals.

Aditya's question showed his eagerness to understand the subtleties of influence beyond mere appeasement or agreement. I clarified this common misconception.

I strongly feel influence isn't about pleasing people just to gain their agreement. True influence involves understanding and resonating with people on a deeper level. It's about building genuine rapport, which can lead to mutual respect and understanding.

The process starts with identifying individuals you can connect with and reaching out to them. Then, you find common ground, which may involve engaging in topics they are passionate about, like football, for example. I also feel it's not about feigning interest but showing genuine curiosity and respect for their interests. This opens a channel of communication and trust. From there, influence grows as a natural progression of a relationship built on shared values, interests, and goals.

Influencing is surely a strategic approach that combines empathy, active listening, and authentic communication. This approach has enabled me to connect with people, explore opportunities, and find success in my endeavors, both personally and professionally.

This explanation aligned with their understanding and cleared their minds.

A thought occurred to me, and I told them about the guiding center example I had given earlier. I wanted to share an interesting anecdote about it.

As I reflect on my journey, a particular encounter stands out, shaping much of my future endeavors. I remember the day vividly when I crossed paths with Mr. Shah, an eminent educationist from Pune. I had known him since my younger days, and he had always recognized the zeal within me to push boundaries and excel with the resources at hand.

Mr. Shah was not just an acquaintance; he was a pillar in the educational community, having founded one of the most prestigious engineering colleges in Pune—a college that continues to hold its stature as one of the top ten in India.

His reputation was one of kindness and mentorship. He possessed a unique charm that made him both approachable and revered. Students from all corners sought his counsel, hoping to glean insights and assistance for their educational pursuits. With his characteristic grace and adeptness, he guided countless young minds through the complexities of college admissions. His willingness to lend a hand was not just a service but a testament to his profound impact on the educational landscape.

Taking a moment to reminisce further, I shared how Mr. Shah, after stepping away from the college, never lost his passion for guiding students. His commitment to education took a new form when he envisioned a center—a hub equipped with comprehensive resources to assist students through the maze of college admissions.

The center Mr. Shah conceptualized was to be a lighthouse for seekers of knowledge, offering vital information on entrance exams, preparation strategies, application procedures, and more.

His aim was to demystify the admission process, making it more accessible and less daunting. By offering this service at a minimal cost, Mr. Shah was not only providing a valuable resource but also leveling the playing field for all aspirants, regardless of their background. The center was his way of giving structure to dreams and creating a pathway to the gates of higher education. This initiative was a testament to his belief that with the right guidance, every student could find their place in the academic world.

Mr. Shah, with his foresight and passion, saw potential in the idea of a guiding center and brought it to my attention. As we deliberated over this concept, we sought insights from various experts in the education sector to gauge its viability and impact. Their feedback was invaluable in refining our approach and strategy.

Sensing the moment was ripe for action, Mr. Shah turned to me and entrusted me with the responsibility of leading this ambitious project. Over the years, I had built a strong rapport with him, demonstrating my capabilities and earning his trust. He saw in me not just an executor of tasks but a visionary who could bring his idea to fruition. This was the essence of influence—having established a connection and trust, I was now in a position where my mentor believed in my leadership and abilities enough to pass the baton to me. It was both an honor and a challenge, and I accepted it with the intent to not just meet but exceed his expectations.

As we prepared to leave the café, Riya's compliment was a pleasant capstone to our intensive conversation. She had known of me through her father's words, but it was only through our direct interaction that she could truly appreciate the depth and application of intelligence.

In response to her earnest remark, I couldn't help but emphasize a point I considered crucial for both her and Aditya. I thanked Riya but also reminded her that intelligence isn't a static measure. It's about how you apply what you know to real-life scenarios. The discussions we had today, the insights we shared, and the questions you pondered—these are all exercises in practical intelligence.

I stressed that intelligence is about adaptability, the ability to learn from experiences and continuously evolve. Every challenge you face is an opportunity to grow smarter and stronger. So, embrace learning as an endless journey.

Their nods told me they understood, and with that, we were ready to continue our journey, armed with fresh knowledge and a shared eagerness for what lay ahead.

As the discussion picked up once more, I was keen to hear Aditya and Riya's reflections on the story I had shared. "So, tell me," I urged, leaning forward with genuine interest, "what have you learned from the story I narrated?"

Their thoughtful expressions and the brief silence that followed indicated they were sifting through the layers of our earlier conversation, searching for the pearls of wisdom they could apply to their own lives. It was these moments of introspection and connection that I hoped would provide them with guidance and inspiration for their journeys.

Riya's response was swift and insightful, reflecting her understanding of the narrative. Her grasp of the importance of genuine influence in forging meaningful connections was heartening. I agreed with her and counseled that influence should be practiced on genuine grounds. Authenticity in your actions and intentions is key. Be righteous, and life tends to reciprocate with its best offerings.

It was crucial for them to understand that while influence is a powerful tool, it must be wielded with integrity. Only then can it truly be a positive force in one's personal and professional life.

After enjoying a delightful break with refreshments, I felt reinvigorated. We promptly continued our journey, eager to see what lay ahead.

Our drive continued in contemplative quiet until Aditya broke the silence with a question: What became of that guidance center? I appreciated his curiosity. To answer, I explained that it was all about utilizing our resources effectively. We had established the guidance center and garnered a modest clientele of students. Our knowledge of the educational landscape had deepened considerably by then.

I recalled how Mr. Shah and I took swift action, reaching out to a network of education professionals from diverse fields—professors, sales and development professionals from various institutes, owners of coaching centers, among others.

It was during this phase that we met a college professor deeply entrenched in management education. His idea sowed the seed for what would later become our own management college, aimed at fulfilling a dual purpose.

One was to continue with the counseling center, and the other was to create a nurturing environment for students to study and flourish. The professor left after laying out his vision, and Mr. Shah found himself at a crossroads, uncertain whether to act on the professor's suggestion.

The period that followed was far from straightforward. The complexities of wrapping up and liquidating my father's business weighed heavily on my mind. Engaging with banks and prospective buyers, fielding their endless inquiries—it was relentless. Yet, my resourcefulness and ability to take command of situations kept me afloat, guiding me through the turmoil. These qualities of perseverance turned me into a victor in the face of adversity.

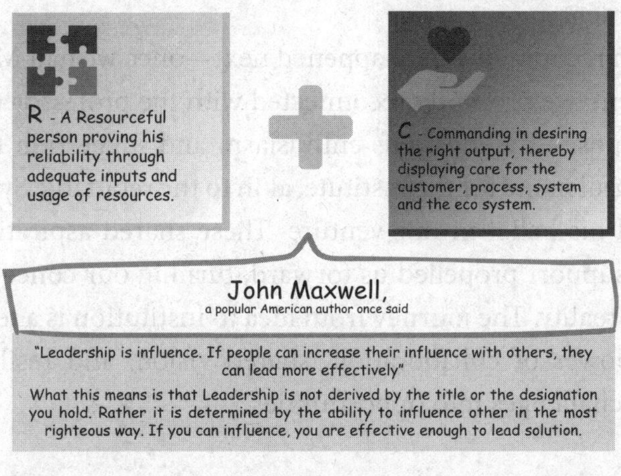

“Then what happened?” Riya asked, her curiosity piqued.

I explained that I took the initiative to build my network of potential buyers, identifying exactly who could help me sell my units. Instead of waiting passively, I reached out proactively. Leveraging my influence, I kept the banks informed of every step I took. They knew I was making genuine efforts to secure their investments. This transparency and proactive communication-built trust and ultimately facilitated the sale.

While managing these tasks, I also put my influence, my ‘I’, to good use by persuading Mr. Shah to embrace the professor’s suggestion of starting a management college. We convened to chart our course of action. After a series of strenuous efforts and negotiations, I successfully sold off my family’s business. The ordeal left me exhausted yet fulfilled. It was gratifying to see that the principles encapsulated in my R.I.C.H.™ model guided me toward a new beginning.

Aditya’s recognition of the effort required to navigate such complexity was heartening. His insight into the power of the R.I.C.H.™ model was spot on—it’s a potent tool when applied diligently. It’s not merely about overcoming challenges; it’s about transforming them into steppingstones for growth and success. This model embodies a strategy that, with the right mindset and action, can lead to profound personal and professional development.

I then recounted what happened next—once we had Mr. Shah’s agreement, we promptly reconnected with the professor who had first proposed the idea. His enthusiasm and suggestion to find a meaningful name for the institute, akin to the reputable Symbiosis, reflected his belief in our venture. These shared aspirations and mutual support propelled us forward, turning our concept into a tangible reality. The journey from idea to institution is a testament to the power of collaboration, shared vision, and resilience in turning challenges into opportunities.

The inception of Synergy Institute of Management Studies marked a pivotal moment in my journey, embodying the essence of collaborative strength and shared purpose. The name 'Synergy' was a deliberate choice, symbolizing the harmonious union of efforts and aspirations foundational to the ethos of the institution we envisioned. The collective agreement on this name highlighted our unified direction and the potential we saw in pooling our expertise for a transformative educational experience. This venture wasn't just a business—it was a beacon for future leaders and a testament to how aligned minds and hearts can make the path to success vibrant and attainable.

There was a momentary pause.

Aditya's sense of wonder was clear; my story had clearly struck a chord. I acknowledged that there were times when everything seemed to crumble around me, yet strength can be found in the rubble of what was once stable ground. The R.I.C.H.™ model was not just a concept; it was my lifesaver, my strategy for turning the tide. Every opportunity that came knocking was a chance to shape a new reality—and I seized them with both hands.

I wanted Aditya to understand that life's trials often serve as a crucible for success. Adversity can be a great teacher. It's in our darkest moments that we discover our true potential. By staying resourceful, commanding situations, being innovative, and influencing the right people, I was able to steer my path from chaos to creation.

Delving deeper into the narrative, I asked them to imagine it like orchestrating a symphony—where each element, from the venue to the curriculum, from the décor to the faculty, plays a crucial note. It took us an entire year of meticulous planning and execution to bring our vision to life. The journey was exhausting yet exhilarating, marked by sleepless nights and marathon days. Every meeting, every decision, every blueprint brought us closer to our goal. It was like a roller coaster—intense highs and nerve-wracking lows—but every twist and turn was thrilling, culminating in a ride full of fulfillment and joy. I concluded, reflecting on the satisfaction that comes from seeing a dream materialize through persistence and teamwork.

R.I.C.H.™ was helping me reach the goals of my dreams. I was resourceful, influential, commanding—and I had made these qualities habits, performing them to the best of my ability. I did not let the dark past of my destiny cloud my vision or the positivity of my life. I stayed true to the core values I believed in.

My Window of Wisdom

Lord Krishna once said, "One who does good work will not come to a terrible end."

Friends, here is the key takeaway:

The R.I.C.H.™ model means be Resourceful, be Influential, command your situation, and make it a Habit.

- Your Resourceful ways make you reliable.
- Your influence inspires you and those around you.
- Your commanding attitude makes you care.
- Your habits make you happy.

Beyond this, there are other subtle teachings to consider—

Throughout the trials I recounted, there were countless moments ripe for surrender—times when frustration and helplessness clawed at my resolve. Temptations lurked, offering false solace in the shadows of vice and escape. Yet, despite my modest experience and the constraints of power—both financial and mental—there remained an unwavering determination. This indomitable spirit was my beacon, guiding me through the tumult to emerge not as a casualty of circumstance, but as a victor in the truest sense.

- For those with ambition's flame burning within, it is essential not to dwell in the shadows of adversity but to channel your energy into transforming challenges into triumphs. Harnessing the essence of the R.I.C.H.™ model can be your compass. Embrace resourcefulness; reach out, expand your network, and cast aside any doubts that cloud your vision or hinder your progress. Exercise bravery. Immerse yourself in learning, gather wisdom, and equip yourself for the journey ahead. By doing so, you set the stage not just for survival, but for resounding success that echoes the depth of your determination.
- The "R" in R.I.C.H.™ stands for Resourcefulness. It means assessing your surroundings and optimizing the resources available. Even when you lack the finest tools, resourcefulness empowers you to gather and utilize what you have effectively, creating value and meaning in the process.
- The "I" in R.I.C.H.™ is closely linked to resourcefulness. Through networking and building connections, you enhance your ability to be Influential—able to sway both people and decisions. The "C" represents Commitment, Determination, and Perseverance in pursuing your goals. Despite obstacles, stay focused and resolute in your journey.
- Finally, the "H" reflects the habits you form through consistent action. Making and practicing good habits is essential, so they become second nature.

Among many accolades, one stood out prominently—an opportunity to present my college's specifics to Consulate Generals from over 160 countries, helping international students learn about us and giving them a chance to join and improve their lives. It sounds like a dream, maybe even unreal. But the fact is, it was very real, and indeed one of the rare opportunities an individual could have had back then.

The R.I.C.H.™ model taught me equally well in both extremes. I am glad I emerged a winner. R.I.C.H.™ can help you rise from the ashes like a Phoenix and guide you steadily towards a better tomorrow.

Tool to embrace learning:

Q. List five major take home /learnings so far:

1.
2.
3.
4.
5.

Q. List three major areas of improvement in yourself that you think will help you:

1.
2.
3.

Q. I have experienced many times that whatever problem I am facing, there are people who can help me out and their names are in my mobile contacts. They could be your first contact or may be your 'contacts'.

So, suppose (God forbid), you have lost your job, list down your 5 resources who can help you get a job and how do you think you will influence them to help you?

1.
2.
3.
4.
5.

Q. In this situation that you read, there was an element of ***C*** that is commanding the situation that I showed. Have you ever commanded a situation? If yes, do you think, after reading the example here, you could have done any better? If yes, why and if no, why?

____

____

____

____

____

____

____

____

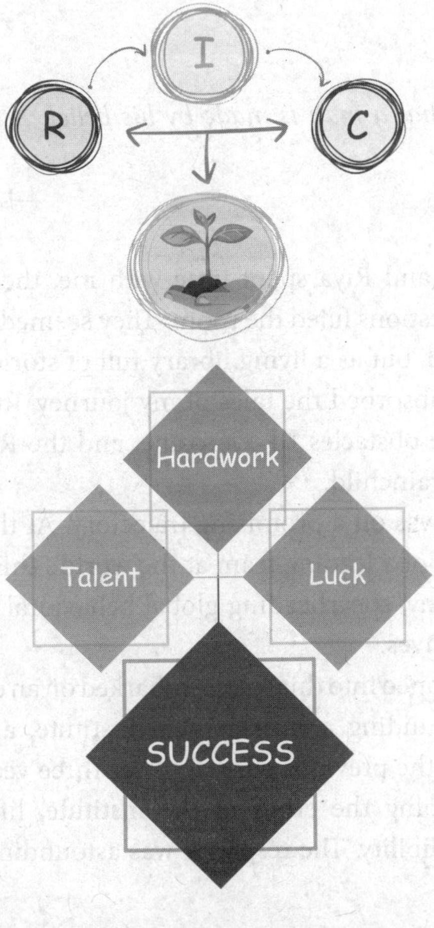

CHAPTER 3

USA Calling

"I believe that a man is made by his belief. As I believe, so I become."

—Lord Krishna

As Aditya and Riya spent time with me, their laughter and eager questions filled the room. They seemed to view me not just as a friend, but as a living library full of stories and insights. Eagerly, they absorbed the tales of my journey, the passions that fueled me, the obstacles I'd overcome, and the R.I.C.H.™ model that was my brainchild.

My career was on a promising trajectory. At that point in my life, I was part of a leading team at the world's third-largest wind energy company, spearheading global behavioral and leadership training initiatives.

Before I stepped into this role, I embarked on an entrepreneurial venture: co-founding a management institute, a venture I had delved into in the previous chapter. Over three years, I dedicated myself to shaping the ethos of the institute, lifting it to new heights of credibility. The response was astounding. My role was often hailed as the 'catalyst' for change. I forged partnerships with over sixty-five consulate generals and collaborated with AIESEC, the global platform known for facilitating student internships. Our alliance was a trailblazer of its time, a synergy that still stands unparalleled.

I was on the cusp of a promising career. At that time, I worked for the world's third-largest wind energy company, where I led behavior trainings in the global behavioral and leadership division.

My three-year tenure with the management institute was marked by steady commitment to shaping the institute's direction and enhancing its reputation. The institute thrived under my stewardship, receiving an extraordinary response from academic and business communities alike.

My 'R' represented resilience, and my 'I' symbolized initiative—the cornerstones on which I built a network that significantly amplified my net worth. Without honing my initiative and nurturing my resilience, these two major opportunities would have remained out of reach. To grasp the essence of my experience, let's look at how Aditya and Riya processed my story.

Since hearing my narrative, Aditya had been wrestling with a question. It surfaced one day during a casual conversation at Riya's home with her parents. Seizing the moment, Aditya asked, "Mehul Sir, many of us know that co-founding an institute and leading it to success from the ground up is no small feat. And you've said you were an average person without a strong support network. How did you manage to accomplish such a remarkable endeavor?"

He paused, then continued with curiosity, "I agree your influence was pivotal—enough to convince Mr. Shah to take a leap of faith with you. But can you explain what distinct factors helped you not just start, but also grow and succeed as you did?"

I listened patiently, then after a thoughtful pause, I replied, "Well, Aditya, the best answer to your question is a story. Let me take you on a little journey with my words."

Far away in a small village lived two brothers, Ram and Shyam. Ram always wanted someone to help him with his chores and tell him what to do next. Shyam, on the other hand, was quite independent. He did have mentors and guides in his life—but only to the extent of learning from their wisdom and becoming wiser himself. Ultimately, he would take charge of his own situations and make his own decisions.

One day, there was a bad storm in their village. Their farmed vegetables started to get destroyed owing to the severe winds and rain showers. Shyam instantaneously leaped forward and quickly got into making a shed to protect them. As the storm was getting mightier, he had to ensure that the shed was strong enough and away from the direction of the wind's wrath. In villages, we have huts which are constructed on desolate land, and the farm ground is mushy and quite ready for cultivation; one can immediately begin to dig.

His imperious attitude immediately gave him the idea to dig a big pit there. He dug and wrapped the cultivated produce in plastic sheets and placed them in the pit. He then covered the pit with a metal sheet so that the rain and wind would not affect it. The storm soon passed and fortunately, his farm produce remained unscathed. All this while, Ram, marooned in his own thoughts and thinking about what should be done instead of doing the deed, ended up being a mere spectator and failed to ultimately respond to the situation.

Before we jump to the conclusion, what do you understand from the story?

____

____

____

____

____

____

"So, Aditya," I inquired, a hint of curiosity in my tone, "what insights do you glean from this story?"

Aditya paused for a moment, his intellect fully engaging with the narrative before he offered a response. "Perhaps… Shyam was proactive, always managing to see opportunities within challenges…" His voice trailed off, uncertainty creeping in at the edges.

Noticing his hesitation, I quickly reassured him. "Don't worry," I said with an encouraging nod, "you've absolutely hit the nail on the head." His eyes lit up with confidence, and I continued to explore the subject further.

I began to explain, "This tale illustrates that adopting the right approach allows us to tackle crises and diverse scenarios decisively, without undue hesitation. It becomes a habit—'H' in the R.I.C.H.™ framework. Shyam's resourceful, influential, and assertive demeanor enabled him to navigate the crisis swiftly. Had Ram been in his place, he might have floundered or watched helplessly as his farm produce succumbed to the unforeseen storm.

I found myself in a similar situation when the opportunity to establish this institute arose. Drawing from my past hurdles, I confronted the challenge without wavering. As I reached various milestones, the R.I.C.H.™ model evolved into a guiding philosophy, strengthening my efforts in co-founding the institute. I was determined to be resourceful, to wield my influence wisely, and not to let my circumstances become obstacles. In essence, I took the reins of the situation, steering it toward the best possible outcome.

Riya confirmed, clearly elated that what I had explained made sense to her. She expressed her belief that the qualities embodied by following the R.I.C.H.™ principles bring a person closer to reality, aid in making wise choices, and empower one with the decision-making abilities needed to amicably solve problems. These qualities become inherent. She looked to her parents and me for a nod of confirmation, which, of course, we gave.

"Of course, you're right, sweetheart," I assured her, and warm smiles were exchanged all around.

"Well, Mehul, it seems the children are quite taken with this newfound 'Walkepedia,'" observed Mr. Roy,

Riya's father, with a hint of amusement in his voice.

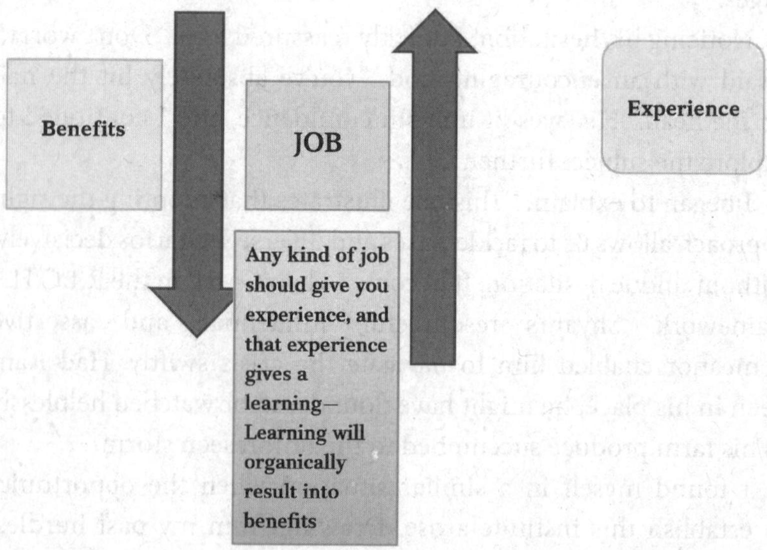

"Walkepedia!" Riya and Aditya exclaimed in unison, their eyes sparkling with delight.

Mr. Roy chuckled at their puzzled expressions and explained, "Indeed, just as we have an Encyclopedia, Mehul is our 'Walkepedia.' He converses with you, imparting his wisdom and offering so much to learn from. He's like a walking encyclopedia—hence the nickname 'Walkepedia' for you kids. I'm delighted to see that, in this first instance of you both engaging with him so eagerly, he has been a valuable resource."

At Mr. Roy's words, a wave of hearty laughter filled the room. Mr. Roy was exceedingly generous with his comments toward me, and I appreciated that he regarded me with such respect. Moments later, Mrs. Roy, who had slipped away earlier to prepare refreshments, returned bearing a plate brimming with treats, which she set down gracefully on the table.

As she poured the tea, Mrs. Roy cast a warm glance at me and the children, remarking on the engaging conversation that had unfolded. "I've been quite captivated by your discussion," she said, "and it's inspired me to share a short story of my own as an illustration, if you don't mind." Of course, we eagerly granted her the floor.

"Warren Buffett, the world's best-known investor by his own admission, credits passion as the sole reason for his achievements. Buffett worked from 1951 to 1954 at Buffett-Falk & Co. as an investment salesperson; from 1954 to 1956 at Graham-Newman Corp. as a securities analyst; from 1956 to 1969 at Buffett Partnership, Ltd. as a general partner; and from 1970 as chairperson and CEO of Berkshire Hathaway, Inc.

In April 1952, Buffett discovered Graham was on the board of GEICO insurance. Taking a train to Washington, D.C. on a Saturday, he knocked on the door of GEICO's headquarters until a janitor let him in. There he met Lorimer Davidson, GEICO's Vice President, and they discussed the insurance business for hours. Davidson later became Buffett's lifelong friend and influence, recalling he found Buffett to be an "extraordinary man" after just fifteen minutes. Buffett wanted to work on Wall Street, but both his father and Ben Graham urged him not to. He offered to work for Graham for free, but Graham refused. This did not deter Buffett, who became the world's most respected investor and businessperson."

"You've hit the nail on the head, Mrs. Roy," I responded with a nod. "Consistency is key to success. Two essential qualities that fuel this journey are integrity and focus. This is well shown in Mr. Buffett's story," I continued, eager to explain.

I went on: Although I consider myself an average person, I have always tried to embody integrity and focus, applying them consistently in my life. These virtues are integral to anyone following the R.I.C.H.™ model. For example, my experience with the U.S. green card. My family urged me to chase the American Dream—a dream that captivates millions in India and beyond. Yet, I was different; the allure of America didn't tempt me. I found satisfaction right where I was.

I was reluctant to take the leap; the idea of leaving my homeland didn't resonate with me. Moreover, such a move seemed at odds with the principles of my R.I.C.H.™ theory. In the end, it simply made more sense for me to stay, I concluded.

Riya was about to ask a question when the doorbell rang. She opened the door to a pleasant young man with a friendly smile. "I'm looking for Mr. Roy," he said. Riya welcomed him into the living room where we were gathered. The newcomer introduced himself with a polite nod. "Hello, I'm Rohan, the Event Manager."

"An Event Manager?" I asked, curious. Riya nodded, her eyes sparkling. "Yes, we're planning a party for my parents' 35th wedding anniversary and want it to be memorable," she explained.

"That sounds wonderful! I'm all in for a great celebration," I said, matching her enthusiasm. The conversation soon turned to the event's specifics, with everyone sharing ideas. But Mrs.

Roy posed a thoughtful question. "Rohan, your expertise with corporate and musical events is impressive," she said, "but this is a personal occasion—a tapestry of cherished family moments. How will you ensure the emotional heart of this celebration is captured and honored, especially with over 200 guests?"

Agreement filled the room. Rohan smiled confidently. "I understand the importance of this occasion," he said, "and I promise to handle every detail with care and attention."

I noted how Rohan, despite his background in managing large corporate events, had a unique talent for engaging with people on a personal level. His ability to connect shone through as he spoke. "Once I feel a connection to the event, that sentiment is shared by my entire team," he assured us.

The youthful and charismatic event manager had effortlessly charmed Mrs. Roy. For a moment, she was so captivated by Rohan that she couldn't look away. The mood in the room grew lighter. Noticing her mother's admiration, Riya playfully broke the spell with a light-hearted comment.

The interview with the event manager, full of probing questions and thorough discussion, ended with a mutual agreement to stay in touch. As Rohan left, a collective sigh of relief spread through the room. Then Riya voiced her concerns, her tone worried. "Dad, I'm worried about his ability to manage our event. We're expecting over 200 guests; it's no small task, and their team didn't seem to have the right experience."

Mr. Roy seemed to have a different view. He believed the event manager had responded well to the concerns raised. "I felt a genuine connection with him," Mr. Roy said, his voice steady and sure. "His answer resonated with me, showing he understands our vision for the event."

Mrs. Roy appeared completely charmed by the event manager's demeanor. Riya, ever observant, caught the subtle signs of admiration on her mother's face and couldn't help but notice her favorable impression of him.

Riya's eyes twinkled mischievously as she teased her mother. "Yes, yes, Mom… I know exactly what you found so likable about him. But really, it should be me who's charmed by him, not you," she said, sparking laughter all around.

Aditya was clearly impressed by the young man's poise and skill. He quickly voiced his support, joining Mr. Roy in his favorable opinion of Rohan.

Attention turned to me as I watched the lively exchange quietly. Riya seized the moment to ask, "Oh, yes, Mehul sir! I've been meaning to ask you," she began with a curious tilt of her head, "I heard you weren't too keen on moving to the USA. So, what changed your mind?"

I offered a gentle smile, choosing not to dig into other discussions during such a warm gathering. Steering the conversation away, I said, "Let's focus on the present happiness, shall we? I'm really looking forward to the party. It'll be a chance for all of us, including myself, to really let loose. Don't you think, Riya?"

Riya kindly acknowledged and even complimented me on my potential dancing skills. I thanked her for the sweet comment and expressed my anticipation for the event.

Aditya, however, seemed slightly amused since I hadn't commented on Rohan, the event manager. He appeared concerned I might not see any value in Rohan's abilities.

I responded immediately, "Well, I've been observing, and I think I can tie this back to Riya's question. Let me explain. I have a question for all of you: Why were you skeptical of the event manager's abilities? Why didn't you take him at his word and trust him?"

They exchanged glances before Mr. Roy quickly said, "I believe it's because he lacked the necessary experience."

As Riya expressed her doubts about the event manager's capabilities, I could see her point. "He just didn't strike me as someone who could handle such a large event," she said. I pondered her words, and Aditya's insight struck a chord with me.

"I guess it's typical to shy away from the inexperienced," he mused. "Risk-taking isn't for everyone."

Riya reacted instantly; she sprang from her seat, conviction clear. "But there's no need for risks when you have trusted alternatives. I much prefer the safety of the known rather than getting entangled with someone who promises the moon but might fail to deliver." I nodded, understanding her preference for certainty over the gamble of the unknown.

Laughing at their playful debate, I interjected, "You know, you're both right. And I was right too when I hesitated to leave my established career in India to venture into an unknown territory in the U.S. Why would I do that? I was in my mid-30s and doing well, yet there I was, faced with an opportunity I wasn't excited about initially."

Gesturing towards Mr. Roy, I continued, "The US didn't truly captivate me. I've always believed India offers equally splendid opportunities. Sure, the US is a progressive country and has earned its status as a superpower for good reasons. That intrigued me, but moving to the US was something I hadn't seriously contemplated."

Aditya, brimming with curiosity, then asked, "But how did you end up there?"

"The decision to move was strategic, guided by what I call the R.I.C.H.™ model. I gave myself a timeline and a clear goal. Standing at a significant crossroads, I had to consider not just my career but also my wife's. She was working for a company headquartered in California, and they had been suggesting she relocate to their main office. While the move seemed right for her, I wasn't ready to uproot my life without good reason. So, I took my time, searching for any opportunity in the USA, even the smallest one, that could serve as a catalyst for the move," I shared.

Taking a sip of coffee, I went on, "By applying my R.I.C.H.™ model again, the work I'd been involved in grabbed the attention of a company in New York I'd been in touch with. They presented me with a two-month assignment in California. That was my moment of realization—my 'BINGO' moment if you will. I said to myself, this is my opportunity to travel and seek out prospects there. At last, I had a compelling reason for my stay in the USA that aligned with my career goals."

Riya's question was tinged with skepticism and wonder. "How did your R.I.C.H.™ model actually land you an assignment? Isn't that practically magic? You wanted to go but had no real prospects, and then suddenly, this opportunity comes up?" she asked.

Smiling at her astuteness, I replied, "You're absolutely right, Riya, and that's an excellent question. Let me break down how my R.I.C.H.™ model played a crucial role in this."

"But before I delve into that, let me share another real-life example to enhance your understanding. A close friend of mine owns an IT firm named iWeb Technology Solutions Pvt. Ltd. This company has weathered many challenges over the years. iWeb began its journey in 2005 with its proprietary ERP, the iWeb Enterprise Suite®. But when they identified opportunities in the education sector, they developed IUMS®. Today, they're actively involved in digitizing both academic processes—like admissions, exams, fees, and attendance—and non-academic functions—including HRMS, payroll, purchasing, inventory, and finance—for universities, colleges, and schools across India."

One of the co-founders, a very good friend of mine, Akshay Shah, admits that the R.I.C.H.™ model has been instrumental in shaping the way he conducts his business. iWeb was performing adequately, but automating educational institutions posed a colossal challenge, as they are often politically governed and managed. It's a tangled web with multiple stakeholders—many of whom are not education specialists—which makes the task of persuading them to digitize even more difficult. To break out of this mold, they embraced the R.I.C.H.™ model and innovated their business approach. They began offering their services on a SaaS platform under a freemium model, transforming a traditional B2B structure into a dynamic B2B2C model. This shift brought in lakhs of students to their student marketplace as a byproduct, allowing them to capitalize on each transaction. The strategy enabled them to provide the core SaaS application free of charge to universities, colleges, and schools.

"The 'R' in the model inspired Akshay to ensure their offerings were dependable. 'Now, we're all aware that "R" signifies being Resourceful, which entails becoming reliable,' I explained. 'That's precisely what Akshay accomplished. He meticulously organized his resources and utilized them in a way that made his services synonymous with reliability.'"

Riya's eyes lit up with understanding and excitement. "Oh, that's impressive! It looks like someone has successfully implemented one of the practical advantages of the model," she remarked enthusiastically.

"Absolutely, and I'm pleased to say that several others have also applied it and reaped the benefits, which I'll share as we go deeper into the model," I continued. "In the same vein, Akshay and his team harnessed the 'I' for 'Influencing,' which, in the R.I.C.H.™ framework, evolves into 'Inspiring.' This inspiration extends beyond the students to their circumstances. Akshay believes their platform enables students to learn and assess in ways that foster growth by creating meaningful connections for them."

Aditya, seeking clarification, chimed in. He said he found it fascinating and agreed that I was suggesting their company had organized its resources to enhance the reliability of its services, which, in turn, contributed to stability and ensured the product's success. He wanted to confirm if that understanding was correct.

I immediately confirmed that he was right.

"But how did they accumulate their resources? What strategy did they use?" Aditya inquired again.

"Excellent question, Aditya," I said, and continued, "Most platforms like iWeb typically sell their solutions for lakhs and crores, making them expensive options for colleges. This is where Akshay applied his 'R.' He gathered the necessary resources and built a platform that was entirely complimentary for these colleges. Their revenue model was based solely on transactions—meaning they would charge the college only if any of the services were used. That's how they developed their product."

"That's really impressive!" Aditya exclaimed.

"Yes, indeed. That's why it's crucial to grasp how you can build your own R.I.C.H.™ to bring your plans to fruition," I explained, taking a momentary pause.

Excited to hear more, Aditya inquired, "Were they able to effectively grasp the other aspects of the model, like the 'I', 'C', and 'H'?"

Anticipating this question due to their evident interest, I explained that the 'I' in their model signifies Influence, stemming from the product's broad appeal to various stakeholders. With over 300 modules, it offers something for everyone—students, parents, academicians, and administrators—making it influential and encouraging widespread adoption.

This influence extends beyond students to their circumstances, embodying the R.I.C.H.™ principle that influence leads to inspiration. Their platform uniquely enables students to learn and create meaningful connections, inspiring them.

Regarding 'C' and 'H', their approach challenges conventional norms, maintaining steadfast dedication to their cause over four years—with visible success, as their user base expanded from 18,000 to over a million students. They realized the importance of leading rather than being led, embodying the R.I.C.H.™ ethos that commanding situations fosters care for themselves, their stakeholders, and those who believe in their vision. Overcoming challenges was crucial to their journey.

The 'H' represents Habit, highlighting the product's design to integrate seamlessly into users' routines, making it indispensable.

Their goal was to make automation and digitization habitual in educational institutions across India, aligning with the R.I.C.H.™ philosophy that good habits contribute to happiness. This approach ensures businesses stay both relevant and content.

Aditya and Riya were deeply impressed by Akshay's application of the R.I.C.H.™ model to his company, iWeb. Aditya speculated whether Akshay was grateful for this framework as a cornerstone of his success. I shared that Akshay's gratitude was profound—acknowledging that by applying entrepreneurial lessons and decisions from a young age, he had woven the R.I.C.H.™ components into the fabric of his life, aiding in both survival and excellence.

Akshay emphasized a critical perspective in my book, cautioning against the allure of entrepreneurship purely for its glamour or out of FOMO (Fear of Missing Out). He warns that starting a business should be driven by genuine passion to solve a real problem, urging potential entrepreneurs to listen to their intuition over logic or emotion.

He resonated with Chris Power, a pioneer in automating space and defense manufacturing with Hadrian, who criticized the focus of many VC-backed startups on inconsequential innovations. Power's assertion—that the disappearance of 90% of these companies would not affect the world—and his critique of the misallocation of talent to trivial tasks echoed Akshay's beliefs. This underscores a widespread misdirection of resources toward solving non-existent problems, highlighting the need for a more impactful and meaningful approach to entrepreneurship.

Akshay's insights affirm the principles of the R.I.C.H.™ model introduced in the book. By embodying Resourcefulness, Influence, Command, and Habit, he believes individuals can achieve profound success and make significant contributions to society.

Impressed with this anecdote, Riya was eager to learn more about how R.I.C.H.™ played a role in securing my assignment in the USA.

I began to explain that, initially, I was inclined to pass up the opportunity. However, I had a change of heart because my wife wanted to take on a leadership role in the California office. A few months before this, I had applied to a New York-based company. They needed mentors and subject experts in various fields of management to help them optimize their resources. But there was one catch: they wouldn't offer any compensation.

Aditya was astonished. "How could there be no compensation for this?" he asked.

I shared his surprise, though I wasn't particularly taken aback by his reaction—8 out of 10 people tend to dismiss opportunities simply because they're unpaid. The thirst for learning is often lacking, and that's exactly what the R.I.C.H.™ model challenges.

I've always believed that one must build their 'R'—Resources. And I did just that. After a rigorous interview process, they assessed my qualifications and soon brought me on board. I seized the opportunity with the clear intention of building my 'R.' I knew I could leverage the experience someday—and indeed, I did.

A moment of silence followed. Aditya and Riya appeared puzzled, while Mr. Roy seemed to sense where my train of thought was heading. I decided to pause, allowing the young minds to reflect without interruption.

Then, Riya thoughtfully asked, "You mentioned that this was to build your 'R.' Does that mean the two-month assignment in the USA was a result of that 'R'?"

"Bingo!" I exclaimed with excitement, and Mr. Roy applauded Riya's astute answer.

I continued, turning to Aditya, "Now, Aditya, imagine if I had let this opportunity slip away solely due to financial considerations, as you mentioned. Given that 80% of people tend to share your viewpoint, what do you think the outcome would have been?"

I had a strong inkling of what Aditya's response would be—and indeed, he answered by suggesting that I might have missed out on the opportunity in the USA.

However, I felt this was more than just a missed opportunity. It was about them never having the chance to even know me—because I wouldn't have approached them if it weren't for my R.I.C.H.™ model. At the crossroads where I stood, declining this opportunity would have meant forfeiting three valuable years of experience in the USA. It would've been unwittingly shutting the door to a life-changing chapter.

Aditya nodded in agreement and asked what lessons I had learned from the experience and whether it had added value to my contributions during that time.

I've always believed that if one wants to experience vertical growth—in scope of work, knowledge, wisdom—and horizontal growth—in stature, monetary gains, and more—they need to constantly present themselves on a pedestal for good and challenging work. One lesson I learned early on is that we shouldn't engage in things solely for the benefits they offer. We should also pursue them for the experience they provide. Ironically, those who focus only on benefits often reap the fewest rewards, while those who prioritize gaining experience tend to benefit far more.

I, too, pursued it for the experience. I wanted to understand how to tackle real-life challenges, how to resolve employee issues, what it's like to work for a New York-based company, and what aspects of myself I needed to refine to match their standards.

I tried to explain to Aditya that the entire decision hinged on the belief that this opportunity would help me build my 'R' and refine myself.

Aditya nodded in understanding and remarked, "Indeed, even if you hadn't secured the opportunity in the USA, you still would have gained valuable experience—and that would have contributed to your learning."

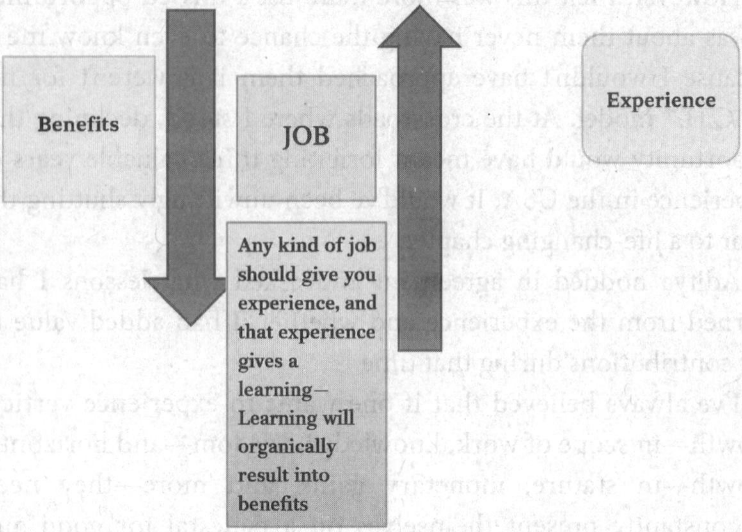

Riya pondered for a moment and asked how I ended up staying for three years when the assignment was originally slated for only two months.

I found their observation intriguing and elaborated. I explained that since the initial assignment was planned for just two months and I was relying on my savings, I knew I couldn't sustain it for much longer. However, that's exactly what my model emphasizes. As I mentioned earlier, while my 'R' was developing through this opportunity that allowed me to learn a great deal, a thought occurred to me.

Considering that my wife was heading to California and my family was eager for me to join them, I decided to leverage the 'R' I had built with this company. I approached them and asked if there were any assignments I could take on, highlighting that I already possessed the necessary visa, eliminating the need for sponsorship. As expected, they readily agreed.

I continued, emphasizing that the R.I.C.H.™ mindset within me was confident in my ability to succeed anywhere, and I had a solid plan to back it up. I was willing to take the risk, even though many hesitate to embrace it. During that period, when I held a green card and had the freedom to travel, I felt comfortable and considered not taking any action regarding the USA. This illustrates the difference between a decision made in a typical scenario and one made when you are R.I.C.H.™-enabled.

Riya readily agreed and understood that this was my 'R'—signifying my readiness to embrace opportunities rather than turning them down due to misplaced expectations.

Aditya also concurred, acknowledging my success in building my 'R,' but he was curious to know how I handled other challenges that may have arisen and whether I felt nervous.

At this point, I want to highlight the importance of our EQ, which stands for Emotional Quotient—a crucial element in personal development. In response to Aditya's question, I emphasized the significance of EQ. It played a pivotal role in enabling me to learn rapidly and take calculated risks. Moreover, I was confident that by instinctively applying the R.I.C.H.™ concept, I would achieve success.

To relate to them, I drew upon the example of the Event Manager, Rohan. Just as in the case of appointing a simple event manager where they preferred their comfort zone and hesitated to entrust an inexperienced individual, I found myself in a similar predicament. I had no prior background, experience, or formal education related to the USA. To add to the challenge, I was headed to Silicon Valley—the global technology epicenter where technology takes precedence, and intense competition prevails.

And here I was, a non-tech individual, filled with uncertainty about whether I was making the right choice. However, as I mentioned earlier, I had faith in my resolve to pursue my goals. Some might label me stubborn or even selfish, but viewed differently, my approach—rooted in my R.I.C.H.™ model—yielded success, and I discovered fulfillment in the domain I had mastered.

You see, in each of our lives, we encounter circumstances we can influence and those beyond our control.

This brings us to a crucial distinction: controllable and uncontrollable events.

Controllable events are those where we have influence over the origin, the process, or the outcomes—any one of these or even all three. For example, I can control my response and reaction to a situation. I can choose to be less dominant, less aggressive, or less angry. That is something I can manage. Furthermore, when I decide to travel from one place to another, I control how I will travel, the travel date, and all details related to the journey.

Uncontrollable events, conversely, are those where none of these aspects fall under our control. To illustrate, let's reverse the previous example and consider it uncontrollable. Suppose someone is coming to your place. You can suggest a date and recommend a mode of transport, but ultimately, you cannot control their decisions. Therefore, I believed that while I had control over how I approached the opportunity in the USA, I had no control over what it would bring me. So, why should I worry?

Aditya and Riya were silent for a few moments, seemingly immersed in my words. It appeared they grasped the clarity of the message I was trying to convey.

I promptly instructed them to jot down their 'controllable' and 'uncontrollable' events. This exercise would help them articulate their thoughts and gain a clear understanding of these concepts.

Aditya and Riya promptly began jotting down their interpretations of controllable and uncontrollable events. Aditya finished his list in five minutes and then took some time to reflect on his notes. Meanwhile, Riya was still writing. I noticed the intense focus Aditya was investing in reviewing his own notes, which seemed to spark his curiosity.

Controllable Events	Uncontrollable Events

I found myself wondering why Aditya was revisiting his responses. He explained that he had realized controllable events are primarily 'internal,' while uncontrollable events tend to be 'external.' He pointed out that most internal factors related to his actions were controllable, whereas external factors often fell into the uncontrollable category.

Riya quickly voiced her agreement with Aditya's observation.

I smiled and walked over to the window behind him, then turned to elaborate on their point. I explained that they were indeed correct—controllable events are largely internal, while uncontrollable events tend to be external. If something is beyond your control, why waste time and energy worrying or getting frustrated over it? Instead, it's wiser to focus on matters more within your control, wouldn't you agree?

They fully agreed with my explanation.

I have a theory about this whole situation. My initial perspective was, "Why focus on Uncle Sam when everything is going well for you in India?" Don't we all tend to think this way? After all, aren't we all overly rational, carefully weighing our options like I did?

But for us rational thinkers, sometimes the future has other plans. As the saying goes, "Man proposes, God disposes."

As I concluded, Aditya and Riya seemed captivated by the insights I had shared. They could now clearly visualize the scenario I described. Observing their confident and serious expressions, Mr. Roy remarked, "Well, young ones, I believe we should grant the event contract to this young man. Let's see if we can truly step out of our comfort zone and take a calculated risk. It's not a big one, so we can certainly afford to take that chance, right?"

"Of course, Dad. I'm now inclined to take that risk. We just need to ensure his commitment level and ability to deliver. I believe he's quite solid in both aspects. But Mehul sir, how did you ultimately decide to go? You mentioned exploring the opportunity later, but you didn't explain how you finally made the decision."

Riya's curiosity was piqued as she wondered whether my decision was driven by family pressure or a path I chose on my own merit.

Aditya nodded in agreement, seeming to resonate with her thoughts. He speculated that there might be layers to the situation not yet apparent. He had a strong feeling there were aspects I wasn't ready to share just yet. Perhaps they were onto something.

"Well, for that, you'll just have to wait," I said, a hint of mystery in my voice. "It's time for me to head out—I have a meeting to attend, so please excuse me. But I promise, the next time we meet, I'll unveil the rest of the story," I concluded, deliberately leaving the reason for my journey to the USA shrouded in mystery for the two millennials.

Shortly thereafter, Rohan, the seasoned Event Manager, secured the contract for the party, which turned out to be an astounding success. Following the directives given to him, Rohan and his adept team orchestrated a spectacular soiree. The event featured a medley of engaging games, a spread of mouth-watering dishes, and breathtaking decorations. In every respect, it was an affair to remember.

Despite arriving an hour behind schedule, the party's vibrant atmosphere quickly swept me into a whirlwind of joy. We danced with abandon, laughter filling the air as we rocked and rolled through the evening. Eventually, it was time for accolades, and Rohan was showered with well-deserved praise from Aditya, Riya, and the Roy couple. His meticulous efforts had crafted an event to remember.

As dinner ended, I prepared to leave. It was then that Riya's fingers curled around my wrist, her grip firm, silently pleading for clarity. She implored me to unravel the suspense that had been lingering in their minds. The matter of my move to the USA had sparked a flicker of intrigue in her eyes—a shared restlessness with Aditya, both eager for the veil of mystery to be lifted.

In the end, I yielded to their persistent entreaties. Reluctance gave way to resolve; I decided there was no merit in prolonging the enigma any longer.

With the ambiance now ripe for revelation, I found my voice and began to unfold my tale. There I was, standing at life's crossroads, beset by uncertainty. I grappled with the allure of what was dubbed a 'golden opportunity'—a U.S. visa—and the gravity of my own aspirations. At that moment of indecision, an email arrived in my inbox, from the very New York-based company I had alluded to earlier.

Riya's intuition was sharp; she quickly pieced together the puzzle, recalling the company known for presenting real-life client case studies. With a knowing smile, I confirmed her connection, revealing that my enigmatic 'R' was indeed a chapter of my journey with the New York firm. The path of an international professional is often avoided by many due to myriad deterrents, yet my resolve was not just to participate but to shine and surpass my own benchmarks. Thus, I navigated the interview gauntlet, showcased my acumen, and earned their nod of approval. That marked the beginning of an enriching two-year tenure with them.

The anticipated day unfolded when they offered me a mentoring role with someone from the Bay Area, California. My two-year tenure had been a period of professional growth, during which the company recognized the extent of my capabilities. The enigmatic 'R' that had guided me proved true north, as the role was extended to me. The feeling of elation was palpable—I was on the verge of not only increasing my income but also immersing myself in the dynamic pulse of Silicon Valley, an adventure full of boundless possibilities.

Within the brief assignment laid before me was an invitation: travel to California and guide a mentee through a maze of challenges. The stint was short, the financial reward modest, but deep inside, a voice declared, "This is the moment." Seizing this chance was my leap into the unknown—a finite venture that promised to satisfy my yearning to set foot on American soil, utilize my green card, and above all, bring joy to my family.

"Wow, seriously? That's incredible! Such chances are rare, aren't they? I couldn't have imagined something like this—only in my wildest dreams. But hearing it from you, it's undeniable," Aditya exclaimed, his voice buzzing with excitement.

Smiling at his enthusiasm, I leaned in. "That's the essence of R.I.C.H.™—embrace the power to build your resources, harbor big aspirations, cultivate vital connections, and take charge of your circumstances. Make these habits, and you'll be unstoppable," I encouraged, affirming their potential.

To temper their growing expectations, I added a note of realism. "There are still challenges ahead," I cautioned, "and one big question remains: Is it wise to upend everything for just a single assignment?"

Yet in a moment of reflection, I considered the delicate balance between what we can control and what we cannot. This realization steeled my resolve to commit fully. "If, by chance, the stars don't align," I mused, "the experience won't be wasted. I can always return home after completing this assignment."

As the evening deepened, I sensed the weight of Aditya's anticipation. He leaned forward, eyes fixed on me with a mix of wonder and impatience. "I'm so curious," he said, "how did you end up staying almost three years when you were initially supposed to be there for just a few months?" His question echoed my own internal musings—a tale of unexpected turns and extended time that even I marvel at in hindsight.

The prospect of struggle in the USA was clear to me. A new place, new faces, and a fresh start awaited. Despite my years of experience, I knew I had to prove myself all over again. I arrived in the Bay Area of California, near San Francisco, ready to tackle a small assignment. I was certain that after two or three months, I'd return home with at least the pride of having embraced a new challenge, if nothing else.

No sooner had I settled in than challenges began to surface—one after another. My housing situation was less than ideal, my car became a constant hassle, and daily expenses quickly piled up. In the USA, especially where I was, having a personal vehicle was essential; public transportation options were sparse and inconvenient. Living in California, with its notoriously high cost of living, only added to the financial strain. Doubt crept in, questioning the wisdom of my decision. Yet, it was my steadfast adherence to the R.I.C.H.™ model that strengthened my resolve, and I embraced the challenge head-on.

"That is so cool. Even in a state of uncertainty, you stood by what you believed in," Aditya said, his eyes reflecting a sense of wonder at my approach. His words felt like a balm to the tumultuous journey I had been on, affirming that the principles I clung to were not mine alone, but resonated with others as well.

I quickly explained that I was confident I would succeed. I had triumphed over numerous challenges before; why would this be any different? And that's exactly what happened. I delved deep into my R.I.C.H.™ model and reflected on its lessons. Starting with 'R,' which stands for resourcefulness—the more you experiment, the more you learn, and the more you grow. People often measure opportunities solely by financial benefits. But when you assess value beyond money, you begin to consider personal gains—the "What's in it for me?" perspective.

If a concept aligns with our reasoning, we tend to embrace it. Many shy away from change, but not me. I knew that financially, it might not seem sensible, yet I pursued it. Embracing that risk was a conscious choice—and, as it turned out, one that soon rewarded me," I shared, a note of affirmation in my voice.

As I recounted these moments from my journey, I noticed Riya's curiosity deepen. She leaned in, eyes wide with anticipation, and asked, "What happened next?"

I knew exactly what to share next—the following layer of the R.I.C.H.™ model. Beyond 'Resourcefulness' and 'Influence' lies 'Command'—the aspect of taking control of your situation. And that's precisely what I did. I used 'Resourcefulness' and 'Influence' to forge connections, immerse myself in the local scene, observe the dynamics at play, and then, strategically, I made my move.

Riya's eyes sparkled with eagerness, silently urging me forward. She leaned in, the word "Then" escaping her lips like a bridge to the next chapter of my story.

I began the next chapter: "Soon after taking command, another opportunity came knocking. I secured a deal to organize a Valentine's Day event for over fifty Indian couples. It was a chance to weave my resourcefulness and connections into something memorable."

Roy chimed in with a memory that seemed to emerge from the mists of the past. "The challenges were daunting," he recalled, "but the resilience in you—the R.I.C.H.™ in your spirit—wouldn't allow you to falter for long." His voice carried a note of admiration as he spoke of my perseverance and how I had, metaphorically, risen from the ashes. In that moment, a vivid memory of my mother's words of wisdom enveloped me, a mantra that had long been my beacon: "Become the kind of person," she had said, "who, when striking a stone, makes water flow."

My ordeal pressed on, and the looming question hung heavy. Days melted into weeks, and weeks stretched into months. I found myself nearing the end of my assignment, with the Valentine's Day event serving as a lifeline for just one more month. But what lay beyond that? Once again, I leaned on my R.I.C.H.™ principles, seizing control of my circumstances. Without any external support, I embarked on the journey of building resources in a foreign land.

Riya's intrigue was unmistakable, and her desire for more details palpable. She leaned forward, her eyes locked onto mine, silently urging me to continue.

Just as the clock struck 1 a.m., I glanced at it and said, "I'm sorry, Riya. I'm sure you're eager to hear more, but it's quite late, and I must take my leave. However, I promise to share more with you. To keep your anticipation alive, let me share something intriguing. I ventured into the world of radio jockeying, led training programs as a vendor for California State's criminal justice department, and successfully completed numerous such remarkable assignments. And all of this was made possible by something I developed—the R.I.C.H.™ model."

The famous social worker and author from the USA, Amy Morin, in her bestselling book *13 Things Mentally Strong People Don't Do*, meticulously lists a few typical characteristics of successful people. It is imperative that, to be successful, you must be mentally strong. So, what do these mentally strong people do?

Among the many things that she lists down, a few are worth a mention here:

Does this not resonate with the R.I.C.H.™ model? One needs to be watchful of how and what one gathers.

- Mentally strong people don't fear taking calculated risks-meaning they will use their common sense, available elements of decision making and their own abilities into consideration and will make that decision and go ahead.
- Further she states that mentally strong people don't make the same mistakes over and over-meaning, failure is inevitable, and one should make mistakes and fail. There is nothing wrong in failing but one must learn from them and not repeat the same mistakes again
- Finally, she states, they don't expect immediate results- meaning, sometimes, somethings take time and one must do his/her bit and leave it to the fate of their goodness to get the desired result. They should for sure not fall into the trap of expecting so much so soon. It's an organic cycle of things and it will happen when its destined and if you get restless for results, it will only jeopardize your fortunes of the possibilities of having the same.

My Window of Wisdom

- I firmly believe that self-confidence and actions are fundamental to achieving success. The R.I.C.H.™ theory, which I've embraced, empowers me to formulate my plans and believe in them wholeheartedly. It acts as a catalyst, driving me to confront challenges head-on. For instance: when you push your limits to align with your vision and empower yourself to overcome all odds, you've already won over 50% of the battle. What remains is smart planning and execution. I could never have imagined—even in my wildest dreams—that I would be consulting and training employees for one of the largest auto interior companies, with clients such as Audi, Tesla, Jaguar, and more.
- I never imagined I would train and consult staff and subcontractors of the world's largest correction and rehabilitation company or become a radio jockey on a California-based channel. And the list doesn't stop there. All these opportunities became possible because I embraced the R.I.C.H.™ model and welcomed change.

- Many of us fear change, often keeping a safe distance from it. When the prospect of change looms, our minds start to whir, prompting us to contemplate deeply before taking the leap.
- Any of the reasons listed here—or others—might cause your reluctance to embrace change. Yet it's important to remember that change is inevitable. You can either choose to initiate it with motivation and a positive attitude to reap the benefits, or it may be forced upon you. When you can't adapt to change thrust upon you, it often leads to even bigger challenges.

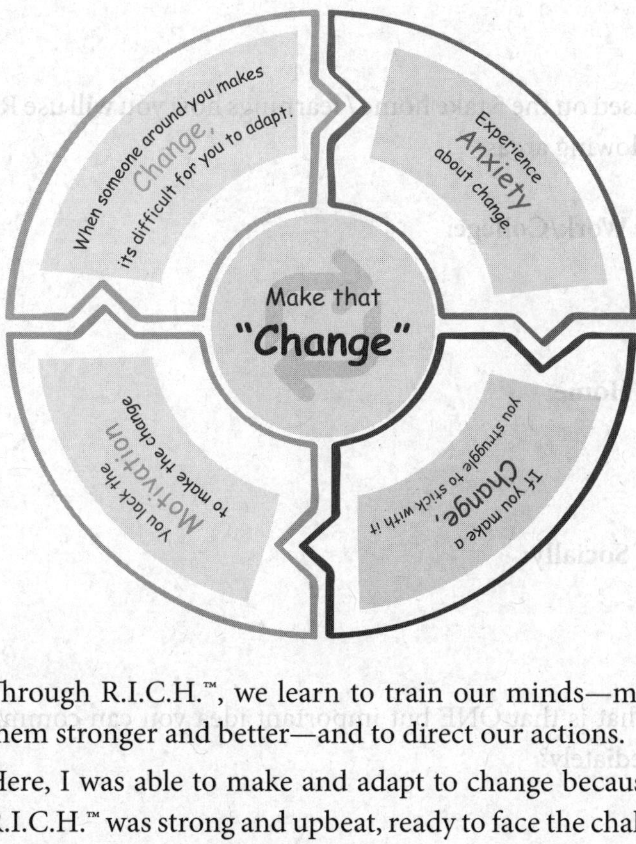

- Through R.I.C.H.™, we learn to train our minds—making them stronger and better—and to direct our actions.
- Here, I was able to make and adapt to change because my R.I.C.H.™ was strong and upbeat, ready to face the challenge head-on and boost my confidence.

- Your learning curve is always in your hands as long as you're alive. We've all heard this, but only a few follow it. I could have chosen not to move to the USA, or even if I did, I could have given up after the first assignment. But I didn't. I persevered and emerged victorious.

Tool to embrace learning:

List five major take home /learnings so far:

1.
2.
3.
4.
5.

Based on the 5 take home / learnings how you will use R.I.C.H.™ in following areas:

A. Work/College:

B. Home:

C. Socially:

What is that ONE but important idea you can commit to use immediately?

CHAPTER 4

The Reformist in You

"Do everything you have to do, but not with greed, not with ego, not with lust, not with envy but with love, compassion, humility, and devotion."

—Lord Krishna

When I shared my story of resilience and bravery—detailing how I not only managed to close my failing business but also created something new—it deeply impressed Aditya and Riya. They had never imagined that someone could be so wise and resourceful as to handle a failing venture, conclude its operations, and simultaneously conceive such a brilliant new idea. They wondered how one could undertake two tasks so diverse and seemingly contradictory at the same time.

This question lingered in their minds. As they continued with their college education and work, they often thought about me. They resolved that the next time they met, they would ask how I managed to handle such contrasting tasks simultaneously.

One day, while Riya was preparing for her arts exam, her phone rang. It was her friend Gautami, sounding disheartened.

Riya immediately asked what had happened. Gautami revealed that one of her relatives had been diagnosed with cancer, plunging her into deep sadness. Riya tried to uplift her spirits and, as a true friend, offered her support and encouragement.

Little did Riya know that the encouragement she gave Gautami would soon become vital for her as well. As she observed her own transition into a Zen mode, attempting to decode the purpose of life, Riya felt unsettled. Learning about Gautami's illness deeply disturbed her and made her reflect on the fragility of well-being.

Riya had her midterms, but she couldn't concentrate; her mind was preoccupied with contemplating life's purpose. Lost in thought, she struggled to find answers to the confusion enveloping her.

That evening, Mr. Roy, her father, had invited me over for a couple of drinks. When we arrived, I noticed Riya in a lost, somber mood. It was clear something wasn't right. After a few drinks and dinner—which Riya skipped—I excused myself to check on her in her room. I found her alone with her thoughts.

"Hey Riya, what's the matter? You don't look good," I asked, noticing the troubled expression on her face.

Riya hesitated before replying, "No, Mehul sir, I'm good… What makes you think otherwise?"

I could see through her facade. "You might be able to lie to yourself, but you can't fool me. It's clear on your face," I said gently, trying to encourage her to open up.

After a moment of hesitation, Riya confided in me about her phone conversation with Gautami. She admitted to feeling despondent, unable to grasp life's purpose or see the worth in doing good when fate could be so unkind.

Understanding her delicate state of mind, I took a few seconds to think and then suggested, "Let's meet tomorrow morning at 9 a.m. Perhaps we can talk about it more then."

"Riya, I understand what you're going through… I think I might have a solution," I found myself saying, a hopeful idea budding in my mind. "Could you meet me at Shivaji Park at 9 a.m. tomorrow?"

"Shivaji Park? Why? What's there?" Riya asked, her voice tinged with surprise.

I tried to inject a bit of mystery to lighten her mood. "Well, it's a surprise for you," I said with a small smile.

Her response was quick and tinged with weariness. "I am in no mood for surprises, Mehul Sir."

I knew she was looking for answers, and I believed I could help. "I'm confident you're seeking answers to your questions, and if you feel the same, please come. Will you come?" I asked, hoping she would agree to what I had in mind.

After pondering for a few moments, Riya gave her consent. We agreed to meet at Shivaji Park the following day at 9 a.m. I've always had my own way of imparting lessons. I'm creative and thoughtful, and I firmly believe that philosophy is most impactful when paired with a practical approach. This, I believed, would be the best method to help Riya understand.

As the morning sun draped Shivaji Park in a warm glow, true to her word, Riya appeared. I greeted her, "Good morning, dear… you look ravishing," complimenting the effort she put into her floral dress and neatly done plait.

She responded with a soft, "Good morning, Mehul Sir, and thank you," her voice barely above a whisper. Her curiosity was evident as she asked, "So, what brings us here?"

I reassured her, "You're here to find the answer you've been seeking," trying to provide her with comfort.

Riya looked around, perplexed. "But there's nobody here. Who comes to a park at 9 a.m. on a working day?" she questioned.

As she settled on a nearby bench, her confusion lingered. That's when she noticed a group of women entering the park gates, armed with broomsticks and buckets, clearly there to tidy up the space before it welcomed its daily visitors.

Noticing Riya's puzzled look, I prompted, "So, what do you see, Riya?"

She glanced over and replied dismissively, "Just a group of women here to clean the park, maybe."

"Is there anything else you notice?" I asked gently.

"No, not really... What else is there to see?" Riya's tone carried a hint of exasperation now.

I encouraged her, "I'd like you to take a closer look at them and tell me what you find," hoping she'd see what I intended her to see.

Riya paused, understanding that if I was asking her to observe, there must be a deeper reason. She concentrated, focusing her gaze on the women with renewed attention. After a moment, a realization began to dawn on her.

"Yes, I see it now. Two of them seem to be pregnant, from their appearance," Riya said, her smile showing a spark of insight.

"Good observation, you're right. But there's even more to it," I acknowledged with a nod. "Have you noticed the smiles and the energy they carry? They know this park will be littered again once it opens to the public, and yet they'll return tomorrow to clean it up. But that's not the main point. The real takeaway is that they show up each day with a smile, with positive energy, and they do their work diligently. What's remarkable is their awareness that no matter how well they clean today, they will need to do it again tomorrow. And still, they come with broad smiles on their faces, radiating happiness—even those who are pregnant," I explained, hoping to impart the lesson of finding joy and purpose in the face of life's relentless cycles.

"But that's their job, isn't it? Why wouldn't they come?" Riya asked, her brows knitting together in thought.

I nodded, understanding the practicality of her question. "Yes, it is their job. But consider this—just because something is your job doesn't guarantee you'll approach it with joy or dedication. They come not only because it's their responsibility but also with a sense of pride and purpose in their work. They find joy in the routine, in the very act of making a difference, however small it may seem. That's a powerful lesson about attitude—about finding meaning in the repetition of our daily tasks and choosing to be happy despite knowing that what you do today might have to be redone tomorrow. They choose to be here with a smile, and that choice makes all the difference."

"Just like these women, it's our duty to do our best with the abilities we have—to give it our best shot, to smile, and to be happy. In doing so, we find contentment in knowing we've done something worthwhile. Moreover, happiness benefits us; it makes us feel better, live better. The purpose you're searching for is to share love, spread kindness, and excel in our work. We are created with intention, and fulfilling that through our actions is what we're meant to do. And yes, just as the park will become dirty again, we will face challenges in our lives. But we must persist in our endeavors and strive for excellence. That's what helps us grow and become more than we were."

Riya reflected deeply on my words, and in a moment of clarity, she grasped the essence of what I was conveying. Yes, this is what life is about: doing the best you can with what you have, learning, growing, and perhaps this pursuit of growth and contribution is the very purpose everyone should embrace.

"Let me share an interesting story with you about a professor and his cup of coffee," I said, seeing that I had piqued Riya's interest with the change in subject.

"Cup of coffee? Wow, that does sound intriguing," Riya remarked, her curiosity clearly awakened by the prospect of a story.

"Yes, it is. It so happened that a professor invited his students over to his house to celebrate their results. When they arrived, he offered them coffee and went to the kitchen to ask his wife to prepare coffee for all the students. After 10–15 minutes, his beautiful wife came in with a pleasant smile. One thing to notice was that she brought the coffee in different kinds of cups—crystal cups, glass cups, ceramic cups, some shining, some plain-looking, some ordinary, some exquisite, and some expensive.

The students thought that since the professor didn't have enough of the same kind of cups, his wife had served the coffee in different cups due to the large number of guests. When all of them had a cup in hand, the professor said, 'If you noticed, all the nice-looking and expensive cups are taken, leaving behind the ordinary, plain, and cheap ones.'

It was a surprising moment, as nobody had noticed there were extra cups of coffee, and while having their cups, no one took the ordinary ones—they were all left on the serving tray. The professor continued, 'Every one of you wanted the best cups. While it's, of course, normal for you to want only the best for yourselves, that can also be the source of much of your dissatisfaction, problems, stress, and tension in life.'

All the friends looked confused and toward the professor, unable to understand the connection between choosing a coffee cup and the stress and tension of life.

The professor smiled at their curious faces and explained, 'Be assured that the cup itself adds no quality to the coffee. In most cases, it is just more expensive; in some cases, it even hides what we drink. What you really wanted was coffee, not the cup! But you consciously went for the best cups—and then you began eyeing each other's cups.'

The professor further said 'Always remember one thing, if life is coffee; and jobs, money, status, or position in society & love etc. are the cups!!! They are just tools to hold and contain life. The type of cup we have does not define or change the quality of life we live. Please don't let the CUPS drive you!! Enjoy the COFFEE ...!!!'"

Riya was captivated by the beautiful story I told her. As the narrative unfolded, I could see a transformation in her demeanor. By the end, she seemed to have shed the weight of her earlier concerns. She turned to me, her expression one of gratitude, and said, "Mehul Sir, thank you so much. That makes so much more sense now. It's remarkably simple logic, isn't it? We are here to create our lives, to experience them. I'll do just that and not worry about the rest... Your way of explaining things is enlightening... I feel much better now." Her words were heartfelt, and I could tell she truly felt relieved and uplifted.

"Thanks, Riya. I'm glad to see you're feeling better," I said, heartened by the change in her. I wanted to ensure the story had not just provided temporary relief but also a lasting insight. So, I asked, "What did you specifically learn from the coffee story?"

Before we explore what Riya learned from the story, pen down your own learnings from it:

____

____

____

____

____

____

"Well, I learned that life isn't about the cup, but about the dreams and passions that give us sleepless nights and stress. But the truth is, life is about enjoying and living every moment. It's about making it pleasurable, accepting things as they come, and learning to live with them," Riya articulated her understanding. Her interpretation of the story resonated deeply with the lesson I had hoped to impart.

"Absolutely, well said. And I'm sure the sorrow is still there, but hopefully, you've come to accept it?" I asked, looking for signs of her newfound perspective.

"Yes, I'm good now… Of course, the pain for her relative diagnosed with cancer is still present, but the heaviness and burden of life that clouded my feelings have dissipated. I understand your point, and I will pray for her well-being and hope for her speedy recovery," Riya replied, her eyes alight with a newfound sense of hope.

She seemed to have one more thing on her mind. "Aditya and I both wanted to ask you something. It's somewhat related to what we've been discussing—about your experience with establishing a management institute. We're eager to learn from you. When do you think we could arrange a meeting for this?" Her inquisitive nature was evident, as was her eagerness to understand.

"Oh, it seems there's another question poised on the tip of your ever-curious mind," I laughed, delighted by Riya's relentless thirst for knowledge.

"Oh yes, and Aditya's just as eager," Riya chuckled in agreement.

"Well, I have a session this afternoon from 2 to 5 pm. Why don't you both come to the hall? You can listen in, and we can talk after it ends," I suggested, thinking it would be a good opportunity for them.

"That sounds like a plan… I'll bring Aditya along, and we'll be there at 2 pm," Riya confirmed with a nod.

"Great, I'll send you the details of where it's going to be," I said, finalizing our arrangement.

Later that day, Riya and Aditya arrived at the session venue. They found me in the midst of delivering a lecture on 'Productivity and Efficiency' to a group of employees from a multinational company, deeply engaged with the topic.

My presentation seemed to captivate them, and they stayed for the entire session.

"That was superb, Mehul Sir. I never imagined someone could explain the concepts of efficiency and productivity so well," Aditya said, genuinely impressed.

"Thank you. The things in life are mostly simple; we humans tend to complicate them," I replied, and we shared a knowing smile.

We made our way to the cafeteria in the session hall and settled down comfortably. "So, tell me, what brings you here today?" I asked, curious about their interest.

Aditya didn't hesitate to dive into their burning question. "The other day, you mentioned winding up your family business while also co-founding a management institute. It really made us think. We're puzzled—how can someone handle two such contrasting situations at the same time and still bring both to a successful resolution?"

I couldn't help but laugh at their earnestness. "You two are quite charming with your curiosity… but it's a good question, indeed. I've been asked this before. Yes, both situations were distinct in their own ways. On one hand, I was grappling with debtors, creditors, issues with plant and machinery, labor disputes, and more. On the other, the institute required me to help design the curriculum, market the institution, and build a solid faculty base, among many other things.

Each endeavor demanded a different approach and strategy. It was certainly exhausting—I won't deny that. However, by applying my own model and drawing on the support of another immensely popular framework, I was able to navigate through both and make a meaningful impact."

Riya leaned in, her curiosity piqued. "Oh really? What is that?" she asked, her eyes wide with anticipation.

Sensing their interest, I continued, "The concept is called Ikigai, a Japanese term that roughly translates to 'a reason for being.' It intrigued me from the start, so I immersed myself in learning everything I could about it—especially how it might help me find balance in the midst of chaos.

The insights I gained brought clarity to a kind of 'theory of everything' that had long eluded me. I realized that Ikigai could also complement my own R.I.C.H.™ model, when applied with thought and purpose."

Both Riya and Aditya looked as though they were hearing about this concept for the first time.

"Ikigai—that does sound intriguing. Can you tell us more about it?" Riya asked, eager to understand.

"Ikigai is about finding a balance that connects the spiritual with the practical. It's about discovering the reason you're excited to wake up every morning. Based on examples and anecdotes from the Ikigai philosophy, I'll outline some key points to help you grasp it better," I said, ready to share the insights that had significantly shaped my life and work.

The Boxer:

A boxer might feel that sometimes the urge to hurl the alarm clock against the wall is overwhelming—but they resist. Instead, they give themselves a metaphorical kick to get up and start the day with a run, I shared, illustrating the daily discipline that aligns with the Ikigai philosophy. It's about finding compelling reasons to greet each day, even when the comfort of your sheets tempts you to stay.

The Dance Teacher:

A dance teacher may feel that their reason for waking up each morning is the joy of seeing students make progress at their dance school, I relayed, connecting the concept of Ikigai to the personal joy found in nurturing others' growth. It's about having a clear and fulfilling purpose that makes every morning worth the struggle of leaving rest behind.

The Horse Trainer:

This trainer's Ikigai lies in embracing the responsibilities they have toward the horses they care for and the people they interact with, I shared, highlighting the sense of purpose and fulfillment that comes from caretaking and meaningful connection. It's about recognizing the value in everyday responsibilities and the relationships they build.

The Craftsman:

When they see their customers are happy, that's when they feel most fulfilled, I conveyed, expressing the joy that comes from making others happy. It's a sentiment that reflects the Ikigai belief: personal happiness is often rooted in the value we bring to others.

The Grandmother:

The grandmother may not have any siblings, but the presence of her many grandchildren fills that space. Their visits—seeing their faces—that's what Ikigai means to her, I shared, showing how deep bonds with family can offer lasting purpose and joy. This anecdote brings to life the essence of Ikigai, emphasizing that our reasons for being often lie in the relationships we cherish.

What is your Ikigai?

This balance is found at the intersection where your passions and talents meet the things the world needs and is willing to pay for, I elucidated, trying to paint a picture of how Ikigai combines personal desires with practical demand.

"Intersection… what intersection?" Aditya asked, his curiosity piqued but clearly bemused by the abstract concept.

Without missing a beat, I reached for a bill counter and came back with a paper and pen. I began to sketch a diagram to illustrate the concept more tangibly, eager to provide a clearer understanding of how the elements of Ikigai interact and create harmony in one's life and work.

This balance is found at the intersection where your passions and talents meet the things the world needs and is willing to pay for, I elucidated, trying to paint a picture of how Ikigai combines personal desires with practical demand.

"Intersection… what intersection?" Aditya asked, his curiosity piqued but clearly bemused by the abstract concept.

Without missing a beat, I reached for a bill counter and came back with a paper and pen. I began to sketch a diagram to illustrate the concept more tangibly, eager to provide a clearer understanding of how the elements of Ikigai interact and create harmony in one's life and work.

Pointing to the diagram I had sketched, I explained, "Do you see this? In the center is Ikigai—the reason for being. Surrounding it are four overlapping circles.

The top circle is 'What you love,' intersecting with 'Mission' and 'Passion.' The overlapping areas also include 'Profession' and 'Vocation,' along with 'What you can be paid for.' The circle on the left represents 'What you are good at,' and the one on the right signifies 'What the world needs.'

Now, if you look closer, apart from the central convergence, these circles also intersect at different junctures, forming 'Passion,' 'Mission,' 'Profession,' and 'Vocation.'"

"Yes, we see that… but what does it mean?" Aditya asked, eager to understand the significance of these overlaps.

"I'll explain," I said, preparing to dive into the essence of the Ikigai model. "If you look at the outer edges of each section, you narrow it down to the following:

- At the top, there's 'What you love'—the activities or tasks that bring you joy.
- On the right, 'What the world needs' prompts you to think about the necessities the world requires—like food, shelter, and clothing.
- Then there's 'What you can be paid for'—the skills or services you offer that can earn you a living.
- And finally, on the left, is 'What you are good at'—the skills you've honed or the talents you naturally possess."

"Okay, got it…" said Riya, nodding in understanding

I further explained that Ikigai is about discovering happiness and joy in the everyday—in small actions and moments—rather than fixating on a distant goal that promises ultimate bliss. It's about finding meaning in the ordinary. In fact, a person's Ikigai gives them a reason to keep going even during moments of unhappiness, emphasizing the value of appreciating life's simplicity.

In Japanese culture, it's believed that everyone possesses an Ikigai. It represents the significance one finds in life—the factors that make life feel worthwhile. It encompasses both the mental state that brings a sense of purpose and the tangible actions or circumstances that provide that meaning, shedding light on the deeper cultural and existential dimensions of Ikigai.

What truly resonates with me about Ikigai is its adaptability. It's a concept unique to each individual and acknowledges the elusive nature of 'happiness.' The beauty of Ikigai lies in its ability to evolve as you do. If one avenue of purpose fades, you have the flexibility to adapt, change, and pursue new passions with intention. It embraces life's constant shifts, allowing for growth and the pursuit of fulfillment in changing circumstances.

"So, what you're saying is that Ikigai is a Japanese concept that revolves around your happiness—identifying what brings you joy, understanding your goals, and aligning them with your skills," Riya summarized.

Aditya added, "Exactly, and it also defines your life's value and helps you pinpoint what you excel at and what your passions are—ultimately allowing you to find avenues where you can earn a livelihood."

I nodded and continued, "Yes, you've both captured the essence of Ikigai perfectly. In my own journey, when I was winding up my business, I had lost my sense of purpose. I wasn't sure what I could be paid for, or where my passions lay. It's a common experience for many of us at different points in life.

While Ikigai has many facets, one fundamental idea that stood out for me is this: even if the present doesn't feel quite right—even if you don't feel valuable in your current state—if you have a strong goal you're striving toward, you can still discover your Ikigai. I found mine in being a part of something important and meaningful because..." I paused, leaving a sense of anticipation in the air, eager to continue the conversation.

- It gave me the passion to be fulfilled, and
- It allowed me to be paid for it," I concluded, emphasizing the dual benefits of Ikigai—finding fulfillment in one's passions and turning them into a means of livelihood. This unique blend of personal fulfillment and practicality makes Ikigai such a powerful concept for living a meaningful life.

I explained to them that during that challenging phase, I had two choices: either get absorbed in the process of winding up my business, lose my spirit and motivation, potentially fall into depression, and feel lost—or make the best of the situation. Ikigai played a pivotal role in helping me rediscover my passion and turn it into my profession. It provided the clarity and direction I needed, showing how Ikigai can serve as a guiding light during difficult and uncertain times.

"But Mehul sir, where does R.I.C.H.™ fit in here? You said Ikigai helped you trigger your R.I.C.H.™ — how did that happen?" Aditya asked.

"That's a great question," I replied. "During that tough phase, I naturally turned to my R.I.C.H.™, which stands for Being Resourceful, having the Influence to affect change, Commanding the situation, and ultimately turning these into lasting Habits. I realized I could leverage these qualities to improve my chances of overcoming the difficulties I faced. So, I began using my R.I.C.H.™ to navigate my way out of the mess."

"As I made progress, a recurring thought started to occupy my mind: What's next? Where do I lead myself from here? How can I make a living and rebuild my life?' According to R.I.C.H.™ principles, I needed to gather more resources and take command of the situation again. It was during this exploration that I discovered Ikigai," I continued, explaining how Ikigai became a guiding philosophy in my life.

Riya thoughtfully savored her donut, while Aditya sipped his hot chocolate, their full attention fixed on my story.

"As I delved deeper into Ikigai, it posed a crucial question: 'What is it that I can be paid for?' My R.I.C.H.™ responded promptly to me. I had accumulated enough resources to seize the opportunity before me. The 'I' in R.I.C.H.™, Influence, had already worked its magic through my dedicated efforts. This opportunity also aligned perfectly with my passion for education. That's when I decided to embrace it without hesitation," I concluded, describing how the combination of Ikigai and R.I.C.H.™ led me to pursue the educational venture.

"Ikigai then posed another important question to me," I continued. "It asked, 'What are you passionate about? What are the things you truly enjoy doing?' Given my background in a business-oriented family, curating business strategies and working on projects like the educational one felt like a natural fit. This alignment with my passion allowed me to become fully immersed in the venture. Each question from Ikigai sparked new thoughts and helped me uncover solutions," I elaborated, explaining how Ikigai guided my journey.

"As I had anticipated, the two models, Ikigai and R.I.C.H.™, worked harmoniously, and their synergy made perfect sense," I emphasized. "Being aware and conscious of my circumstances, I recognized that this opportunity had come my way. I immediately understood the importance of seizing it instead of dwelling on missed chances," I affirmed, highlighting how the alignment of these models prompted me to take decisive action.

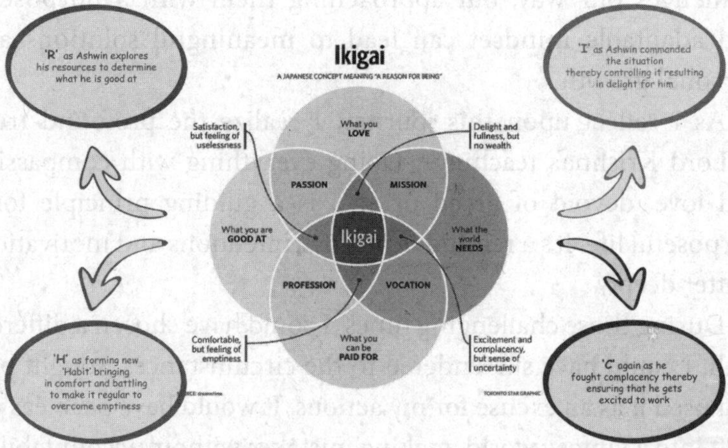

"That's exactly right," I responded to Riya's question. "My R.I.C.H.™ model was more of a subconscious foundation—I hadn't explicitly structured it. Ikigai acted as a catalyst, prompting me to evaluate what I love, what I'm capable of, and more. It not only helped me formalize my model but also guided me through that difficult period. So, to clarify, this entire process helped me prioritize and ultimately succeed," I explained, emphasizing Ikigai's pivotal role in my journey.

I continued, sharing my perspective. "You know, this kind of mindset comes from your attitude and outlook. For me, personal development was key, and that meant reforming, improving, and upgrading myself. Essentially, I consider myself a reformist. To live a fulfilled life, you have to start by reforming yourself. Many people don't have clear goals at all. So, the key is to reform yourself and find your purpose. Once you do, commit to it. To maintain discipline and stay on course, it's essential to seek support. For me, R.I.C.H.™ was the vehicle that helped me reach my goals, and Ikigai was the path that guided me," I concluded, underscoring the importance of growth and purposeful living.

It was heartening to see that Aditya and Riya found the discussion insightful and valuable. Life can indeed throw challenges our way, but approaching them with a purposeful and adaptable mindset can lead to meaningful solutions and personal growth.

As I reflect upon this journey, I realize the profound truth in Lord Krishna's teachings. Doing everything with compassion and love, devoid of greed or ego, is a guiding principle for a purposeful life. It's a reminder that our intentions and motivations matter deeply.

During those challenging times, I could have chosen a different path. I could have surrendered to the circumstances, sought pity, and used it as an excuse for my actions. It would have been easy to drift into a fantasy world, making mistakes without accountability. But I knew that wasn't the path to fulfillment.

Instead, I decided to stay true to myself. I made a conscious choice to face the situation head-on, with compassion and love guiding my actions. I refused to let external circumstances define my character. That decision led me on a transformative journey of self-discovery, resilience, and ultimately, success.

The lesson here is that, in life, we always have a choice. We can choose to be passive victims of our circumstances or active architects of our destiny. By embracing the values of compassion and love, and by staying true to our authentic selves, we can navigate life's challenges with grace and purpose.

I knew I wouldn't stop—and probably no one would have stopped me either. But it was my reformism that kept me from going down that path. I wanted, at any cost, to be a good and direction-oriented professional. That's how it all began—and it helped me, I said, giving Aditya and Riya something new to learn and apply.

"You know, I get what you're saying… as humans, we're mostly finding excuses for ourselves more than for anyone else. These models keep you in check—and if you help yourself, they'll help you. It's your willingness that's the only requirement," Aditya remarked.

"Of course, if there's no willingness, then nothing can help you. And what is a person who has no self-control, desires nothing, and cannot work toward anything? What's the difference between a human and a vegetable? They both live—but what distinguishes them is the willingness to change the stride," Riya exclaimed.

"For now, my vegetable is calling me—and I need to eat dinner," Aditya quipped, and we all laughed before heading to our respective homes.

My Window of Wisdom

The Ikigai model, a renowned Japanese concept, has proven to be tremendously beneficial to those who have embraced it. It empowers individuals to pursue their goals and assists them in identifying the path they should follow.

The combination of Ikigai and R.I.C.H.™ enabled us to learn the below in this chapter:

- To succeed, one must adopt a reformist mindset, which means having the capacity to constantly reinvent oneself and remain open to change.
- The Ikigai model assists in identifying key factors such as your strengths, what is financially viable, what the world requires, and more. On the other hand, the R.I.C.H.™ framework helps in understanding how to gather resources once you have defined your goal. Additionally, R.I.C.H.™ helps in discerning effective influencing techniques and enables you to establish rapport with individuals, ultimately facilitating impactful decisions that enhance your life.
- Ikigai delves into the realms of passion, vocation, and mission, while R.I.C.H.™ provides guidance on how to reach and achieve these facets, provided you have control over the situation.

- As Lord Krishna wisely stated, achieving our goals necessitates compassion and love, rather than succumbing to greed, ego, or negativity. Similarly, these models are effective when driven by the right intentions, enabling individuals to reach the heights they have envisioned. However, if one harbors malicious intentions, these models may prove ineffective. Therefore, it is crucial to maintain clear, virtuous, and righteous intentions to derive maximum benefit from them.

It is vital to distinguish between what you enjoy doing and what has the potential for financial reward. The Ikigai model aids in understanding your passions, motivations, and objectives. Additionally, the R.I.C.H.™ model reinforces this knowledge by teaching you how to gather resources and apply influencing techniques to manage and navigate various situations.

Being willing to improve your surroundings is crucial, and one should actively strive for it. Any model, theory, or tool can only be effective if you are willing to act and help yourself. Therefore, it's essential to overcome boredom and focus on constructive ways to reinvent and reform yourself.

Please fill the diagram for your own understanding:

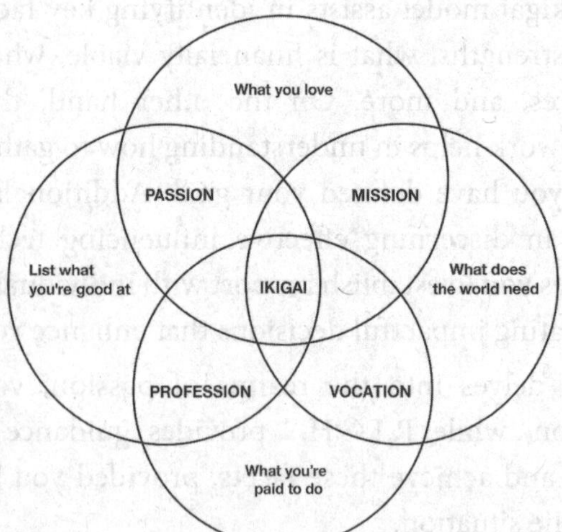

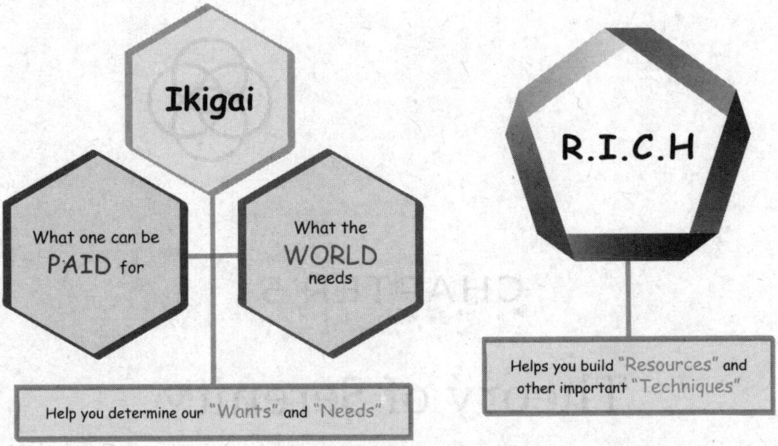
Ikigai
What one can be PAID for
What the WORLD needs
Help you determine our "Wants" and "Needs"
R.I.C.H
Helps you build "Resources" and other important "Techniques"

CHAPTER 5

Theory of Serenity

"Meet the transient world with neither grasping nor fear, trust the unfolding of life, and you will attain true serenity."

—Lord Krishna

I meticulously explained the Ikigai and R.I.C.H.™ models to both Riya and Aditya, briefly sharing the challenges I had faced and how I managed to overcome them.

As days passed, Aditya and Riya deepened their understanding of Ikigai, discovering how they could uncover their purpose and, with the help of R.I.C.H.™, put their plans into action.

Aditya, an engineering student, and Riya, an arts student, took time to reflect on their journeys and consider what they truly wanted to achieve in life.

This pressing question stayed with them as they struggled to find answers.

After explaining this aspect of my model and its correlation, I became engrossed in my work, which had brought me to India. I had some property-related matters to attend to outside the city, so I traveled there and stayed busy for a few days.

Riya and Aditya, each caught up in their own commitments, hadn't seen each other for some time. Eventually, they reunited at a mutual friend's birthday party.

Aditya and Riya greeted each other warmly and engaged in small talk. To their surprise, they soon realized they were both on a quest to discover their Ikigai. It was quite a revelation that they shared the same goal—finding their true purpose in life.

They recalled that I had recently explained the concept of Ikigai and how it could be connected to finding answers through the R.I.C.H.™ model. This shared interest brought a new sense of purpose to their conversation.

Knowing I was out of town, Aditya and Riya found themselves unsure of how to proceed in their quest. While lost in thought, an idea suddenly struck Riya. She suggested making a video call to me, believing it could offer valuable insights and guidance. After all, in this modern age, technology often proves to be a helpful tool for seeking advice.

"Hey there, Riya," I greeted from the other side of the call.

"I'm doing well, Mehul Sir, and Aditya is here with me," Riya replied, and Aditya joined in with a greeting.

"You both seem a bit tense… what's with the music in the background?" I asked.

"Oh, that's from a friend's birthday party; they're all dancing to the music," Riya explained.

"A friend's birthday, that's great! Your friends are having a blast, and you're calling me… come on, enjoy the party," I suggested.

"We'd like to, but we can't… there's something bothering us," Aditya admitted.

"Hahaha… oh, come on, you two… there can't be anything bothering you when you're at your friend's birthday," I chuckled.

However, I soon realized they were genuinely serious and eager to discuss their concerns with me. Sensing the urgency, I suggested they call me at 9 am the next day, which seemed to ease their minds. After reassuring them we would talk the next morning, they returned to enjoy the party.

The following day, Riya arrived at Aditya's house around 8:45 am and found him still finishing his breakfast. She promptly insisted that it was nearly 9 and he should hurry up. They exchanged some light-hearted banter before getting ready for our eagerly anticipated call. Both were excited about discovering their Ikigai.

As the call began, I expressed amusement at their eagerness. Riya admitted it had been a real concern for them and they were eager to uncover their Ikigai.

I reassured them there was no need to be anxious, pointing out that they had already identified part of their Ikigai and just needed to discover the rest.

"What do you mean?" Riya asked, curiosity piqued.

"What is it that you're currently pursuing in life?" I asked.

"Well, I'm studying arts," Riya replied, sounding a bit hesitant. "And what about you, Aditya?"

"I'm studying computer engineering," he answered.

"So, do you both genuinely love what you're studying?" I asked again.

"Absolutely. I've always been passionate about arts… you know me—the paintings, the drawings, the architecture of these marvelous places… not to mention my music. All of these are essential to me. They excite me," Riya exclaimed with enthusiasm.

"And what about you, Aditya?" I inquired.

"Well, yes, I love technology… the world today is driven by computers, and there's so much you can accomplish with this tool. You just have to think, and you can make it happen… it holds the power of invention," Aditya responded with enthusiasm.

"Yes, you're both absolutely right. So, if I were to break down Ikigai… what does the first part mean?" I asked again.

Without hesitation, Riya replied, "What you love."

"Exactly… so you both genuinely love what you are pursuing, right?" I confirmed.

They both nodded in agreement, and then I asked, "What's the second part of Ikigai? Tell me, Aditya."

Aditya replied, "Ah… I believe it's 'What the world needs?'"

"Exactly," I confirmed. "So, do you both believe your chosen fields are in demand?"

"Yes, absolutely. I mean, who doesn't need technology? We've become so reliant on it, and it's practically intertwined with every aspect of our lives. However much we may try, we won't be able to do without it. Moreover, computers are a treasure trove and have been helping to solve many global issues," Aditya said excitedly.

"That's wonderful, Aditya. And what about you, Riya?"

"Of course. I mean, arts, paintings, and more are the taste buds of millions around the world. They are a manifestation of your personality and your thoughts, and they also provide that wonderful feeling of experimenting with your fantasies… it helps you become the person you've always aspired to be. So, for me, the world will always have a need for these forms of expression—to soothe themselves, enrich their lives, and simply find happiness in it," Riya explained, her eyes lighting up with passion.

"Well said. Now, I suppose you have answers to two of the most crucial aspects," I remarked.

"Yes, and I know what the remaining two are… first, 'What you can be paid for,' and second, 'What you are good at.' And again, in our first two answers, we already covered those. We're proficient in our respective fields—at least I believe so—and since we excel, we'll also be compensated for our expertise," Aditya affirmed.

"I agree. We're still students, but one day we'll complete our education and apply it, and at that point, we will indeed be compensated for our skills," Riya added optimistically.

"Yes, both of you are absolutely right. You already had a sense of what you want. It just needed to be brought to the surface from your inner intellect, which is why I said you already partly know your Ikigai," I affirmed.

Riya then said, "Yes, that's true… thank you for this. But the question is, how do we make the best use of our abilities? I know I'm learning art and that one day I'll be a good artist, but to reach that level, I need something more. There's a reason why not everyone can be Picasso. Picasso was Picasso, maybe because he did something differently…"

It was clear they were eager to explore how to fully realize their potential and purpose.

With a smile, I replied, "Yes, Riya, you're absolutely right. Picasso was Picasso because of a mix of luck and exceptional talent. Sometimes, even with great talent, success eludes us due to factors beyond our control or lack of effort. Conversely, some with less talent succeed because they work hard or luck favors them."

Aditya chimed in, "Yes, that makes sense."

"Now that I'm making sense to you both," I continued with a mischievous twinkle in my eyes, "let me introduce you to an exercise by the renowned author Jeremy Sutton. Let's build our mindset by answering some questions he suggests. Would you be willing to try? We can discuss your answers once you're done."

Upon hearing this, Aditya and Riya quickly shifted into exercise mode, ready to engage with the new questionnaire I had prepared.

Tool to embrace learning:

Jeremy Sutton, a recognized author, discusses this theory on the Positive Psychology portal and offers guidance on assessing your own circle of passion.

1. What do you love?

- What do you never get bored with?

____

____

____

- When do you feel happiest?

____

____

____

- What were you doing when you lost track of time?

- In the past, what has left you feeling energized?

- What would you continue to do even if you did not get paid?

2. What are you good at?

- What do people approach you for help with?

- What skills or talents come naturally to you?

- What do you excel at even when you are not trying?

- What parts of your current job come to you easily?

- In what activity do you excel in your social circle, workplace, or community?

3. What can you get paid for?

- What would you be doing if you were not in your current job?

- Can you make a good living doing this work in the long term?

- What does the competition look like? Can you spot a niche?

- Which jobs, positions, or tasks spark your interest?

- Are you already making a good living in your line of work?

4. What does the world need?

- What can you do or offer that would bring meaning to others?

- What problems in your society would you like to help solve?

- Will your work still be relevant a decade from now?

- What is the world lacking?

- How could you be more involved in your community?

____

____

____

"Wow! That was quite an intense exercise. It really makes you think," Riya remarked, clearly satisfied.

"Yes, indeed, it was remarkable. It taught me a lot and encouraged introspection. Well done, Mr. Sutton," Aditya chimed in, applauding.

"Now that we've aligned our Ikigai and had some thought-provoking moments through this exercise, I feel we're on the right track. It's reassuring, but I still want to make sure I'm sustaining well. What are your thoughts on this, Aditya?" Riya asked.

"Of course, I feel the same. I don't aspire to be number one—I don't believe in the number game—but my goal is to improve every day in what I do. Mehul sir, does Ikigai help me with that?" Aditya inquired.

"Individuals who are self-aware often make better decisions because they understand the underlying philosophy of Ikigai. You'll naturally discover the answers as you walk this path. Unfortunately, over 70% of people don't even realize which direction they're headed in life.

They don't truly reflect on their actions. Those who do, continually push their limits, but the biggest mistake is competing just for the sake of winning. I call this a mistake because, as Aditya rightly pointed out, your aim should be to improve yourself—not to outdo others. That's not what any model will teach you," I explained.

"Okay, so what you're saying is that as we make progress, we'll eventually figure out how to sustain ourselves and keep going," Riya summarized.

"Yes, and if you want to speed up the process, as I explained the other day, you could use my R.I.C.H.™ model, which will help accelerate your journey," I confirmed.

Aditya added, "Yes, that was my intention. Based on what you told us about how you effectively use those two models, I've been trying to apply the same concept to my own situation to see how I could make it work."

Hearing him, Riya chimed in, "I guess I was thinking along the same lines. Perhaps this will help us complete the circle of confusion and give us better clarity."

"I'm afraid you two are rushing ahead a bit too fast. It's good to have these thoughts, but you still have time to work things out and figure them through. Nevertheless, here's what I'll do—I'll be back in town the day after tomorrow, and since you're both eager to connect the dots between the two models for your own lives, let me give you an exercise. Are you willing to give it a try?" I proposed.

"Of course, we're willing to do anything that helps us gain clarity," Aditya responded, and Riya immediately echoed his enthusiasm. "Yes, we're ready."

"Great, let's get started then. So, what does my theory say? R… I… C… H. Now, you both know what each stands for and their purpose, so I won't explain that again," I began.

"Now, Aditya, what you need to do is connect each of these elements with your computer engineering course. For example, what resources will you need after you graduate to move to your next step, like finding a job or starting a business? Similarly, what will your quotient of influencing be, and how will you ensure you keep the situation in command?" I instructed.

"Same goes for you, Riya. After graduation, how do you envision proceeding, and what will be the 'R', the 'I', and the 'C' that you will need?" I asked, encouraging them to think ahead.

"Yes, that sounds easy, but I'm sure it won't be… after all, figuring things out with yourself can be a bit challenging," Aditya remarked with a smile.

Laughing, I replied, "Well, I'm confident you both are intelligent enough to figure it out. (After a pause) Okay, guys, let's catch up the day after tomorrow and see what you've come up with. Alright?"

"Sounds good," Riya and Aditya replied before hanging up.

As expected, they both needed to dive into the details and work on their plans. Utilizing R.I.C.H.™, they sought answers to critical questions many of us often overlook or aren't even aware of—questions crucial for charting a roadmap.

The two-day window was a race against time to figure things out, but somehow, they managed. Now, what they were searching for was a way to bring it all together.

The awaited day had finally arrived. I was back in town after handling some property matters in my hometown and eager to meet Aditya and Riya to discuss their progress.

A little while later, both Aditya and Riya arrived at my home, ready to share their thoughts. I greeted them warmly and asked, "So, how are both of you, and how was the process of figuring things out?"

"It was good! We had to put in some effort to find the answers, but overall, it was fine," Aditya replied, and Riya echoed a similar sentiment.

Sensing their excitement and nervousness, I was glad they had taken the initiative to complete the exercise. "So, who would like to go first?" I asked, eager to hear their thoughts.

"I'll go first. I want to get this done… although I'm a bit nervous," Aditya volunteered.

"Come on, you'll do great," I reassured him. Aditya then began to explain his R.I.C.H.™ plan.

"As I mentioned, I'm looking to establish my career in the world of technology, and I'd love to dive deep into it. Now, following the standard process that most of us typically follow, an ideal career path would be—" Aditya started to outline his plan.

He continued, saying that upon graduating from college, the typical path involves pursuing campus placements or applying for jobs at multiple locations, actively seeking employment through various channels to secure a job as soon as possible. Next, the usual stage involves working for 2-3 years in that job. If you're driven by entrepreneurship, you can begin laying the groundwork for your startup during this time, alongside your regular job. Eventually, with the help of your co-workers and your own research, you can set the stage for your startup.

I listened attentively as he laid out his plan.

Reflecting on Aditya's words, I found myself engrossed in the natural progression he described—one that resonates deeply with my own aspirations. Growth is an organic process, where investment and expansion become integral as you aim for lateral development. This ambitious journey seems almost straightforward when you're riding the wave of success, where seeking funding and scaling up feels like the next logical step. But it's in the face of failure that the true challenge emerges.

If my endeavors were to falter, would I retreat to the safety of a regular job? Or, bolstered by courage and whatever resources I have left, would I take another leap into the uncertain world of startups? This is the cycle through which progress is made — not just in business, but in personal growth as well. As Aditya shared the trials and tribulations of an entrepreneur's path, I noticed Riya was completely captivated too. His insights were a beacon, guiding us through the fog of our entrepreneurial journey.

When Aditya's presentation ended, I sensed his unease. His words had stumbled, not once but twice, and a veil of uncertainty clouded his usual confidence. I needed to understand the crux of his argument—the core of his ambition that was clearly pushing against the norms. "Okay, maybe what you're saying could make sense… but what exactly are you getting at?" I asked, genuinely curious.

Aditya's response came with a determination that filled the room. "I don't want to follow the traditional or conventional path. I want to build my startup from the ground up, starting today," he declared.

The surprise must have been clear on my face, but it was Riya who voiced the skepticism we both felt. "From today? You're only 19, in your second year of engineering. What do you really know about starting a business?" she asked.

The question hung in the air, heavy with anticipation — a response that could either quell our doubts or fuel the flames of Aditya's dream.

Aditya's retort was sharp. "Mark Zuckerberg started Facebook when he was 19 too," he said, frustration and defiance mixing in his voice.

Riya, ever the realist, wasn't convinced. "But he was Mark Zuckerberg," she emphasized, as if the name alone was explanation enough.

"And he might have been planning his platform long before he launched it," she added confidently.

Aditya's frown deepened. "What makes you think I haven't prepared? Mark Zuckerberg became 'Mark Zuckerberg' after he became famous. Before Facebook, he was just another college student," he shot back, his tone revealing a hint of feeling underestimated.

Riya turned to me, seeking an ally in reason. "Mehul, Sir, please make him understand. He doesn't get it. How can he just work on something without any knowledge or experience?" she pleaded.

I couldn't help but smile—not out of amusement, but because I saw something in Aditya that perhaps Riya hadn't recognized. "I'm sorry, Riya, but you're mistaken. It's not that your logic is flawed; it's just that there are many paths to achieving one's goals. That's where the beauty of Ikigai comes in—it helps you discover your purpose. And with R.I.C.H.™, you have a framework to execute that purpose. Remember when I mentioned this earlier?" I tried to bridge the gap between Aditya's fiery ambition and Riya's practical concerns with a dose of wisdom that transcended age and experience.

Riya, still skeptical but willing to entertain the possibility, composed herself. "Of course I remember. Okay, tell me—how do you think he'll be able to do this?" she asked, seeking concrete steps rather than abstract concepts.

"That's precisely why we're gathered here today," I said, turning to Aditya with a mix of mentorship and challenge in my tone. "So, Aditya, why don't you walk us through what you've developed that instills such confidence in you? Come on, sell us your plan."

With a nod, Aditya stood up, a new resolve in his posture. He approached the flip chart with determination, marker in hand, ready to lay bare his vision. "Okay, so we're talking about R.I.C.H.™, right? Let me begin," he said, and with those words, he was ready to outline the Resources he envisioned as the cornerstone of his startup plan.

Aditya's confidence was palpable as he began scribbling on the flip chart, outlining the framework of his resources.

"Firstly, I've delved deep into the domain I'm working on. I've acquired substantial knowledge in this area, which is fundamental

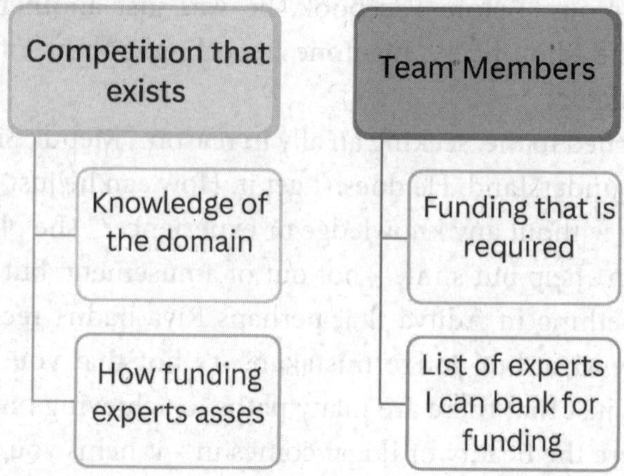

to the success of my venture," he said, his marker squeaking as he jotted down key points.

"Next, I've analyzed the competition—or rather, the lack of it. My research suggests there's a gap in the market that my startup can fill," he continued, a hint of pride in his discovery.

"I've also considered the team aspect. I've already aligned a group of co-founders who share my vision and are ready to embark on this journey with me," he added, ticking off another crucial box.

"As for funding, I understand the magnitude of what I'm undertaking. I've outlined a detailed plan to make us an attractive proposition for potential investors." Aditya's voice was steady, reflecting his preparedness for the financial hurdles ahead.

He took a breath before diving deeper. "I've researched how funding experts think—their assessment criteria, the questions they typically ask, and what they look for in a startup. This insight will be invaluable in navigating that landscape."

"And finally, I've identified potential investors. I've studied their backgrounds, investment styles, the startups they've backed, the sectors they focus on, and the trends currently shaping their decisions," Aditya concluded, stepping back from the chart to let us absorb the breadth of his groundwork.

It was a comprehensive list, no doubt, and I could see Riya processing the information, perhaps reassessing her earlier skepticism. Aditya had not only prepared—he had done his homework with a thoroughness that demanded respect. Whether it would be enough to secure the support he needed, only time would tell. But for now, he had our full attention.

Aditya, unfazed by Riya's interjection, responded with a touch of exasperation, almost as if he had anticipated her reaction. "I'm surprised you're questioning the level of detail, Riya. It's about gathering everything you can. Sometimes, you don't know what you need simply because you don't know it exists. That's how thorough we need to be," he said, his tone firm—this was only the beginning.

Riya, perhaps overwhelmed or unconvinced, could only muster a resigned sigh.

Aditya turned back to the flip chart, ready to advance to the next phase of his plan. With a slight sigh, mirroring Riya's, he continued, "Now, let's proceed to the 'I' in R.I.C.H.™—My Influence—which will focus on—" He paused, then began outlining how he planned to sway stakeholders and market forces to back his vision, undeterred by skepticism.

Aditya confidently moved his marker across the flip chart, detailing his plan for Influence:

"To build influence, I'll begin by connecting with people in my domain through networking on social media platforms. It's crucial to immerse myself in the ecosystem by attending meetings, seminars, and other relevant gatherings," he explained, outlining a strategy to become an integral part of the industry community.

"Furthermore, I'll cultivate relationships with experienced startup professionals—individuals who've been through the journey, who've seen both success and failure, and can provide invaluable insights into how things work at the ground level," he added, stressing the importance of learning from those who've already walked the path he's embarking on.

"And by slowly and steadily engaging with people, I'll be able to understand their thought processes, which will"—he paused for effect—"enable me to anticipate their needs and extract something tangible from our interactions."

The word Rapport stood out on the chart, underlined twice. It was clear that Aditya perceived building relationships not just as a means to an end but as a crucial element of his entrepreneurial strategy—a way to influence and be influenced by the movers and shakers of the startup world.

Aditya continued, highlighting the pinnacle of his Influence strategy with fervor:

"And the most crucial element is cultivating my own image within the community. I plan to do this by actively participating in events, offering my help to associations, and contributing to startup bodies in the most impactful ways possible. It's about giving before you get, establishing goodwill, and making sure my name is recognized for the right reasons."

His plan wasn't just about traditional networking; it was about becoming a valued member of the startup ecosystem—someone known for their contributions as much as their aspirations. This was Aditya's way of laying the groundwork for a reputation that could open doors and build the trust necessary for a successful venture.

I listened intently as Aditya laid out his strategy, impressed by his foresight and how he was connecting the dots between his resources and influence to achieve his goals.

"My Resources will arm me with a comprehensive understanding of the market, the technology I'm focused on, and the global dynamics at play. I'll be up to speed on the successes and failures of others in this space. The goal is to mitigate the risk of being caught off guard by any unforeseen market dynamics. While it's impossible to predict every variable, we can certainly aim to prepare for as many as possible to draw the most informed conclusions," Aditya explained, a sense of resilience in his words.

He paused briefly, ensuring his points had landed before continuing. "As for Influence, it's about articulating my idea clearly, connecting with key decision-makers, expanding my network, and establishing the right communication channels. Essentially, it's about positively swaying those who have the power to make or break your venture. The more effectively you can reach and connect with the right people, the greater your chances of success," he concluded.

Aditya's response reflected not only his plans but also the mindset with which he intended to pursue them. It was clear he aimed to build a strong foundation to rise to the challenges of entrepreneurship.

I listened as Aditya outlined the precautions one must take when exercising influence. "Influence, while powerful, comes with its own set of risks and requires a careful approach," I interjected, affirming the weight of his insights.

"Indeed," Aditya nodded. "It's crucial to identify and engage with stakeholders who align with our objectives. Targeting the right individuals is a delicate process—one must balance making meaningful connections with avoiding the trap of seeming overbearing."

I leaned in, encouraging him to elaborate, eager to hear how he planned to walk this tightrope.

Aditya continued, his tone a blend of caution and enthusiasm. "Persistence is key in our quest for influence, but it must not cross into the territory of intrusion. Every interaction should add value—not just serve our own ends."

His points resonated with me, reflecting my own experiences in the industry. It was imperative to communicate effectively—to be clear and consistent—to avoid misunderstandings that could jeopardize long-term relationships.

"And protecting one's own interests is a crucial aspect of influence," Aditya added, almost as a reminder to himself. "We must engage with an open mind yet remain vigilant, always aware of the balance between sharing and safeguarding our vision."

I appreciated the thoughtfulness Aditya was applying to his approach. It wasn't just about the mechanics of influence but also the ethics and strategic thinking it required. His foresight was impressive, revealing a maturity beyond his years and an understanding that influence, when handled with care, could be a cornerstone of entrepreneurial success.

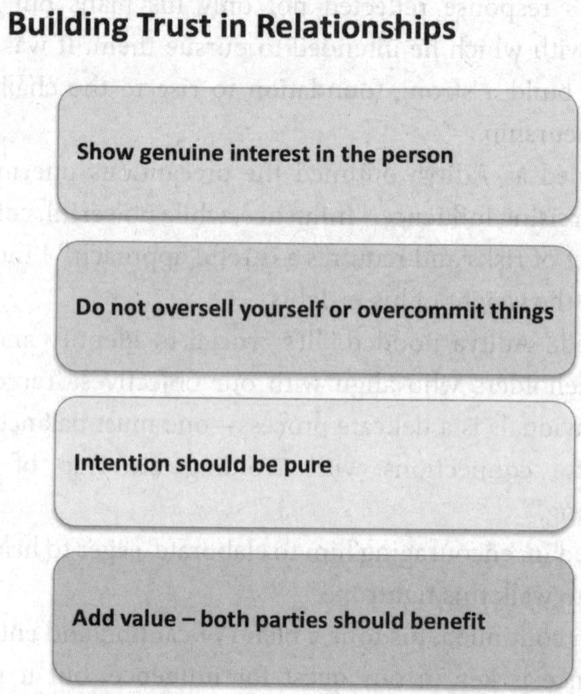

Aditya's acknowledgement of the fundamental role of genuine interest struck a chord with me. "Yes, I recall emphasizing that point," I said, reflecting on the essential nature of authenticity in building influence. "Genuine interest in the people you engage with is the bedrock of any lasting relationship. Pretense isn't just transparent—it's counterproductive. If you feign interest, it will inevitably be exposed, and the damage to your reputation could be irreparable."

He nodded, absorbing the weight of that truth. Authenticity wasn't a tactic but a core value that would define his entrepreneurial journey and the integrity of his venture. Seeing this understanding in Aditya reassured me that his vision was grounded in principles that foster trust and credibility.

Aditya's points aligned with the core values of any successful relationship, and I found myself nodding in agreement. "Absolutely," I affirmed. "Having the right intent is as crucial as showing genuine interest. It's important to promise only what you can deliver. Overcommitting or overselling sets unrealistic expectations and can tarnish your credibility."

Watching Aditya, I could see the gears turning, ideas clicking into place. It was critical for him to understand that true influence wasn't manipulation but the creation of shared value. This understanding would be the keystone not just of his current ambitions but his entire entrepreneurial career.

Aditya's grasp of the concept of mutual value was commendable. "Understand this point and always give the other person a reason to value their association with you," I affirmed, impressed with his preparation.

"Bingo! You are well prepared, and yes, most of what you've articulated is correct. The 'R' and the 'I,' as I mentioned, will aid you in these endeavors. It's like what I've experienced in my own career, and I've shared some of those lessons with you," I said, feeling proud of his diligence.

Riya, who had been critical at first, couldn't help but express her admiration. "Wow, Aditya, you've actually taken the effort to understand these concepts thoroughly," she complimented with newfound respect. She elaborated that in the latest season of Shark Tank India, Season 3, she observed numerous entrepreneurs who, despite being bootstrapped, managed to achieve profitability from their first year. She attributed this success to the entrepreneurs' thorough planning and strategic thinking, akin to the guidance provided by Aditya. Their ability to anticipate every minute detail was commendable, and their profitability and success impressed the Sharks as well. To me, Shark Tank exemplifies how young entrepreneurs can drive change by organizing their operations effectively to turn visions into reality.

Before concluding the discussion with Aditya, I decided to share another anecdote to add even more value to our conversation. *This story comes from a well-known and highly respected news anchor, Mr. Vineet Malhotra. Vineet is a senior consulting editor and a prime-time anchor at a leading news channel. His experiences and insights, drawn from a career in journalism, promise to enrich our understanding and perspective on the matter at hand.*

When I asked him what R.I.C.H.™ meant to him, he quickly retorted that there is a popular album—a classic—titled Get Rich or Die Trying. As extreme as it may sound, the phrase does have some granular realities that signify the tenets of success. Having been part of the media for almost two decades, he said it is only fair to say that without certain rules, it is difficult to sustain, survive, and succeed in a world where new stakeholders are popping up incessantly.

He felt that my mantra for success—or as he likes to call it, successful survival—has been a 'Ram Baan' (Ram's Arrow) for him. In it, he found some easy fallback options when he was confused and some disciplines to remember when things went wrong. It is abbreviated as R.I.C.H.™, and rightly so, it made him richer in every way. He further states that wealth is not always about money. What good is a billionaire in a grave? He then explains how it helped him.

Vineet is a news and sports anchor, and as such, he constantly deals with multiple challenges. The media—and news media in particular—can be ruthless at times, requiring one to always be on their toes to perform at their best.

In his words, the industry is good and great, but there are some key challenges news anchors face:

1. ***Intense competition***: *The news industry is highly competitive, with multiple channels vying for viewership and ratings.*
2. ***Rapid news cycle***: *Keeping up with the fast-paced news cycle and delivering breaking news accurately is a constant challenge.*
3. ***Maintaining credibility***: *News anchors must uphold the highest standards of journalism and credibility in an era of fake news and misinformation.*

Vineet wanted to share a particular case. A couple of years ago, he had to interview a well-known politician who was doing exceptional work in his constituency. Unfortunately, a few weeks before their scheduled interview, the politician had appeared on a different channel. That interview was manipulated through clever editing, portraying him in a shallow and demeaning light.

Because of this experience, the politician was hesitant about proceeding with Vineet's interview and had almost decided not to participate. When Vineet learned of this, he knew he had to act. First, they had already announced the exclusive interview to their viewers; secondly, they couldn't allow someone else's mistake to harm their channel's reputation.

Vineet immediately sprang into action and contacted the politician's Personal Assistant (PA) to request a meeting. Thankfully, the PA agreed. During their meeting, the PA provided Vineet with all the details surrounding the previous interview incident, which reinforced Vineet's belief that the situation was unfair. After careful consideration, Vineet scheduled a meeting with the politician for the following day, which the PA graciously arranged.

The next day, Vineet met with the politician as planned. The politician was curious about the "magic" that had compelled the correspondent from the rival channel, who had mishandled his previous interview, to call and offer an apology. Furthermore, they had promised to promptly remove the interview from all social media platforms.

Vineet was elated that the politician was now at ease and readily agreed to proceed with the interview on their channel. He kept his promise and appeared for the interview two weeks later. The interview was a resounding success, restoring the recognition he deserved for his commendable work.

Throughout this process, the R.I.C.H.™ model played a pivotal role for Vineet. Firstly, consider Resourcefulness (R). Vineet's ability to establish a good rapport with the politician's PA proved crucial. He had always maintained a positive and cordial relationship with the PA, recognizing the potential need for such assistance in challenging situations. Additionally, his resourcefulness helped him to be well-prepared with exclusive information—akin to a gold mine in the news industry. Thanks to Vineet's resourcefulness, media professionals from rival channels also reached out to him, realizing the value of maintaining contact with Vineet.

This leads us to the Influence (I) aspect. Vineet's ability to influence the decision-making process of the PA, the politician, and even the correspondent from the rival channel played a significant role in resolving the situation. Without his resourcefulness and established relationships, such influence might not have been possible.

When Vineet engaged with the correspondent from the rival channel, he adopted a commanding position. This is where Commanding (C) came into play. Vineet says he emphasized the importance of cooperation between their channels. His commanding presence, backed by the strength of his resourcefulness and influence, was evident to all parties involved. He was determined not to accept a 'no' for an answer, especially when the situation warranted a fair resolution.

To Vineet, the R.I.C.H.™ principles were instrumental in this successful outcome, and he feels grateful that they have become ingrained as habits (H) in his professional approach. He naturally thinks in this direction, and it consistently yields positive results.

Imagine the scenario if Vineet hadn't cultivated the resourcefulness, influence, and commanding abilities that he had. He might have lost this valuable opportunity, given that the politician was a prominent figure and his presence on their channel held significant importance. These were the words of Vineet himself.

Vineet says that my concepts and the R.I.C.H.™ philosophy represent a state of mind that must be cultivated through daily practice. The beauty of this concept lies in its simplicity and effectiveness. While one may not apply it consistently to every aspect of life, it is a life skill and a tool that helps individuals reach their desired goals. He further says that in his role as a TV anchor and as someone who has been part of historical events through news channels, maintaining a sense of grounding and discipline is impossible without embracing a tenet such as R.I.C.H.™

"Wow! That was insightful. I'm even more confident in our R.I.C.H.™ approach now," Aditya exclaimed. Riya, too, felt uplifted by the anecdote, seeing it as a morale booster for their endeavors. The story strengthened their resolve and belief in their project's potential.

Aditya's face lit up with a mixture of relief and gratitude. "Thank you, Mehul sir, and Riya," he said just as the doorbell interrupted their discussion.

I excused myself to answer the door and returned carrying food packets, the aroma immediately filling the room. "Okay, guys, break time. Come, let's enjoy your favorite thin-crust pizza," I announced, ready to shift our intense discussion into a more relaxed atmosphere over a shared meal.

"Wow, pizza… are we really having a mid-morning snack?" Riya asked, excitement clear in her voice.

"Absolutely," I smiled. "I figured you'd all be hungry by now, so why not throw a little pizza party? Besides, after Aditya's exceptional and insightful presentation, it seems only fitting to celebrate."

We eagerly tucked into the hot, crispy thin-crust pizza, the cheese melting decadently with each bite.

As the mid-morning gathering wound down, Aditya, beaming with satisfaction, couldn't hide his excitement. "I can't express how grateful I am for your support with the 'R' and the 'I' components," he said. "And I have a hunch you're going to appreciate the 'C' and the 'H' just as much."

"Wait, wait, wait—while I appreciate your compliments and I'm tempted to pat myself on the back, I must emphasize that these are merely guidelines. It's essential to remain flexible and resilient, adapting them to different situations. Achieving this requires dedication and hard work. So, while it's great to feel happy, it's crucial not to become complacent and to always be prepared for any circumstance," I cautioned.

"Point taken," Riya said with a smile.

We soon returned to the living room, where I urged Aditya to continue his explanation. Now fully in his element, he began enthusiastically.

"So, after that delightful and rich pizza, I'm even more charged up to delve into my 'C' and 'H.' With the 'R' and 'I'—those two mischievous little mischiefs—now tamed and in sync, the 'C' and 'H' should be relatively straightforward. However, they do require a strong sense of discipline, as we saw in Vineet's anecdote," Aditya explained, gearing up to elaborate.

"Now, my 'C' will, of course, be to..."

"I need to ensure that I'm following the direction I'm meant to. If I find myself straying off course, it's critical to notice and realign with my intended path. Commanding is about control, which, in turn, is about caring for the situation. Like Vineet did when he refused to accept 'no' for an answer—he wanted to keep the situation under his control. That is exactly what I intend to do.

I will make sure that I care for both myself and the purpose of my activities. For instance, if I'm unable to connect with a person or navigate an unfamiliar situation, I won't let my focus and energy waver. Instead, I'll harness my resources to find alternative solutions.

This is where my 'R' becomes invaluable. With the resources I've accumulated, it's likely I have a substantial reserve to draw upon as I progress, and this will assist with my 'C.' Am I on the right track, Mehul sir?"

"Yes, you've grasped it well," I confirmed. "Command is about maintaining composure—resisting jitters or nerves when faced with unexpected challenges. It's about having your resources ready, using them effectively when one approach fails, and being prepared to address any issues swiftly without losing sight of the overall goal."

Aditya's understanding reflected the principles I was trying to impart to him and Riya. He was nearly done, and within a few more minutes of discussion, he had completed his explanation—a perfect illustration for any newcomer eager to understand the R.I.C.H.™ model.

"Well, Aditya, I must say I'm quite impressed. You've absorbed everything I've shared, and now we're sailing in the same direction. With your permission, Mehul Sir," Riya said, glancing at me for approval, "I'd like to add that I'm planning to open my own art studio. My vision is to blend technology with art and create a platform where people can freely express their creativity. I imagine an app that lets users design whatever they envision and transfer it onto a digital canvas—free from the pressure of public approval. It wouldn't just be a gateway for imagination, but would also offer a suite of design features to elevate their creations."

"Good initiative, Riya," I responded, intrigued. "It sounds like you've given this some serious thought. The idea is compelling. Could you elaborate a bit more so we get a fuller picture?"

Riya nodded, ready to share her vision. "Mine might not be as detailed as Aditya's just yet, but let me give you the essence, as it's along similar lines." She paused, collecting her thoughts.

"Now that I've discovered my Ikigai, it's time to roll out my R.I.C.H.™ For the 'R', I need to gather all the resources relevant to the field of art I want to pursue.

That includes deciding exactly what I want to do, and identifying the means to ensure I have the necessary tools—for example, basic art supplies, understanding both domestic and international market trends, and pinpointing platforms where I can showcase and sell my work."

Continuing from where Riya left off:

"Similarly, my 'I' involves building a network with other artists and immersing myself in the art community. This kind of networking is vital for my growth and deeper understanding of the art world."

"And when it comes to 'Command,' I must maintain control, much like Aditya is doing. It's one thing to talk about plans and another to execute them. I need to be ready for the many challenges ahead and navigate through them with resilience and adaptability."

"Hmmm… that sounds promising. Of course, you'll need to flesh this out more thoroughly, but I understand the essence of what you're saying. The critical point here is identifying at least three main areas within the art field that you wish to pursue. Art is a broad concept, so you'll need to pinpoint what you're truly passionate about—this will become your central focus."

"You can then ensure your resources are aligned. They must be relevant and purposeful," I advised, emphasizing the importance of strategic planning.

Aditya chimed in supportively, "Exactly, that's the first step. Once you've gathered your 'R' resources, starting your 'I'—the integration and networking—won't be such a hassle. By then, you'll have a clearer understanding of the landscape, making the process more intuitive."

"Yes, Mr. Einstein," Riya quipped, casting a playful look at Aditya, her voice tinged with mirth. "I'll get right on that."

Aditya, energized by the exchange, sought affirmation. "Thanks to both of you for listening so patiently. I'm pretty sure I've earned a brownie point now, haven't I, Mehul Sir?" His enthusiasm was evident.

I laughed along with them. "Of course, you both have earned your points. And Riya, since you're still in the planning phase, you get one point. Aditya, you get two points for your progress," I declared, appreciating their efforts and the friendly competition unfolding.

Receiving a round of appreciative hoots from Aditya and Riya, I felt a sense of accomplishment. "I'm pleased to see you both aligning with this model—recognizing how it can best serve your individual needs and guide you forward. This level of comprehension and understanding," I said, pausing for effect, "is what I like to call the 'theory of serenity.'"

"'Theory of serenity'—what is that?" Riya inquired, her curiosity clearly piqued.

I took a moment before answering, wanting to express the concept as clearly as possible. "Serenity refers to a state of being calm, peaceful, and untroubled. When you reach a point in life where you have clarity about what you want to do and how you intend to progress, it's akin to achieving a state of serenity. Believe me, most people wander through life without truly understanding what they want, where they're going, or how to reach their goals. But you two have attained that clarity. That's why I call it the 'theory of serenity,'" I elaborated, hoping to convey the deep sense of peace and direction that comes with such understanding.

"Oh, wow… that's an intriguing concept… I'm on this path of self-reformation," Aditya said, sparking a wave of laughter among us.

Reflecting on our journey together, I shared my thoughts. "You know, there's an essential principle we should always remember: the value of a friendly attitude. From the moment we started our conversation that day at the airport, when you both picked me up and showed your eagerness to learn and grow, I was genuinely taken aback. Initially, I thought it might be a short-lived enthusiasm—something that would last a week or two at most," I confessed, appreciating the depth of their commitment.

"Short-lived? Could you clarify, Mehul sir?" Riya asked, a hint of confusion in her voice.

With over two decades of experience to draw upon, I knew she needed a thoughtful response. "Throughout my career, I've observed that it takes a remarkable level of dedication and perseverance to truly turn aspirations into reality. It's not something everyone can sustain. Many begin their journeys full of enthusiasm and bursts of positive energy, but too often that initial spark fades. They lose focus, fall into monotony, and eventually give up on their goals. That's what I meant when I said you might 'lose it'—the drive, the steady effort, the persistent dedication," I explained to Riya, hoping to impart some wisdom about the endurance success demands.

"Ha-ha… I'm glad you didn't either. It's been months since we began working with this model, and you both have shown remarkable dedication. You're not just learning; you're adapting and evolving, aiming to harness this model to its fullest potential—to program yourselves for success and achieve your goals," Aditya said, his commitment clear.

"Yes, and I'm grateful for all the knowledge we've gained. It has indeed provided us with a clear path to follow. I'm with Aditya on this," Riya added, her voice reflecting a sense of accomplishment and determination.

"Thanks, guys! I'm delighted to have been of assistance. Now, because I'm really impressed with both of you, let's dive into a quick exercise. Are you up for it?" I asked.

"Absolutely! If it's related to our learning, then Aditya and I are all in," Riya responded with an eager nod.

"Great! I've spoken about attitude. You two have demonstrated a remarkable attitude, which is why you've been able to stick it out this long and absorb so much," I acknowledged their perseverance and then segued into the task at hand. "In keeping with that spirit, let's evaluate how well you truly understand the concept of attitude. I'd like you both to engage with this little exercise I've prepared."

Saying this, I laid out a sheet in front of them containing the exercise below.

Tool to embrace learning:

A. What are the factors that determine our attitude? OR how do we really develop our attitude?

B. What are the consequences of a negative attitude?

@Home

@Work

@Social

C. What are the pros of a positive attitude?

@Home

@Work

@Social

What in your opinion are the steps to build a positive attitude?

"I'm done," Riya exclaimed, a sense of accomplishment in her voice.

I glanced over her work and, with a nod of approval, gave her a thumbs-up. It's always gratifying to see eagerness and determination come to fruition. We then turned our attention to Aditya, giving him space to concentrate.

After a few more minutes, Aditya also announced his completion. "Finished," he said with a confident smile.

I gathered their sheets, eager to see how they had applied their understanding to the exercise. This was more than just a test of knowledge—it was a showcase of their attitude and growth. The sense of achievement was palpable as both Aditya and Riya reflected on the exercise.

"Phew! That really made me think hard. Yet, it was incredibly valuable. It's fascinating how much you can learn about your own attitude," Aditya said, rubbing his temple but smiling.

Riya shared her insights as well. "It's been revealing to observe how my attitude shifts in different environments—whether at work, at home, or in social settings. It's like seeing a mirror of my cognitive patterns and how they adapt without me even realizing it," she said, her voice filled with wonder and understanding.

I felt a surge of pride. "I'm glad you both found the exercise valuable. Keep these insights in mind and continue cultivating your attitude. Remember, it's a process of 'rethinking'—unconsciously molding yourself to rise to the level where you can tackle any challenge head-on," I said earnestly. "As professionals, being ready to embrace challenges is key."

Watching Aditya and Riya, I could tell they felt fulfilled, knowing today had added another layer to their growth. It was clear they were building a strong foundation for future success.

My Window of Wisdom

"Lord Krishna said, 'Meet the transient world with neither grasping nor fear, trust the unfolding of life, and you will attain true serenity.'"

- This teaching encourages an attitude of openness and acceptance, suggesting that peace comes from embracing life's flow without excessive attachment or aversion. It's about finding balance and harmony within the ever-changing tapestry of existence.
- To cultivate serenity, one must approach life with positivity and right thinking, without succumbing to fear. This mindset creates an environment where calmness and peace can thrive, both within oneself and in one's surroundings. It's about letting go of negative patterns and embracing a more affirmative outlook on life's journey.

- Life will inevitably unfold in unexpected ways, and the best approach is to meet it with preparedness. Surprises catch us off guard when we are unready or fail to anticipate potential outcomes.
- While it's true that unforeseen situations cannot be entirely avoided, developing a wide range of options for yourself offers a sense of control and the ability to choose how to respond, which fosters greater serenity.
- By preparing and understanding what you want from life, fear diminishes, placing you in the driver's seat, better equipped to navigate life's challenges.
- Aditya and Riya utilized the R.I.C.H.™ framework to clarify their desires and focus their efforts effectively, envisioning their paths with precision and care.
- This strategic approach prepared them not only for the enjoyable aspects of their journey but also significantly boosted their confidence. Knowing how to capitalize on opportunities expands possible outcomes, leaving them better equipped to handle life's varied scenarios.
- Conversely, imagine facing challenges unprepared—life's hurdles come at you haphazardly. You might catch some, but others slip by, or you may find yourself stuck, leading to confusion, indifference, or despair.
- Equipping yourself and being ready by developing your personal theory and stage of serenity is essential.
- This approach calls for taking initiative to shape your experiences and reactions to life's events, fostering a tranquil state of mind. It's a call to create a personal framework that guides you toward inner peace and resilience.

CHAPTER 6

Alley of the Silicon Valley

"Set your heart upon your work, but never its reward."

—Lord Krishna

That night marked a significant milestone for both Aditya and Riya. It was a time of profound discovery when they not only identified their own raison d'être but also crafted a well-structured plan for the journey ahead. Often, we get tangled in the idea that meticulous planning is the key to success. On one such occasion, I told them that while planning is important, it's not the be-all and end-all. What truly matters is understanding the 'why' behind our actions, which naturally guides the 'how' of our plans.

The confusion on their faces was clear, and I realized my message might have been a bit perplexing for Aditya and Riya.

"Let me clarify," I said, trying to ease the furrows of confusion between their brows. "We often believe that to succeed, we must plan meticulously. While planning is a valuable tool, it's not the sole determinant of success. What's truly indispensable is the purpose behind your actions—your 'why.' It's this purpose that gives your plans meaning and direction, not the act of planning itself."

I paused to let that sink in, hoping to bridge the gap between confusion and understanding.

"See, planning without a clear intent is like setting sail without a compass. Yes, you're moving, but where to? The clarity of your destination—the reason you embark on the journey—is what matters most. That's the key to not just planning, but planning effectively," I continued, hoping to turn their confusion into a moment of revelation.

On a radiant, sunlit day, Riya found herself among a gathering of art industry connoisseurs. She had carefully cultivated her resources and used her influence to carve out a niche within this creative circle. The assembly, made up of active experts, met quarterly to engage in robust discussions, share insights, and exchange groundbreaking ideas in the art world. For Riya, these meetings were more than just informational—they were invigorating. They gave her a chance to expand her network, stay abreast of industry trends, and most importantly, interact with some of the most esteemed and innovative artists in the field. Each conversation, each new connection, was a brushstroke on the canvas of her growing career.

The enigmatic statement, "Planning is important but not essential," continued to occupy Aditya and Riya's thoughts. It was a question that persisted, nagging at them day by day. They couldn't help but wonder why I had emphasized this perspective. What deeper layers of wisdom lay beneath these words? They were driven by a fervent desire to uncover the true significance of this message and how it intertwined with their personal journey.

Meanwhile, Aditya found himself caught in a whirlwind of academic responsibilities—vivas and assignments—while tirelessly advancing his entrepreneurial venture. Together with Riya, he grasped the importance of unwavering focus—a concept they had previously explored when they introduced themselves along with their R.I.C.H.™ framework. They were acutely aware that having the right ingredients was pivotal to the successful realization of their plans.

Unable to bear the suspense any longer, Aditya decided to visit Riya. He was eager to share his thoughts and seek her help in decoding the cryptic statement that had been weighing on their minds. To his surprise, Riya was just as perplexed as he was.

"You know, Aditya," Riya began, her brows furrowing in confusion, "I'm not entirely sure either. I mean, I understand the importance of planning, but I can't grasp why Mehul sir said it's not essential. Aren't we always taught that having a well-structured plan is a fundamental principle, especially in management?"

As their mentor, I introduced this concept intending to spark thoughtful reflection and encourage them to explore unconventional approaches to achieving their goals. While I firmly believe in the value of planning, it was crucial to convey that rigidly adhering to a plan might stifle adaptability and hinder creative problem-solving.

I was heartened by their determination to decipher the message's meaning and its relevance to their journey of self-discovery and the pursuit of success. It was a testament to their growth and willingness to embrace new perspectives. I recognized that this journey of exploration would ultimately contribute significantly to their personal and professional development.

Sitting comfortably in a cozy bean bag, I was deep in my own world, engrossed with my phone, patiently waiting for Aditya to reply. Despite my intense gaze and gentle prodding, he seemed miles away, completely unaware of my presence. My frustration was building when suddenly Riya's sharp, commanding voice cut through the silence, almost physically jolting him awake.

"Aditya, are you even listening?" Riya demanded, her irritation obvious as she echoed the question I had in mind.

Aditya was visibly startled by Riya's loud voice; his body jerked as if snapped back to the present by a rubber band. "Oh, sorry," he fumbled, clearly embarrassed. "I was lost in thought. Yes, I'm listening now, and I agree with you both—planning is indeed important."

Riya couldn't hide her exasperation as she confronted him. "You weren't even listening, were you?" Her irritation was clear as day.

Aditya's demeanor shifted quickly, a spark of enthusiasm igniting in his eyes. "I'm confident that Mehul sir can make sense of this. But let's shift gears for a moment. What if we organize a quick weekend getaway? It's been too long since we've all been together. We'll have a chance to catch up, and we could even bring this up with Mehul sir. How does that sound?" he proposed, palpable excitement in his voice.

Riya's response came with a hint of sarcasm tinged with amusement. "Sounds like a plan… oh god, more plans…" And with that, laughter shared between them cut through any lingering frustration.

The excitement was contagious as we delved into the plans for our weekend escape. Mr. and Mrs. Roy were immediately on board with the splendid idea. Even I felt a surge of anticipation for the upcoming adventure.

Then came Sunday, and we all gathered at Riya's place, buzzing with the thrill of what lay ahead.

"Good morning, friends! How are we all doing today?" I greeted everyone as I arrived at the Roys' doorstep.

Mr. Roy returned my greeting with a warm smile, his tone light and teasing. "Ah, Mehul, great to see you! It seems you've become closer friends with these two than we are. We barely get the chance to catch up, buddy," he joked, nodding towards Aditya and Riya, who were brimming with enthusiasm for the weekend plans.

As we settled in at the Roys' residence, the atmosphere brimmed with the warm familiarity of friendship. I couldn't help but remark, with a twinkle in my eye, that Aditya and Riya certainly knew how to keep me actively engaged. Aditya casually mentioned that we still had more to discuss, and I couldn't resist teasing them about their apparent scheme to tap into my insights once again. Riya's laughter, light and knowing, echoed my sentiments, confirming the playful conspiracy in our midst.

As I overheard Mrs. Roy chiming in from the next room, her words piqued my interest. She urged us to put aside our serious discussions in favor of the lighthearted spirit of our trip. I couldn't help but laugh along, assuring her that I'd make sure our conversation stayed in the realm of fun. I turned to Riya, curiosity alight in my eyes, and playfully asked what topic they were planning to explore with me this time.

Mrs. Roy's interjection from the other room caught my attention, reminding us that this trip was about fun, not serious discussions. With a chuckle, I reassured her that any discussion we had would be enjoyable. Turning to Riya with a smile, I asked her to enlighten me about what they were eager to delve into.

Riya, with a slight furrow in her brow, brought up a phrase I had once mentioned: "Planning is important but not essential." She was puzzled by the idea, as they had always valued planning as a key part of starting any endeavor.

I pondered her question for a moment and then, steering the conversation toward our immediate adventure, asked where we were headed for the day.

Aditya, catching on to where I might be going with this, answered with a hint of amusement that we were heading to a beach spot to unwind and perhaps enjoy some delicious seafood.

In response to the quizzical looks from Aditya and Riya, I proposed a small challenge to shed light on the conundrum they had presented me. "Okay, I'd like you both to detail our trip to the beach," I said. "Tell me the mode of transport we'll use, account for the expenses including fuel, tolls, and wear and tear, estimate the time it will take, and consider any other factors you believe will contribute to the enjoyment of our trip."

Aditya and Riya seemed stumped, unsure of where I was leading. Riya's confusion was evident when she asked why this exercise was necessary and how it related to their initial question.

With a reassuring tone, I promised Riya that the relevance of this task would soon become clear. I gave them both five minutes to plan and jot down the details I requested on a piece of paper, instructing them to keep their plans secret until they handed them to me.

Mr. Roy's enthusiasm was infectious as he anticipated the outcome of my little experiment. "This is going to be great… the fun has already started," he laughed heartily.

Aditya and Riya set to work immediately, furiously scribbling down their thoughts and plans, each fully absorbed in the task. The ticking clock added a sense of urgency, while Mr. and Mrs. Roy watched with eager curiosity, trying to catch a glimpse of what was being written. They seemed as excited by the process as by the outcome.

Soon enough, Aditya and Riya handed me their papers, their faces a mix of expectation and uncertainty. I glanced over their plans with a growing smile. "So, you both believe these are the perfect plans for our trip?" I asked.

Aditya, seeking validation, asked if there was something wrong with his plan. Still smiling, I assured him that we were all set and that any gaps in our planning would reveal themselves in due course. With that assurance lingering in the air, we set off for the beach, ready to enjoy whatever the day might bring.

The engine of the sleek SUV purred to life as we made our way out of the housing society, the city's silhouette receding behind us. Mr. Roy was at the wheel, lost in melodies from the 60s and 70s, his enjoyment evident as we hit the open highway.

The journey took a playful turn when Mrs. Roy proposed a game of Antakshri, a classic Indian game where participants sing songs based on the last consonant of the previous one. We all leapt at the idea, thrilled to join the musical contest. The teams were swiftly decided: Mr. and Mrs. Roy versus us 'millennials' and me.

Mr. Roy, brimming with confidence, teased that they would surely be the victors, especially when it came to Hindi songs. He looked at me with a triumphant grin, almost certain of their impending victory.

Our singing was interrupted by the chaos of traffic; an overturned dumper ahead had caused an unexpected delay. Riya and Aditya, growing frustrated, couldn't help but recall the planning exercise I had given them earlier. They glanced at me, perhaps questioning their own preparations, as they remembered the papers they had handed over. Their expressions mixed confusion with irritation, and when I met their gaze with a calm smile, it seemed only to deepen their exasperation.

Eventually, we broke free from the traffic snarl. Thinking quickly, Mr. Roy decided to take a detour onto another road, hoping it would be faster. However, after driving a few miles, we encountered a toll booth. It dawned on us that this alternative route, though possibly avoiding more traffic, resulted in higher toll fees due to its longer distance. It was a practical lesson in the unforeseen turns even the best-laid plans might take.

As we pulled away from the toll booth, Aditya, curious about the unexpected expense, asked Mr. Roy about the toll we had just paid. Mr. Roy explained that while the usual highway route cost 80 rupees, this alternative road had a higher toll of 115 rupees because it was longer. Hearing this, Riya and Aditya exchanged glances, their thoughts inevitably returning to the chits they had written. When they looked at me, I offered the same knowing smile as before—a silent acknowledgment that this outcome was different from their written plans.

Despite the bumps and shakes on the road and the detour from our original plans, the journey was filled with laughter and songs, making the experience enjoyable. Upon finally arriving at our destination, Mrs. Roy noticed the slightly disheartened expressions on Aditya and Riya's faces and commented on the apparent unraveling of their plans, pointing out that the reality of our trip seemed quite different from what they had anticipated.

Riya's irritation was palpable as she blamed the traffic for any deviations from their plans. Mr. Roy, observing the exchanged smiles between the younger members of the group during the drive, hinted at his awareness of an underlying story. Mrs. Roy, sensing the tension, suggested they take some time to settle in and then reconvene at the beach shack to reflect on the day's unfolding events.

Once everyone had freshened up in their rooms, the group gathered at the shack by the beach, now enveloped in the approaching dusk. The tides were growing stronger, and the air was warm, reflecting the day's shifting moods. Dressed in shorts and t-shirts appropriate for the beach setting, Riya and Aditya joined Mr. and Mrs. Roy and me. Despite the casual, fun environment, it was clear that the outcome of our earlier planning exercise continued to weigh on the younger couple's minds.

Aditya's patience seemed to wear thin as he voiced his frustration. He insisted that the unforeseen events, including the detour and extra toll, weren't a result of his planning. He was confident that if they had taken the usual route, everything he had written down would have proven accurate.

Mr. Roy, Mrs. Roy, and I shared a moment of silence—a pause that seemed to stretch between us. Suddenly, the quiet was broken as we all erupted into laughter. This unexpected reaction left Aditya and Riya baffled, wondering what could have prompted such a merry outburst.

It was then that Riya began to grasp the lesson amidst our laughter. She quietly echoed the phrase I had mentioned earlier, realizing the truth in the words through their own experience. With a sudden burst of excitement, she exclaimed, finally understanding the concept that "planning is important but not essential."

Aditya's surprised expression at Riya's exclamation made me pause. It was clear he was still grappling with the day's unexpected twists. When Riya affirmed her new understanding, I sensed a teachable moment unfolding before us.

I prompted Aditya to revisit our morning conversation and describe the plan he had written. He explained his thorough calculations: a five-hour drive time, an 80-rupee toll cost, fuel expenses for 300 kilometers totaling a bit over 2,000 rupees, and even a lunch break at a specific spot. But reality diverged from his calculations, leading to a string of unplanned events and decisions—a stark contrast to the well-ordered plan he had envisioned. It was a firsthand demonstration of the lesson I hoped to impart: while planning is important, the ability to adapt is essential.

Riya echoed Aditya's sentiment, saying her plan was much like his. Still visibly perplexed, Aditya questioned the relevance of my earlier statement about planning.

When Riya volunteered to try unraveling the meaning, I nodded in agreement, intrigued to hear her take. Mr. and Mrs. Roy settled in, equally interested.

Clearing her throat with a touch of nervousness, Riya began. "The statement suggests that while planning is important, it's not the be-all and end-all. Today's events illustrated this perfectly. We meticulously planned our route, the costs, the timing, and even where we would take our break. From the standpoint of preparation, we did everything we could."

Her explanation unfolded, and I saw the beginnings of understanding in Aditya's eyes.

Riya grew more confident as she elaborated on how we had relied on two key resources for our planning: our past travel experiences and common sense to make educated guesses—essentially hypotheses.

Aditya added that he had also incorporated a friend's experience into his plan.

Riya continued, excitement growing as she reached the crux of the lesson. She proposed that while planning is a critical step, it's not the ultimate factor because even the best-laid plans can fall apart under unforeseen circumstances—just as ours did today. She looked to me for confirmation, eager to have grasped the concept I had introduced earlier.

Riya was on the right track, her understanding almost complete. "Yes, you are... although there is more to this, yet a good job... please continue," I encouraged her.

She took a deep breath, gathering her thoughts before proceeding. "Planning allows us to anticipate possible scenarios, which is certainly helpful. However, it doesn't prepare us for the actualities life may throw our way, which are often unpredictable. So, while planning is not the essential part, being prepared for the unexpected is. The ability to adapt to unforeseen events, sudden changes, and unpredicted outcomes—that's where the true essence lies." I nodded in agreement, pleased with her interpretation. It was a lesson well learned.

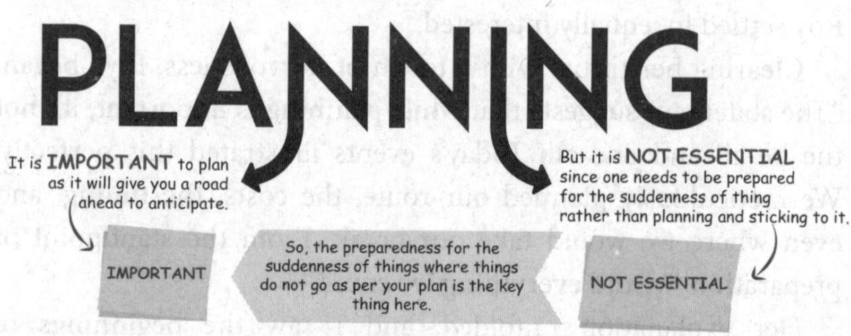

Aditya's realization dawned on him, his face reflecting a mixture of relief and understanding. "So, the statement isn't dismissing planning entirely. It's emphasizing that while planning is a useful guide, it's not infallible. Circumstances, like the ones we encountered today, can disrupt even the best plans. Instead of scrambling to devise a Plan B, it's more about being resourceful and adaptable to whatever situation arises," he summarized, looking between Riya and me for affirmation.

I smiled at them both, acknowledging Aditya's grasp of the concept. It was satisfying to see the lesson come full circle, understood and appreciated through the day's unexpected journey.

To further explain my earlier statement about planning, I decided to share an anecdote from Layth Gafoor, Founder of Lucentem Media. He neatly corroborates the failure of planning in crisis situations. He says it's interesting because we often talk about planning for a crisis and the best way to do that. However, in his experience managing these situations, the problems often stem from the culture within the organization. Even when plans are in place for different crises, a frenetic culture amplifies the crisis and worsens the situation regardless of the plans.

For that reason, we must focus on developing an approach rather than just a plan. This approach needs to be holistic and rooted within the organizational structure. Part of the importance of this methodology is that you can only plan for what you can see—what is inevitable or predictable. Crises, by nature, contradict these ideals. They are unpredictable and unique in how they develop and unfold. These are things you can't plan for because you often don't know what you're planning for. There are intricacies and nuances you can't predict. Therefore, preparedness for failure and the ability to immediately respond effectively is far more critical and necessary.

Mrs. Roy, following the thread of our conversation with keen interest, introduced a new angle—questioning the importance of having a contingency like Plan B. Her point was valid: being prepared for the unexpected is a form of planning.

Riya, recognizing the complexity of the question, playfully passed the baton back to me.

I chuckled, appreciating the depth of our discussion. "You're absolutely right, Mrs. Roy, and you've touched on the core issue. I'm not discounting the value of planning—it's an essential part of managing any aspect of life. The distinction I'm making is that it's not just about planning for a specific event, task, or project. It's about being prepared for life as a whole—being resourceful and adaptable so that when life inevitably throws a curveball, you're ready to catch it. And beyond that, it's about having the mindset and skills to not only manage but thrive, no matter what comes your way."

That's why Dwight D. Eisenhower's famous quote, "In preparing for battle I have always found that plans are useless, but planning is indispensable," is so relevant to the business decisions of law firms. It's often used to illustrate the importance of flexible thinking in the face of change.

The conversation remained lively, stirring thoughts about planning and adaptability as essential life skills.

Mr. Roy took a moment to reflect on everything that had been said. "I've seen Mehul face many challenges and setbacks over the years. Despite his talent and integrity, opportunities were often limited. But rather than dwell on disappointment, he forged his own path. He created and seized opportunities—showing what it truly means to plan for life. It's about being resilient and resourceful enough to thrive in any circumstance, as long as you're prepared to face it."

His words echoed the heart of our discussion: that life planning isn't just about preparing for what we expect, but being adaptable enough to create new paths when the unexpected arises.

Reflecting on the conversation, I decided to offer an example that might resonate with everyone. "Consider Thomas Edison," I began. "Famously, he didn't succeed in inventing the light bulb until his 10,000th attempt. When asked about his repeated failures, he said, 'I did not fail. I found 10,000 ways of not doing it.' What Edison meant was that he was always prepared for every outcome. Life isn't always straightforward or easy. For example, when I moved to the USA, there was always a part of me that felt uncertain. My logical mind was hesitant—but I went anyway, and ended up making a difference. And believe me, none of my plans unfolded the way I had imagined. What truly mattered was my readiness to adapt and face whatever came my way."

The group seemed to absorb this illustration, quietly mulling over the deeper significance of preparedness versus planning.

Aditya, intrigued by the brief glimpse into my past, asked me to share more about my time in the USA. Riya echoed his request—both eager to understand the real-life application of this philosophy. They wanted more than just theory; they wanted to know what it meant to be prepared when plans fall apart.

"I'll definitely share my experiences, but let's save that conversation for dinner," I suggested, glancing around at the group. "For now, let's all head to the beach and enjoy the waves," I added, signaling a shift from our deep discussion to some well-earned relaxation.

As we made our way to the shore, the evening unfurled beautifully before us. The sun dipped toward the horizon, casting a warm golden glow, and the waves danced rhythmically to the tune of the gentle sea breeze. After soaking in the sunset, we returned to the shack, ready to indulge in some delicious seafood.

Aditya, a true connoisseur, eagerly anticipated the spread before us. The prawn masala, grilled fish, and his specially ordered mojito—with just the right hint of lemon and ginger stirred into a fizzy blend of soda and ice—were exactly the kind of tropical delight he savored.

Mrs. Roy, noticing Aditya's enthusiasm, couldn't help but smile and comment on the joy evident in his demeanor as we all settled in for the evening feast.

Aditya's response to Mrs. Roy was filled with genuine appreciation for the feast before us. His comment drew a collective smile as we settled into the warmth of good company and good food.

With everyone tucking into their meals—Mrs. Roy with her vegetarian pasta and the rest of us enjoying the varied flavors of the coast—Riya, between bites of her fries and burger, prompted me to talk about my time in the USA.

I took a moment to collect my thoughts, savoring a spoonful of the rich chicken soup before speaking. "The last time we touched on this topic, I gave you a brief overview of my move to the USA. As you know, it was initially meant to be a short-term, two-month assignment. But as it turned out, that stint extended, and I found myself embracing life there for nearly three years," I recounted, ready to share more about that transformative period in my life.

Riya's enthusiasm for my story was clear, and her question about the practicalities of my stay was a fair one. With a light chuckle at her eagerness, I clarified the misconception.

"My family never pressured me to migrate; they encouraged me to seize the opportunity to explore and enjoy the experience. They knew I was doing well here, so the idea was more about broadening my horizons than settling abroad. I was content with my life and wasn't looking to leave everything behind without a good reason. But then, as life would have it, an unexpected opportunity arose that changed my perspective," I reminisced, hinting at the serendipitous event that led me to make the leap.

Mr. Roy, adding his perspective, highlighted what he called the R.I.C.H.™ concept—a framework I'd lived by without realizing it. It stood for Resources, Influence, Command, and Habit, all of which I had relied on. He emphasized my preparedness and readiness to seize the moment when opportunity arose.

"Yes, you've got it right, Roy," I agreed. "When it comes to the saying 'Planning is important but not essential,' it's about recognizing that while I had plans, they weren't set in stone. I couldn't predict the future. The brief assignment in the USA didn't promise much financial stability—not even enough to cover my rent. But I saw it as a chance to enrich my R.I.C.H.™—to expand my influence, to learn, to grow my resources through knowledge. That's why I went, and that's why I stayed open to possibilities—because sometimes, that's what life planning is all about."

My journey in the USA was about more than just a change of scenery—it was about expanding my horizons, meeting new people, and increasing my influence. The certainty I needed came from my own skills and my ability to handle whatever came my way. I had to be clear on what I wanted to achieve and how I planned to go about it.

Aditya, momentarily distracted from the culinary delight before him, raised a valid question about whether I had a plan when I first set out, and how that plan unfolded.

I smiled, acknowledging his curiosity. "Yes, I had a plan—everyone does when they embark on a new chapter. But the reality was that the situation on the ground was fluid, constantly changing. The plan served as a starting point, a guide, but flexibility and adaptability in the face of new challenges were paramount. When I say planning is not essential, I mean that rigidly sticking to a plan isn't the key; it's about using a plan as a roadmap while being ready to take detours as needed. It was this adaptability that allowed me to navigate the unknowns and uncertainties of a new environment."

That adaptability, that readiness to face unexpected challenges, ultimately made the difference for me. It wasn't just about having a plan, but about modifying it, learning and growing with each new experience, and using every resource at my disposal to create opportunities for success.

Riya's curiosity was evident as she pressed further on how I navigated the challenges in the US and managed to accomplish significant work despite the odds.

Mrs. Roy, having finished her meal, interjected with a gentle tease about the kids' enthusiasm overshadowing the conversation, playfully suggesting they give me a chance to tell my story. I couldn't help but smile at their eagerness. "In truth, I didn't have a detailed plan. I knew my objectives and the broad strokes of what I needed to do. Dublin, where I was to complete my assignment, lies in the heart of Silicon Valley—one of the most expensive regions to live in. The financial aspect was challenging; my remuneration barely covered living expenses. However, I saw this as an opportunity to implement and test my R.I.C.H.™ model—embracing learning, exploration, and the chance to validate my ideas. So despite the financial constraints, I dove in with the intent to adapt and make the most of the situation."

If it had been someone else in my shoes, they might have assessed the opportunity in the US solely in terms of financial gain and possibly declined it, given the need to dip into personal savings. Indeed, I ended up using some of my savings from India because the cost of living was steep, and the salary didn't cover all my expenses.

That was precisely why I couldn't rely on a rigid plan. I had to be flexible and adapt as circumstances arose. My experience proved the truth of the adage I often mention: "Planning is important but not essential." My initial plan was to work in the US for three months, using my savings to sustain myself and gain as much experience as possible before returning home.

But the essence of why planning wasn't essential in my case lay in the dynamic nature of life, especially in a new and unfamiliar environment. You can't predict how things will pan out, so you must be ready for any eventuality. This is where my R.I.C.H.™ model came into play, making the journey not just bearable but intriguing.

As our meal concluded and a gentle breeze began to tousle our hair, Mrs. Roy remarked on the pleasantness of the wind—a refreshing change from the stifling city air. She suggested we continue our conversation with a walk along the beach, letting the meal settle as the evening unfolded with the soothing sounds of waves accompanying our steps.

Mr. Roy's comment about his beer belly lightened the mood further, and we all gathered ourselves, ready for a leisurely walk on the sand.

Riya summarized my journey succinctly, understanding that I had ventured to the US with a singular assignment in mind, relying on my savings to keep afloat and prepared to return if things didn't pan out. She was curious about the turning point in my stay.

As we trod along the cool sand, I began to share the continuation of my story. "Once I found my footing with a place to stay and became acquainted with my work, I leveraged my R.I.C.H.™ model to expand my opportunities. However, this wasn't without its fair share of challenges." I was ready to delve into the obstacles I faced and the pivotal moments that marked my time in Silicon Valley.

Walking along the beach, with the sound of the waves in the background, I recounted the initial struggles I faced upon arriving in Silicon Valley. "I was the new guy in town and barely knew a handful of people. Unfortunately, the few acquaintances I had weren't very welcoming. It seems these days, people are reluctant to extend a hand unless there's something in it for them," I explained, reflecting on the cold reception I received.

"The second challenge was my non-tech background. Here I was, a guy skilled in sales, marketing, and training, trying to make it in the tech capital of the world. It was daunting, considering how heavily the Valley leans toward technical expertise."

I then touched on the issue of transportation, a logistical hurdle that affected my daily life. "Without a car, I relied on public transit and ride-sharing services like Uber to get around. The buses and trains weren't reliable due to infrequent schedules, and constantly using Uber was prohibitively expensive—especially on a tight budget."

I sighed, feeling the cool night air against my face, reflecting on the resourcefulness required to overcome these challenges. "The dilemma was balancing the need to be economical while ensuring I could get around to pursue potential job opportunities. I had to be careful not to deplete my savings. It was a test of managing limited resources while striving to build a life in a new and demanding environment."

The stakes were high, but my determination to make the most of my time in the US was higher. Subconsciously, I began applying the principles of my R.I.C.H.™ model—Resources, Influence, Command, and Habit. This mindset led me to an unexpected opportunity on social media. I connected with an Indian leader of a large community group who organized events for Indian festivals and cultural celebrations. He was looking for collaborators, and I saw a glimmer of possibility.

Aditya, ever enthusiastic, jumped to the conclusion that this was my big break. But Mr. Roy, with the wisdom of experience, cautioned him to wait and hear the full story.

Indeed, it wasn't that straightforward. The individual I met was cautious and wanted to assess my abilities before committing to anything substantial. He offered me a chance to assist with a Valentine's Day event—a task that wouldn't be financially rewarding but promised rich experience and valuable networking. This was a chance to expand my Resources by meeting new people and grow my Influence within the community. It was an opportunity without immediate monetary benefits but with the potential to pave the way for future success.

Meeting this leader in person, I managed to make a positive impression with my enthusiasm and energy. He decided to take a chance on me, tasking me with organizing the Valentine's Day event on a tight budget and ensuring all arrangements were completed. Despite my lack of local logistical knowledge, I embraced the challenge wholeheartedly, and after a thorough and demanding vetting process, I secured my first project.

Aditya couldn't hide his excitement at the thought of me taking on such a significant event, especially given the location and occasion.

"It was truly an exceptional experience," I confirmed. "The event attracted nearly a hundred couples. To handle all the logistical tasks—like acquiring decorations and setting up the venue—I borrowed a car from a generous friend. Public transportation simply wasn't going to cut it. The schedules were unreliable, and I needed the flexibility to move efficiently to prepare for the event."

The experience was about much more than planning; it involved managing resources and logistics, improvising solutions, and building a network—critical elements that contributed both to the event's success and my growth in Silicon Valley.

The success of the Valentine's Day event was a testament to the power of the R.I.C.H.™ model. I put together an engaging program with interactive games, delicious food, and great music, creating a vibrant atmosphere for the couples who attended. Serving as the Master of Ceremony, I facilitated the evening's festivities, making sure everyone had an enjoyable time. This event didn't just provide a paycheck; it extended my stay and opened new doors.

The rewards went beyond finances. The event organizer became a vital part of my network, a resource himself, as he began recommending me to other event planners in the area. This ripple effect of networking, sparked by my willingness to leverage Resources and Influence, marked my first major milestone in Silicon Valley. It was a clear example of how building relationships and delivering results can create opportunities and pave the way for future success.

Mr. Roy's words, filled with pride and reflection, offered a candid glimpse into his initial skepticism about my decision to move to the US. His confusion was understandable; I had a well-established career in India, and leaving it behind in my late 30s didn't seem to make much sense to many. He had voiced his concerns, wondering aloud why I felt compelled to embark on such an adventure—more like a young adult's rite of passage than a seasoned professional's calculated career move.

But as he spoke that day, with the benefit of hindsight, Mr. Roy acknowledged the bigger picture. He recognized that my journey was about more than just finding a job; it was an expedition of self-improvement and professional growth. In Silicon Valley, I not only broadened my experience by collaborating with leading brands but also grew personally, taking on challenges that once seemed unimaginable.

Mr. Roy's admission that he was proud of what I had achieved was a gratifying moment—affirming that the risks taken and challenges faced were not in vain. It reinforced the belief that sometimes, stepping out of one's comfort zone is essential for greater personal and professional growth.

Grateful for Mr. Roy's words, I thanked him for his kindness. His recognition meant a lot, especially considering the doubts he had expressed earlier about my move to the US.

The conversation energized everyone, particularly Riya, who was eager to hear what came next in my story. But just as I was about to continue, Aditya interrupted, grimacing as he pointed to his foot. He complained about the discomfort caused by sand in his shoes—an issue that could have been avoided, as Riya playfully chided him, had he followed our lead and walked barefoot.

Mrs. Roy, smiling and sensing an opportunity to ease the light-hearted bickering, spotted an ice cream parlor nearby. She suggested we take a break from our walk and enjoy some ice cream. It was the perfect moment for a sweet interlude, and her idea was met with nods of agreement—after all, a scoop of ice cream was a delightful way to cap off our beachside conversation.

As we made our way to the vendor, the cheerful spirit of our outing continued. Everyone picked their favorite flavors, and as we savored the treats, I picked up the thread of my story.

"While I was nearing the end of the assignment that originally brought me to the US, and after the Valentine's event had concluded, I found myself facing a drought of opportunities," I recounted. "It seemed increasingly likely that I would have to return to India. However, I chose to persevere, trusting in the principles of R.I.C.H.™—to stay in control of my situation and keep seeking opportunities."

My persistence paid off when a leading US telecommunications company approached me. Despite having no direct experience in US retail, they offered me a position managing three of their retail stores and training their staff in sales techniques.

Riya's surprise was clear in her question. She was right; it was a field I hadn't worked in before. But I was ready to learn and adapt, to apply my existing skills in a new environment and rise to the challenge. That adaptability and willingness to step outside my comfort zone were key parts of the R.I.C.H.™ mindset, playing a significant role in this new chapter of my career.

Aditya's understanding was spot-on. The telecommunications job was more than just another opportunity; it was pivotal—a real turning point. It was a chance to solidify my place in the US professional landscape, and I embraced it fully.

"Yes, it was exactly that—a 'no turning back' moment," I confirmed. "The offer from the telecommunications company validated my belief in the R.I.C.H.™ principles and my adaptability. It wasn't just about landing a job; it was about establishing myself in a new market, a new country, and an industry that was unfamiliar yet exciting. It was a step forward that opened many more doors for me and set the course for the rest of my stay in the US."

My journey illustrated how determination, preparation, and the ability to effectively sell oneself are crucial, especially when venturing into uncharted territory. The success of this opportunity clearly showed that when you are in command of your resources and abilities, your potential for growth is limitless.

Though the telecommunications role wasn't as financially rewarding as one might expect, it offered something equally valuable—continuity and the possibility of a long-term engagement. It wasn't just a short-term project; as long as both parties remained interested, it had the potential to last.

Mrs. Roy's memory served her well, bringing up another unexpected chapter in my story: my stint as a Radio Jockey. Her question sparked disbelief and intrigue in Aditya, who was soon joined by Riya in their curiosity. It seemed almost inconceivable to them that I had found such a unique role in a tech-centric place like Silicon Valley.

"Yes, it's true," I confirmed, a hint of nostalgia in my voice. "Becoming a Radio Jockey was one of the most unexpected turns in my career. I stumbled upon the opportunity, and it was as surprising to me as it is to you now. The role allowed me to connect with a wide audience—to entertain and inform—and it was a stark contrast to anything I'd done before. It was one of those moments when life throws you a curveball, and you just go with it, proving once again that adaptability is key."

The experience was more than just a job; it was a testament to the core of the R.I.C.H.™ model—leveraging every opportunity, no matter how unconventional, to grow and learn.

I chuckled to reassure everyone, explaining that while it was significant, it also illustrated the 'I' in my R.I.C.H.™ journey. I had been actively engaging with various social media platforms when I came across two young entrepreneurs deeply involved in financial planning.

While continuing to broaden my horizons, I also focused on building the 'R' by exploring different opportunities. That's when I stumbled upon a radio channel. I reached out, sharing my profile and detailing my creative experiences and what I could bring to the table. To my surprise, their marketing head contacted me, expressing interest in getting to know me better. During our conversation, she proposed hosting a radio show featuring my clients. They were even willing to pay for this collaboration and offered a contract. It piqued my interest—but the challenge was finding clients, as I had limited connections.

Aditya and Riya exchanged glances, and Riya asked, "So how did you go about it? I mean, in a new place with new people, how did you find your first customer?"

"Well," I said, "I've always believed that where there's a will, there's a way. My 'will' is embodied in R.I.C.H.™, so I was determined to find a solution. I was part of an online social forum meetup when someone noticed my profile and reached out, offering their financial planning services for individuals and companies. Since I had just started and wasn't planning any investments at the time, I politely declined the offer."

I then observed that this gentleman was a young entrepreneur, brimming with energy and enthusiasm. He requested a meeting, and I agreed. A few days later, we met at his office, where he and his partner explained their company's structure and operations. During our conversation, he mentioned that his brother handled all the marketing responsibilities for their company. This immediately sparked an idea in my mind — these individuals were newcomers in the industry, eager to expand their business. My radio show could undoubtedly contribute to their growth," Mehul explained as he continued. "Now, I'd like to emphasize the key takeaway from this experience.

I could have easily dismissed their proposal as just another random marketing offer. However, I recognized a potential opportunity for myself. I was determined to benefit from it. I observed that they were youthful, full of dynamism, and committed to growing their business. This indicated to me that they would likely be receptive to forming partnerships. And indeed, that turned out to be the case.

Shortly thereafter, I presented the proposal to them, suggesting they feature on a special radio show. I elaborated on the potential benefits for them and provided a comprehensive explanation of how the collaboration would work, along with all the necessary details. After some deliberation and their careful assessment, they eventually agreed. It took about two weeks, but they finally came around. We were then seated in the radio channel's office, signing a six-month contract for our radio show," I recalled.

Aditya asked if becoming an RJ was the result of my previous efforts.

I explained that it wasn't part of the original agreement. Initially, my role was limited to referring them and designing their marketing plan. However, the radio channel faced a situation where some of their regular RJs couldn't work, and our secured Saturday morning slot had no available RJ due to prior commitments. Consequently, the radio station asked me to step in.

Apparently, they saw something in me they liked and offered me the opportunity. Despite my initial apprehensions, I decided to give it a try. Being an RJ and engaging with an audience on air was a completely new challenge for me. After receiving training on managing the console, controlling voice modulations, selecting appropriate songs, and more, I eventually became an RJ for them. This role involved playing music, discussing the client's financial products, engaging in lively conversations with listeners, and I did this for six months. During this time, a significant portion of California's population tuned in to my voice.

Riya expressed her amazement at the transformation, acknowledging how I had faced substantial financial challenges with my family business and debts, yet had now achieved such a remarkable feat.

Mr. Roy added his agreement, saying that even he had been skeptical at first, but when he observed my approach and determination, he realized it could indeed be possible.

Curious about their perspective, I asked them for their thoughts on the key takeaway from this experience and how they believed I managed to make it happen.

Aditya took a moment to reflect before saying, "I think the first thing you did was to build your 'I.' You went out networking, getting to know people, and that helped you build your 'R' as well."

Riya immediately chimed in, "Moreover, you were attentive to how you could secure a client for your radio show. When you met those entrepreneurs, you instinctively saw them as potential clients. Your alertness and preparedness were crucial.

If you had dismissed them, this opportunity might never have come your way."

I acknowledged their insights. "Wow, I'm impressed. You're getting closer to understanding things. Well done. Yes, you're right. One must build networks, resources, and skills. I could have shied away from becoming a radio voice, but I embraced the opportunity and invested in building the skills required to be a Radio Jockey. That level of preparedness was crucial, and we had a suitable response for our show. The best part was that the show helped improve the sales figures for my client."

I noticed Mrs. Roy turning to address the children after her kind words. "Yes, Mehul, you're a true inspiration," she said. I felt humbled and a bit bashful with the spotlight on me. She continued, "But there's more to his story. Mehul was involved in some significant endeavors during his time in the USA."

I was humbled hearing this, but quickly steered the conversation toward an even more remarkable story — that of Ms. Vaishali Shadangule, who at 18 walked out of her parents' home in a small town in Madhya Pradesh with no money or belongings. Today, the designer runs a fashion brand in Mumbai that employs 65 people. This is her rags-to-riches tale.

Aditya and Riya were eager to know more. I explained to them that, according to a leading online educational portal, Propel Steps, it was a little past 3 a.m. when Vaishali walked out of her parents' home in Vidisha, a small town about 56 km northeast of Bhopal in Madhya Pradesh.

She walked furiously toward the local train station, with just the clothes she was wearing—no baggage, no cash, nothing.

As she sat on the platform, ignoring the curious and unwelcome stares, she hoped for a train to take her away from her hometown.

When the first train arrived, she didn't know if it was going to Bhopal—the largest town near her home—or away from it.

All she wanted was to get out of Vidisha. Forever.

A little over 12 years later, she employs over 65 people at Vaishali S, a design house of some repute in Mumbai. Her flagship store is a sprawling 2,000 sq. ft. multi-level outlet in the upscale northern suburb of Juhu.

Vaishali recently made her debut at Lakme Fashion Week, her designs a pleasant departure from the heavily embroidered clothes she usually retails.

The line—Virus Free—drew inspiration from pleasant childhood memories and used Chanderi, a delicate handwoven fabric from her home state, as its base fabric.

"That's insane!" Aditya exclaimed.

"Yes, and incredibly inspiring," Riya agreed.

I elaborated on the idea that many successful individuals embark on their journeys without meticulous planning, driven by confidence in themselves. These individuals often achieve significant success because they instinctively practice the right approaches to their endeavors.

Feeling the cold sand beneath her feet, Riya said, "I think it's time for us to head back to the hotel."

Mr. Roy, ever one to cherish moments like these, suggested, "Sure, let's go. But before we call it a day, how about some steaming hot coffee to reflect on the lessons we've learned from Mehul?"

The idea of discussing my journey over coffee was comforting and seemed like the perfect setting to share my experiences and insights.

Amused by the memory of their recent indulgence in ice cream, Aditya playfully suggested he preferred it over coffee. However, given the chilly weather, Mrs. Roy thought coffee was a more fitting choice, and the group agreed, heading toward the hotel. Once inside the tranquil lobby, they made their way to the 'Amara' coffee shop, where Mr. Roy ordered five cappuccinos, specifying extra shots for two.

As they settled in, Riya was eager to learn more about my time in the USA, a topic her mother had lightly touched upon earlier.

Mrs. Roy deferred to me, indicating it was my story to share. I downplayed it with a touch of humor, attributing my achievements simply to surviving the intense competition as a non-technical professional in the US. I concluded that focused dedication was the key to navigating such a rigorous environment.

Aditya's curiosity was piqued by the mention of a particular assignment Mrs. Roy had referenced, something significant in my journey. Having spent several months in the USA, I was actively seeking consulting roles. By then, I had secured a position training retail employees for a multinational telecommunications company and was also representing my client on a radio show—a topic we had just discussed.

These roles, while fulfilling and bringing some recognition, were not quite enough to sustain me in the notoriously expensive San Francisco Bay Area, part of Silicon Valley. Despite the success, it was clear I needed to secure additional work. The cost of living in such a prestigious region demanded that I step up and find a better position to ensure financial stability.

Continuing my pursuit, I persistently applied to various companies. This perseverance paid off when I received a call from a multinational Correction and Rehabilitation Company, listed on the New York Stock Exchange and valued at 23 billion dollars as of 2020. They asked about my training experience.

After detailing my qualifications, they invited me for an in-person meeting. I accepted without hesitation. On the day of the interview, I arrived precisely on time and was greeted by three interviewers—two men and one woman—who thoroughly appraised me. They asked me to elaborate on my background, clearly eager to understand my origins as an Indian. It seemed they were not only interested in my professional experience but also in gauging my English-speaking skills, though they never mentioned it explicitly.

During an intensive 45-minute interview, I was rigorously questioned about my training expertise, personal background, and more. The interviewers outlined the scope of their work, which, to my astonishment, was related to the criminal justice system in California. They were looking for someone to oversee part of the programs—or contracts—they held with the federal and state governments of the United States. These contracts included specific responsibilities for helping soon-to-be-released prisoners transition back into society by providing necessary resources, support, and assistance as part of a government initiative.

The primary objective was clear: to ensure the inmates would not revert to criminal behavior upon release. If they required educational assistance, the company and its subcontractors would provide it. Similarly, if they needed help securing employment, the company and its partners would step in. Support extended to other areas as well, including mental health and financial guidance, with the company and its allies providing necessary resources.

My main responsibility would be to train the company's staff and subcontractors in implementing a 'Behavior Change Plan' grounded in a scientific approach known as 'Evidence-Based Practices.'

After the interview and hearing all the details, I was certain I wouldn't be chosen for the role. I lacked formal education and experience in this field, which made me feel unqualified. However, to my astonishment, they later called to inform me that I had been selected. The news was completely unexpected and left me quite taken aback.

Aditya's reaction was sheer astonishment; the idea of working within the criminal justice system as a trainer was unlike anything he had encountered before. Mrs. Roy, equally excited, said that was why she encouraged me to share my story.

Faced with their wonder and questions about how I managed without direct experience, I explained that this had been the essence of my approach for years: maintaining an open mind, being ready to learn—and, when necessary, unlearn—to thrive. To make the most of the opportunity, I dedicated myself to thorough preparation. This involved not just understanding the technical aspects of the job, but also mentally equipping myself to handle the challenges of such a unique role.

Acknowledging the weight of the challenge before me, I understood that immediate results were unlikely, as such deep-seated changes would take time to manifest. I knew I couldn't fear the risks involved; failure would not only tarnish my reputation but also erode my self-confidence. I had to navigate the situation with authority while accepting the elements beyond my control without complaint. Ready for what promised to be a tumultuous journey, I embraced the challenge with resolve.

Riya's question about my surprise at receiving such an opportunity was natural. Indeed, I was taken aback, and upon joining the company, I sought to understand their decision. Their response was simple yet affirming: they were drawn to the enthusiasm I exhibited and impressed by my comprehensive background in training. This combination kindled their confidence in me.

As time passed, I quickly assimilated the scientific principles underlying the rehabilitation programs. This knowledge became pivotal for the case managers and counselors who devised the Behavior Change Plans for the inmates. My role in delivering these trainings soon made me a notable figure within the organization, as I began to make a significant impact.

I methodically trained not only the company staff but also subcontractors, state officials, and eventually earned a commendable reputation. My efforts did not go unnoticed, culminating in an award for my meticulous service—an achievement Mr. Roy mentioned with pride in his friend's accomplishments.

Inspired by this, Aditya reflected on the broader implications of determination, resourcefulness, influence, control, and ownership. He realized that with these attributes, one could accomplish nearly anything—a point to which I wholeheartedly agreed.

As we finished our coffees, Mrs. Roy showed signs of fatigue from the day's activities and excused herself. Her intention to retire early was clear; even the coffee, she joked, hadn't helped stave off her sleepiness. Noticing the fatigue setting in after a packed day of travel and fun, Riya supported her mother's decision to rest, understanding the importance of being refreshed for the adventures ahead.

Before parting, Mrs. Roy encouraged me to continue sharing my stories, believing in the value of inspiration for the younger generation. I expressed my readiness to recount more experiences, provided the audience was as interested in hearing them as I was in sharing.

Aditya and Mr. Roy were indeed eager to listen. Mr. Roy, familiar with my journey and capabilities, was particularly keen, having followed my social media updates and posts, which gave him a glimpse into various chapters of my professional life. His knowledge of my experiences sparked anticipation for what I would share next.

Riya's curiosity about her father's certainty prompted Mr. Roy to explain his trust in my skills and how staying connected to my social media presence kept him informed about my professional journey. Amused by his interest in my career, I responded with light-hearted appreciation.

Encouraged by the Roy family's enthusiasm, I shared how I had the chance to collaborate with the corporate wing of a prominent university known for placing consultants and trainers in various assignments. Selected by this institution, I was soon given the opportunity to conduct leadership training for employees of a multinational company—a supplier of interior aesthetics for luxury automobile brands such as Audi, BMW, Tesla, and Mercedes—marking another distinguished chapter in my career.

Riya asked about another milestone: the publication of my book. I confirmed, reflecting on the extraordinary experience of interacting with some of the most esteemed professionals in Silicon Valley. They had generously participated in a panel discussion I hosted, which was met with an enthusiastic audience and an engaging Q&A session.

The significance of launching my book among such influential Silicon Valley entrepreneurs was not lost on us—especially considering it all happened within less than three years. The transformation from being relatively unknown and relying on savings from India to achieving notable success was striking.

Aditya expressed admiration for the boldness of my venture. Despite having a comfortable life before, I had taken a considerable risk. This leap of faith, as he saw it, was commendable, and my approach once again proved to be my salvation. His gesture of respect underscored the impact of my journey on those around me.

Grateful for the accolades but preferring humility, I emphasized that passion and willpower are the true essentials. I shared the importance of my personal mantra, R.I.C.H.™, which had not only helped me find my will but also execute it—much like how IKIGAI is used to discover one's purpose.

Riya, reflecting on a previous discussion about the importance of planning, sought to understand its role in my success. I reiterated my belief that while planning is crucial, one must also be prepared for plans to fall through. It's common to have multiple backup plans, but the real challenge arises when all plans fail. My experiences taught me that life's dynamic nature can render any plan obsolete. My adherence to the principles of R.I.C.H.™ was, in essence, my true plan. Thus, planning was vital but not the only requirement for success; adaptability and resilience were just as important.

Riya grasped the concept of adaptability beyond mere planning, understanding the necessity of being prepared for the unexpected and moving forward without mental hindrances. Preparedness for the unforeseen was indeed key.

Aditya, reflecting on my diverse roles—sales trainer, radio jockey, corporate trainer for an auto multinational, contributor to the criminal justice system, and author—all accomplished in under three years, felt reassured about the effectiveness of the R.I.C.H.™ framework for achieving success.

Grateful for Aditya's remarks, I affirmed that success would come as he defined and pursued it. Noting the late hour, I suggested it was time to end our gathering.

Mr. Roy playfully hinted that our discussion had given everyone enough to ponder, perhaps even serving as a topic for their morning riddle. Riya confirmed her newfound insights and excitement for future learnings from my experiences.

With mutual acknowledgment of the evening's rich exchange of ideas, we agreed it was time to retire and made our way to our respective rooms.

My Window of Wisdom

In India, I had established a comfortable position for myself; there was no pressing need to branch out internationally. Nevertheless, a unique assignment beckoned me to the United States. It was an opportunity I embraced—not just to test the efficacy of my professional model but also to make an impact where many might have considered my chances slim, given the challenges I would inevitably face.

I took these challenges head-on, and with a clear vision and relentless will, I embarked on numerous projects. In the competitive landscape of Silicon Valley, I proved that with a strategic approach and the readiness to put in the effort, substantial results are within reach. My experiences there reinforced a lesson I hold valuable: success is attainable anywhere, against any odds, provided you have clarity in your methods and an unwavering commitment to your goals. These experiences highlight the following points:

It's essential to plan because it is important, but more important is being prepared for the unpredictability of life. Having a comprehensive life plan with strategies for various scenarios is crucial. However, it's equally vital to cultivate resilience so that one is not easily overwhelmed by challenges.

As the teachings of Lord Krishna suggest, one should focus on the task at hand and not be preoccupied with potential rewards. Success often comes from perseverance, a well-thought-out plan, and the ability to realize one's ambitions.

People tend to rely on multiple fallback plans, which is a prudent approach. However, these plans may not always suffice, as the future is inherently uncertain. The key to moving forward lies in the behavior one chooses in the face of adversity.

Behavior stems from thoughts, which are influenced by one's education and experiences. It is important, then, to seek knowledge that promotes ethical conduct and sound judgment. This learning process is crucial for breaking mental barriers, challenging the status quo, staying adaptable, and being open to new experiences. Ultimately, it is this willingness to learn and adapt that empowers individuals to make a meaningful impact.

Despite my lack of a technical background, and without any formal education or work experience in the USA, I managed to thrive—something I attribute largely to my determination to make a difference. My adherence to the R.I.C.H.™ model served as a cornerstone of this success, providing a structured approach to overcoming the challenges I faced.

List five major take home /learnings from this chapter:

1.
2.
3.
4.
5.

Based on the 5 take home / learnings how will you use Planning is important but not essential in following areas:

Work / College

Home

Socially

What is the one most important idea you can commit to using immediately?

CHAPTER 7

Fly on the Wall

> *"For one who has conquered his mind, a mind is best of friends, but for one who has failed to do so, a mind is the greatest enemy."*
>
> —Lord Krishna

It is a fine sunny day in the forest, and a lion is sitting outside his cave, lounging in the sunAlong comes a fox, out on a walk.

Fox: "Do you know the time? My watch isn't working."

Lion: "Oh, I can easily fix the watch for you."

Fox: "Hmm… but it's an extremely complicated mechanism, and your enormous claws will only destroy it further."

Lion: "Oh no, give it to me, and it will be fixed."

Fox: "That's ridiculous! Any fool knows that lazy lions with great claws cannot fix complicated watches."

Lion: "Sure they do. Give it to me and it will be fixed."

The lion disappears into his cave, and after a while, he comes back with the watch—now running perfectly. The fox is impressed, and the lion continues to lie lazily in the sun, looking incredibly pleased with himself.

Soon, a wolf comes along and stops to watch the lazy lion basking in the sun.

Wolf: "Can I come and watch TV with you tonight? Mine is broken."

Lion: "Oh, I can easily fix your TV for you."

Wolf: "You don't expect me to believe such rubbish, do you? There's no way that a lazy lion with big claws can fix a complicated TV."

Lion: "No problem. Do you want to try it?"

The lion goes into his cave, and after a while, comes back with a perfectly fixed TV. The wolf walks away amazed and happy.

***The actual scene inside the lion's cave*:**

In one corner are half a dozen small and intelligent-looking rabbits, busily working with unbelievably detailed instruments. In the other corner lies a huge lion, looking incredibly pleased with himself.

***Moral*:**

If you want to understand why a manager is renowned, examine the work of their subordinates.

This story carries a valuable management lesson for the professional world: if you're curious about why someone seemingly undeserving has been promoted, look at the accomplishments of their team.

It offers not only amusement but also deeper reflection. It reminds us of those often told that certain achievements are beyond their reach—yet they defy expectations and accomplish remarkable feats. For them, this becomes a source of inspiration and personal satisfaction.

However, not everyone responds to such challenges in the same way. Some take the advice to heart and choose not to try, while others become passive non-performers who complain without acting. This story illustrates how someone can position themselves as capable and leverage teamwork to showcase their ability to drive results.

On the flip side, there are those who act as passive spectators—perched on the sidelines like flies on a wall—lacking the belief or will to act. They're easily swayed by others' opinions and become mere bystanders in their own lives. This kind of passivity often appears unwarranted, even absurd, and is perceived as a sign of weakness.

Riya found herself in a situation that highlighted these contrasting attitudes and behaviors.

After their enjoyable weekend getaway, she and Aditya returned to their regular routines with a renewed sense of enthusiasm and determination. Aditya immersed himself in his project, while Riya refocused on her responsibilities.

Not long after, Riya's dear friend Simmi paid her a surprise visit. Simmi, a budding fashion designer in her second year of college in Delhi, was preparing to embark on a six-month internship with a prestigious fashion house in Mumbai. Eager to share the exciting news, she decided to surprise Riya with an unannounced visit.

When Simmi suddenly appeared at her doorstep, Riya was momentarily stunned. It felt like a dream—Simmi standing before her, unannounced.

"Is that really you?" Riya exclaimed, disbelief and excitement lighting up her face.

Simmi responded with a warm hug and a playful remark, "Of course—who else can surprise you like this, my sweetheart?"

The two had been close friends since school and had even shared a hostel before Simmi's father, a customs officer, was transferred to Delhi.

Overwhelmed by the unexpected reunion, Riya beamed, "I can't believe it's you. Pinch me!"

Simmi playfully obliged, giving her a gentle pinch that made Riya shriek with laughter. She was genuinely thrilled to see her old friend again.

As the initial excitement settled, they decided to catch up over a cup of coffee. Riya fondly recalled Simmi's daily ritual—dark coffee with a single cube of sugar and a dash of milk, always at 4 p.m.

"I still remember your 4 p.m. coffee," Riya said with a smile, surprised that the memory had stayed with her all these years.

Simmi chuckled and replied, "I didn't expect you to remember after all this time."

Sipping her coffee, Riya eagerly asked, "So, what brings you here?"

Simmi couldn't contain her excitement as she shared her news. "You won't believe it! I've been offered an incredible internship with the renowned fashion brand Shanaya as part of my fashion designing course in Delhi. I'm over the moon!" she exclaimed, dancing on the couch with pure joy.

Riya was genuinely impressed. "Shanaya? That's one of the most renowned brands, not just in India, but globally," she remarked.

Simmi nodded happily. "Yes, sweetheart, it's a big deal."

As their conversation continued, Riya couldn't help but ask how Simmi had managed to secure such an amazing opportunity. She playfully teased her about her past academic performance. Leaning in with a mischievous grin, Simmi shared a secret. "You're right; I wasn't a star student. But here's the catch—my dad knows someone at Shanaya. He works at the international airport customs, and they couldn't refuse his request. So here I am, ready to embark on this exciting journey," she explained, her excitement still shining through.

Riya smiled and said, "Wow, I must say, you are one lucky girl."

Simmi just grinned. "That I am."

Feeling the need to celebrate both the reunion and the exciting news, Riya suggested a get-together with her friends. She planned to introduce Simmi to her close circle, including Aditya and me, whom she described as wonderful company.

Simmi agreed enthusiastically, and Riya quickly got to work organizing a small celebration at her home. She reached out to her friends, gave them a brief introduction to Simmi, and everything was set for the evening.

Riya's excitement was palpable—her old friend's visit had been long overdue, and she was about to embark on a new adventure. As the evening unfolded, guests arrived and the music got everyone moving.

Introductions were made, and Simmi, who had briefly crossed paths with Aditya during childhood, was thrilled to reconnect with him after all these years. I also had the chance to strike up a conversation with Simmi. Riya's college friends, Rinki and Sameer, both art students, added to the lively atmosphere of the party.

Mr. Roy returned from work with a cheerful entrance, commenting on the festive gathering. We exchanged greetings and pleasantries, and I couldn't help but share my excitement. The enthusiasm and liveliness of the younger crowd were infectious, adding to the pleasant atmosphere.

The party took on a life of its own as they danced to the latest tunes and savored pasta and garlic bread from the newly opened Italian restaurant, Buonasera—which fittingly means "Good evening" in Italian.

I savored each moment, sipping my beloved Shiraz red wine and enjoying the festivities.

The dance floor was alive with energy as everyone danced, sang, and grooved to the music. But as the lively hustle began to fade, tired feet pleaded for a break. They begged for mercy and eventually settled down for conversation.

After catching my breath following the spirited dance, I found myself reminiscing about my college days. I turned to Simmi, genuinely happy for her and wishing her the best on her journey at Shanaya.

"Thanks, Mehul Sir. I'm just thrilled to have the opportunity to be there for six months and add it to my profile. Who cares about the experience? I'm going to have fun," Simmi exclaimed, surprising everyone with her candid response. I was taken aback by her straightforward, carefree attitude.

As the conversation continued, it became clear that Simmi's father, a customs officer, had used his influential connections to secure her internship. More than merit, it seemed privileged connections were at play. Simmi's nonchalant revelation cast an awkward silence over the group. To break the tension, Riya quickly changed the subject.

"Wow, Rinki, I really like your dress, and those shoes are amazing!" Riya complimented, steering the conversation toward lighter topics.

The laughter had ebbed, and the warmth of the gathering cooled as friends slowly left Riya's place. Night was closing in when she asked Aditya and me to stay back. There was a tension in the air that hadn't been there before—an undercurrent pulling down the remnants of the day's joy.

It was late, and I noticed the change in Riya. The lightness of the day had vanished from her face, replaced by a crease of worry that deepened with the night. I couldn't help but ask, "Hey, what happened? You don't look good."

Mrs. Roy suggested that Simmi's attitude had cast a shadow over Riya, but to me, it was clear that Riya's thoughts were caught in a storm far bigger than Simmi's snobbery.

"No, it's not that," Riya replied, her voice heavy with the weight of her thoughts. She spoke of Simmi's seamless integration into Shanaya, how things seemed to be handed to her while they struggled and toiled, only to receive a nod of 'just about fine.' I could feel the frustration simmering in Riya's words—a mirror to my own thoughts about the unfairness of effort and reward.

Mr. and Mrs. Roy tried to soothe her, offering words they hoped would heal. They spoke of individuality and the importance of walking one's own path, of not measuring one's worth against another's journey. They were trying to light a candle in her darkness, to guide her back to a place of self-recognition and peace.

But it seemed all for naught. The room was filled with the echoes of their motivational sermon, yet the air remained heavy, untouched by the optimism they tried to impart. Riya stayed locked in her somber mood, unmoved by their words.

As I stood there, a silent witness to this family scene, I couldn't help but share a quiet hope with Aditya—that the coming days would bring back the Riya we knew: the one whose spirit was as infectious as her laughter, who saw her worth clearly beyond the shadows cast by others.

Aditya chimed in, his tone diplomatic though unable to fully mask his agreement with Riya. "Well, I guess Riya's not completely wrong. She may be overanalyzing things now, but her fundamental concern is valid, and anyone in her place would have thought the same," he said, his words falling into the room like cautious steps on thin ice.

I was halfway through my wine, more spectator than participant in this unfolding drama, when Mr. Roy caught my eye with a pointed question. "Hey Mehul, you seem to be enjoying this?" His query, edged with curiosity and challenge, prompted a grin from me. I couldn't help it—it was an odd moment, hovering somewhere between concern and absurdity.

Riya, not quite catching the subtlety of the exchange, continued her soliloquy unabated. Mrs. Roy, however, cut through with a question that carried the weight of wisdom. "Well, Riya, I think you're overreacting. Why do you need to compare yourself with her? You've accomplished a lot yourself, and you have big plans, which you've shared with us. Why feel low and jeopardize your chances of doing even better?" Her statement was formidable, meant to fortify Riya's faltering self-assurance.

Riya's response came swiftly, a mix of defiance and a plea for understanding. "I'm not low, Mom. I feel dejected. I know I may be doing it all wrong by comparing myself to her, but 'Shanaya'—people invest years of hard work to get into that brand, and here she gets it just like that? Isn't she a privileged child born with a silver spoon in her mouth? Are you serious?" The questions hung in the air, a reflection of Riya's struggle with life's inequalities that even parental wisdom couldn't easily soothe.

The room's atmosphere shifted with Mrs. Roy's laughter, a ripple of amusement at the evening's earnest debate. I remained detached from the fervor, a silent bystander nursing a glass of Shiraz. The wine's subtle complexities seemed to mirror the layered conversation unfolding around me.

Aditya's curiosity about my silence lingered, a question mark expecting some revelation or profound insight. Yet, I was content in my quietude, finding simple pleasure in observation. There's a unique tranquility in being the 'fly on the wall'—an unobtrusive witness to the passionate discourse of others.

My friends' animated exchange painted a vivid tableau of concerns and convictions—a tapestry I viewed with the detachment of an outsider. The role of observer suited me, allowing me to soak in the nuances of their interactions, the varying shades of their arguments, without feeling compelled to partake.

Mr. and Mrs. Roy, seasoned in the ebb and flow of such discussions, seemed to wait with bated breath for me to add a twist to the narrative. But I found solace in my passive stance. There was freedom in detached observation, a serene acceptance of the moment as it was, uncolored by personal investment in the outcome. In this quiet space of watching, I found my haven—amidst the warmth of companionship and the rich tapestry of dialogue that night.

Curiosity about my silence began to stir among my friends, especially Riya, who found my quietness puzzling. Without a word, I rose from my seat, momentarily drawing the room's focus.

I walked over to the bar; the clink of the wine bottle against the glass filled the space where their questions lingered. I refilled my glass and settled onto a high stool, a silent sentinel observing from my perch.

The concept of being a 'fly on the wall' hung unspoken in the air. Aditya's light-hearted interpretation of the idiom added a moment of levity—a brief respite in the evening's earnestness.

Amusement at his jest was shared, a mutual acknowledgment of the wit. It was understood that my role that evening was not to contribute verbally but to observe quietly. My stillness amidst their animated discussion was a conscious choice, allowing them the space to voice their thoughts while I simply listened.

The idea of delving into the mind of the fly was amusing but unnecessary. My silence was my contribution, a quiet affirmation of my friends' need to express themselves, with me as their audience. In that quietude, I found a sense of peace, an observer's solace amid the vibrant tapestry of their conversation.

Amid the ongoing discussion, my gaze settled on Riya, prompting her to question the merit behind Simmi's recent internship acquisition. Riya's realization dawned silently; no words were needed for her to acknowledge that Simmi's own efforts were nonexistent—it was her father's influence that secured the position for her.

I watched as Riya pondered what Simmi's experience at the internship might entail. It was clear from Riya's contemplative silence that she suspected Simmi would contribute little to the work. She likely surmised that Simmi was more interested in the prestige the role would add to her résumé than the knowledge or experience she might gain. Riya's reflections seemed to come from a long history of understanding Simmi's approach to life and work, stretching back to their school days.

From my perspective, the conversation was not about casting judgment on Simmi but about guiding Riya to recognize the contrasting values between her own dedication and Simmi's apparent disinterest in substantive professional development. It was a silent contemplation on the nature of success and the paths we take to achieve it.

Reflecting on the exchange with Riya, I considered the probing question I had posed about Simmi's ability to handle challenges. Riya's response was quick and certain, a recognition that Simmi's default was to seek assistance rather than confront problems independently.

I gently steered Riya to understand that while Simmi might be present in experiences, her lack of ownership and accountability was evident. This realization seemed to resonate with Riya, who agreed with my assessment.

At the heart of the matter was the role Riya envisioned for herself. I challenged her to consider whether she wanted to remain passive in the face of obstacles or actively break through barriers, building a solid foundation for herself. The shift in Riya's perspective was palpable; she no longer felt overshadowed by Simmi's apparent advantages and instead embraced a newfound sense of positivity and self-worth.

However, my analogy of being a 'fly on the wall' puzzled Riya, and before I could clarify, Mrs. Roy interjected with a light-hearted comment on the nature of our discussion. It was indeed an intellectual after-party, a contrast to the usual revelries, where the vibrant exchange of ideas took center stage. It was clear that everyone was not just engaged but also enjoying the depth and turn the conversation had taken.

Mr. Roy chimed in, emphasizing how our conversation, while intellectually stimulating, served as a refreshing departure from typical after-party revelry. It was an opportunity not just for enjoyment but also for breaking free from stereotypical thinking.

Aditya, equally intrigued, shared his initial confusion about my line of questioning and how it had later revealed its deeper meaning. He, too, recognized the value in exploring unconventional perspectives.

Expressing gratitude for their kind words, I proceeded to clarify the analogy of the 'fly on the wall.' I explained that it referred to individuals who preferred not to exert themselves, secretly hoping that others would take care of everything for them. They were passive observers, reluctant to act. In the context of marketing, the term might carry a different nuance, but its essence remained consistent—a symbol of passive observation without proactive participation.

Riya, captivated by the concept, sought clarification on why Simmi was considered a 'fly on the wall.' She was eager to understand whether it was due to Simmi's lack of effort or her perceived inability to manage challenges in the future. Her curiosity illuminated the room, prompting a deeper exploration of the analogy and its application to Simmi's character.

Before I could respond, Aditya eagerly interjected. He shared his perspective, questioning why someone would choose to be so dependent on others. Aditya suggested that Simmi might indeed fall into the category of individuals who preferred to have everything done for them.

Furthermore, I pointed out that Simmi missed an opportunity to demonstrate modesty and gratitude for the opportunity presented to her. Instead of seizing the chance to learn and grow, she appeared disinterested and unengaged. I stressed the importance of having a strong will to drive actions and achieve one's goals, highlighting that this was an area where Simmi fell short.

As Mr. and Mrs. Roy listened attentively to our discussion, Mr. Roy shared his own observations, drawing from his life experiences. He expressed his familiarity with individuals who exhibited the 'fly on the wall' attitude—people who lacked the drive to plan, think, work, or strive for their goals. He characterized this attitude as rather pitiable.

Riya, however, offered a contrasting perspective, pointing out that individuals born into affluent families with abundant resources might not find the concept of being a 'fly on the wall' relevant. She suggested that such individuals might prefer to enjoy life without worrying about their level of engagement or effort.

In response, I acknowledged Riya's point of view and conceded that it wasn't the fault of those born into privilege. However, I introduced a thought-provoking scenario for consideration. I asked Riya to imagine a situation where the smooth sailing of their lives suddenly encountered turbulence, and they had to navigate challenges and uncertainty.

Puzzled by my questions, Mr. and Mrs. Roy wore expressions of intrigue and curiosity. Mr. Roy stepped in to clarify, emphasizing that my intention was to prompt reflection on what individuals with abundant resources might do if faced with adversity. The essence of the discussion revolved around the ability to adapt and thrive in different circumstances, beyond the comfort of privilege.

Aditya questioned the likelihood of such scenarios occurring, prompting Mrs. Roy to offer a thoughtful explanation. She emphasized the unpredictability of life and the importance of preparing for unforeseen circumstances. Drawing an analogy with life insurance policies, she explained that preparing for the unexpected was a prudent approach. Her detailed explanation resonated with Riya, who expressed understanding.

I appreciated Mrs. Roy's analogy and added to the discussion by introducing the concept of being "R.I.C.H.™" I explained that while privilege might provide a sense of security, it was still valuable to be ready, informed, confident, and prepared. Even if one's privilege remained intact, practicing these principles could lead to better decision-making, improved outcomes, and increased satisfaction.

Aditya then sought clarification on whether individuals who were less privileged or struggling were inherently self-sufficient. I clarified that this was not the case. People from all backgrounds can demonstrate the 'fly on the wall' mentality—those who lack the drive to pursue their passions or goals and prefer passive observation over active engagement.

Seeing their puzzled expressions, I elaborated further. I pointed out that some individuals frequently say things like, "I'm confused about what to do," "I know what I need but don't know where to start," or "I have challenges that prevent me from taking action." The issue isn't these statements themselves, but the irony that even after months or years, these individuals still make the same excuses.

Riya, clearly contemplating these thoughts, rose from her seat and began pacing around the living room. After a moment of reflection, she asked whether people with goals, wishes, or aspirations should act instead of making excuses.

I responded affirmatively, emphasizing the importance of taking that initial step toward addressing challenges and pursuing goals. I acknowledged that as humans, we all face problems and often struggle to break free from them. However, I stressed that the key is to begin somewhere—to try to understand and overcome obstacles. Taking that first step is crucial to setting the wheels in motion.

Aditya chimed in, summarizing the idea that rather than continually postponing action, it's essential to start somewhere and see how one can progress. He connected this concept to "R.I.C.H.™," highlighting its role in facilitating this process.

I further clarified that "R.I.C.H.™" is not just a model but a fundamental behavior. It encourages individuals to view their lives through the lens of readiness, information, confidence, and preparedness. This perspective enables them to act and bring closure to their goals and challenges, rather than procrastinating indefinitely.

I continued by highlighting an amusing aspect of this behavior. I pointed out that individuals who observe others succeeding or making progress often feel depressed, complain, or blame their destiny. Yet, they frequently fail to give their best effort to genuinely try to achieve similar results. These are the people who resemble the passive fly on the wall—observing but taking no action.

Mr. Roy then shared experiences from early in his professional life, when he was naive and lacked access to today's technology. He explained that back then, they relied on traditional research methods and faced less global competition. He confessed that he used to be one of those who pondered, blamed others, but took little concrete action.

However, as competition grew and circumstances evolved, he and I recognized the need to become more competitive and self-reflective about our goals. He noted that although I hadn't yet formulated the R.I.C.H.™ model at the time, we often discussed our strategies. Together, we worked to make the best of what we had—adjusting our mindsets and following a path that eventually led to success. Mr. Roy emphasized the importance of correcting one's mindset and pursuing a path that ultimately leads to achievement.

Aditya and Riya found inspiration in the discussion and began to grasp the concept more clearly.

Aditya expressed his understanding, stating that he shouldn't remain a passive observer but act. He related this idea to his startup plans, emphasizing the importance of not waiting for the "right time" but instead taking the initiative to make things happen.

I agreed with Aditya's perspective and appreciated his use of the phrase "unless you try." I stressed the importance of not making assumptions and following a path aligned with what R.I.C.H.™ enables them to achieve. To further illustrate the point, I shared a story to highlight the value of taking action.

"Once upon a time, a daughter complained to her father that her life was miserable and she didn't know how she was going to make it. She was tired of fighting and struggling all the time. It seemed that just as one problem was solved, another soon followed.

Her father, a chef, took her to the kitchen. He filled three pots with water and placed each on a high flame. Once the water began to boil, he placed potatoes in one pot, eggs in the second, and ground coffee beans in the third.

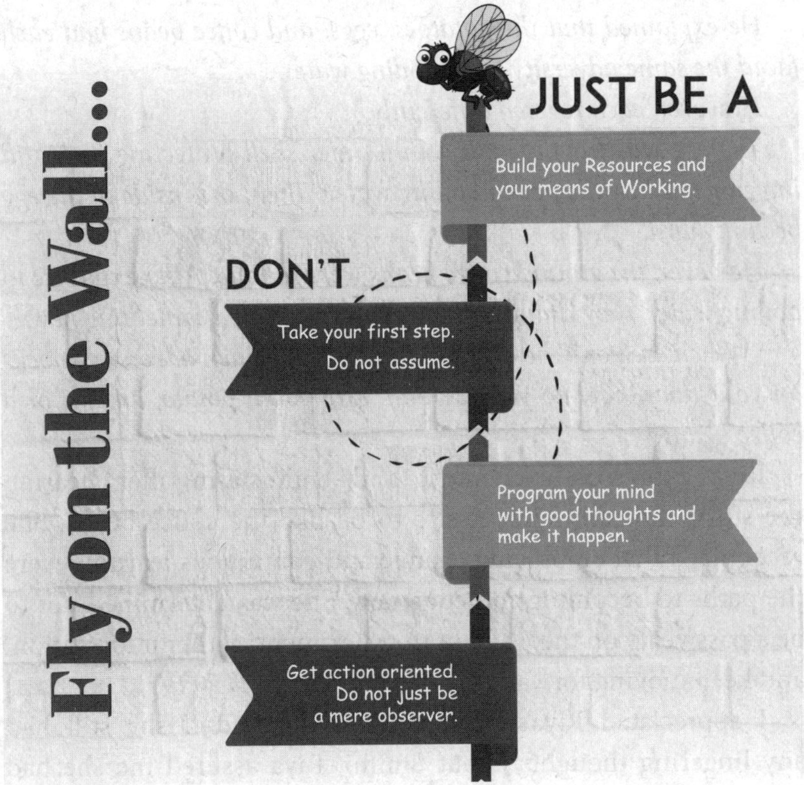

He then let them sit and boil without saying a word. The daughter moaned and impatiently waited, wondering what he was doing.

After twenty minutes, he turned off the burners. He took the potatoes out and placed them in a bowl. He pulled out the eggs and placed them in another bowl.

He ladled the coffee into a cup. Turning to her, he asked, "Daughter, what do you see?"

"Potatoes, eggs, and coffee," she replied hastily.

"Look closer," he said, "and touch the potatoes." She did and noted they were soft. He then asked her to take an egg and break it. After peeling the shell, she observed the hard-boiled egg. Finally, he asked her to sip the coffee. Its rich aroma brought a smile to her face.

"Father, what does this mean?" she asked.

He explained that the potatoes, eggs, and coffee beans had each faced the same adversity—the boiling water.

However, each reacted differently.

The egg was fragile, with a thin outer shell protecting its liquid interior until it was put in boiling water. Then, the inside of the egg became hard.

However, the ground coffee beans were unique. After exposure to boiling water, they changed the water and created something new.

"Which are you?" he asked his daughter. "When adversity knocks on your door, how do you respond? Are you a potato, an egg, or a coffee bean?"

Riya expressed excitement and enthusiasm after hearing the story, indicating her desire to be like the coffee beans. She recognized that embracing change and continuous learning were the paths to becoming someone new. She was determined not to be a passive fly on the wall but to experiment, gather information, and keep moving forward.

I appreciated Riya's perspective and asked if she still had any lingering thoughts about Simmi. Riya assured me she had no hangover from the past and was committed to adopting the R.I.C.H.™ mindset to prosper.

As the clock struck 1 am, I requested to be excused and bid farewell, leaving behind a fulfilling and enlightening discussion with these eager learners.

Tool to embrace learning:

Based on this chapter, can you make a note of an incidence in your life where you were just a fly on the wall, and you did nothing in that situation? And what were the repercussions?

Make a note of incidence which you /or your friend is facing and what you can do to not be a fly on the wall (remember R.I.C.H.™)

My Window of Wisdom

Indeed, the story and this chapter offer valuable lessons about taking initiative rather than merely being observers in our own lives. The analogy of the potatoes and eggs highlights the importance of our inner disposition and how we respond to the challenges life presents.

The moral—"in life, things happen around us, things happen to us, but the only thing that truly matters happens within us"—reminds us that our attitudes, actions, and choices shape our experiences and outcomes. To create a positive and fulfilling life, it is crucial to actively work on ourselves and gather the resources and skills needed to build the life we desire.

The quote from Lord Krishna, "For one who has conquered his mind, a mind is the best of friends, but for one who has failed to do so, a mind is the greatest enemy," emphasizes the importance of mastering our thoughts and emotions. A disciplined and focused mind can be a powerful ally in achieving our goals, while an undisciplined mind can hold us back.

Incorporating these insights can lead to personal growth, resilience, and the ability to overcome challenges effectively. It reminds us that we have the power to shape our own destiny through our actions and mindset.

The R.I.C.H.™ model extends beyond goal achievement to include preserving mental well-being and cognitive abilities. A healthy, focused mind is essential for making sound decisions and taking effective action. There are no fixed methods for this—it varies from person to person.

At its core, the principle is self-reliance: learning to safeguard oneself against life's unpredictability. As Lord Krishna's wisdom suggests, neglecting the pursuit of a fulfilling life is a personal failure. To succeed, one must stay focused and have a clear purpose that drives their actions.

Continuous improvement and personal development are vital on this journey. By cultivating qualities and skills, individuals transcend the role of mere observers and become dynamic forces—ready to soar to new heights and embrace bolder challenges. This transformation is essential for personal growth and realizing one's full potential.

CHAPTER 8

The Blue Ocean Strategy of Your Own Life

"Happiness is a state of mind that has nothing to do with the external world."

—Lord Krishna

Over the past few months, I have had the fulfilling opportunity to mentor Riya and Aditya, guiding them through life's multifaceted lessons. It has been gratifying to see them absorb knowledge, untangle their confusions, and stride toward improvement under my tutelage. The practical examples I provided set a clear tone for their growth and understanding.

Aditya, following the plan he shared with Riya and me, embarked on the journey of his tech startup. I recall the presentation he gave us on how he intended to implement the R.I.C.H.™ framework within his business model. Both Riya and I were impressed by the foresight and detail in Aditya's projections at that time.

Embracing the R.I.C.H.™ tenets as his compass, Aditya began actualizing his vision. His active participation in various startup platforms brought him into contact with like-minded tech enthusiasts and potential funders. This engagement proved invaluable—not only in building his resource network but also in enhancing his influence, enabling him to make strategic decisions as he forged ahead with his project.

However, Aditya harbored some doubts. Despite his proactive efforts, he couldn't shake a nagging sense that something was missing. His inability to pinpoint the issue cast a shadow over his endeavors. Juggling startup development with the demands of his final year in engineering was no small feat. He aspired not only to graduate with distinction but also to have his startup operational by the time he donned his graduation cap.

The mounting anxiety led Aditya to seek my guidance once more. Yet this time, he was determined to approach the meeting with a clear agenda—not as a seeker of approval but as an equal in a meaningful dialogue. He meticulously documented his work in a workbook, compiling every detail to present a comprehensive picture of his progress.

This time, Aditya aimed not just to impress but to engage in a thorough discussion with me. He sought clarity and answers, aware that this conversation could be pivotal in addressing the elusive gaps he felt in his venture.

Meanwhile, I had been in India for an extended period, my stay prolonged by work and commitments. The proximity to family and friends was a welcome change, and I managed to oversee my U.S. work remotely. My latest venture was particularly close to my heart—a finishing school offering management and leadership courses for adolescents and young adults.

My ambitions for this project were high, and I was deeply invested in its development. Alongside this, I had also been addressing some property matters, methodically organizing and setting everything in order.

Riya bumped into Aditya at the jogging track after not seeing him for over two weeks. Surprised by his absence, she greeted him with a playful query about his whereabouts, noticing he was engrossed in his laptop.

Aditya explained that he had been preoccupied with his final semester and laying the groundwork for his tech startup. Riya expressed curiosity, checking if he was still following the plan he had once shared. Aditya affirmed, noting some changes but maintaining his commitment to the original strategy.

Riya recalled my advice on the flexibility of planning, prompting Aditya to elaborate on his progress. He acknowledged that while he had made significant strides in gathering resources, a certain unease about the deployment strategy persisted—concerns about finding the most effective way to launch his startup.

Riya found herself puzzled by Aditya's doubts. To her, he had always been the one with a meticulously crafted plan, clear not only in his own mind but also impressive to me. Observing this shift in his confidence unsettled her, as it seemed a marked departure from the person who had once laid out his vision with such clarity and conviction.

As her concern grew, Riya confronted Aditya, puzzled by his hesitancy. She reminded him of the impressive presentation he had delivered, brimming with confidence about using his R.I.C.H.™ framework to fulfill his ambitions. She asked what had changed to make him so hesitant now.

Riya, failing to grasp the root of Aditya's problem, pressed him for clarity. Aditya explained that their team had divided roles, and since he was adept at marketing, he was tasked with crafting a compelling marketing strategy. The responsibility of being the startup's public face and convincing potential customers to choose their app weighed on him. He expressed uncertainty about how his resources and influence would help in this new phase, where the product and its presentation had to be exceptional to attract buyers.

Riya sensed that Aditya's underlying fear was not just about the marketing plan but also about his ability to communicate the product's value to consumers. She suggested that his doubts might reflect a lack of confidence in the product itself, despite his earlier conviction.

Aditya, with genuine concern, insisted that his confidence in the product wasn't the issue. The product had performed well during a test run with a randomly selected group through their marketing tools, which bolstered their confidence in its viability. His true predicament was the prospect of becoming the face of the company—the primary communicator. There was a stark difference between building R.I.C.H.™ within a small, controlled environment and being the marketing figurehead responsible for articulating the company's vision to a wider audience. The transition from a behind-the-scenes role to front-and-center marketing leader was the crux of his anxiety.

Riya, with a hint of understanding in her smile, diagnosed the situation—it wasn't about the product or company dynamics, but Aditya's own confidence. She observed that his self-assurance seemed to waver when it came to public representation and assuming that responsibility. Her insight prompted Aditya to reflect, and after a moment, he acknowledged her point. He confessed his fear was rooted in uncertainty about whether he could carry his ambition to the market and that he was still searching for a launch strategy worthy of their unique value proposition. He hoped he was making sense in expressing his dual concern: the challenge of public representation and formulating an effective launch strategy.

Riya couldn't help but snicker, amused by the irony of Aditya's predicament. She pointed out the contrast between his usual confident demeanor at social gatherings and his current trepidation about leading his startup's marketing campaign. To her, it was a curious shift—Aditya, the ever-confident individual, now daunted by the responsibilities of his own venture. She suggested that perhaps the strategy was simply a topic for further discussion.

Aditya paused to consider Riya's observations and conceded she was right. It struck him as odd that he would feel such apprehension. The realization that he was hesitating in the face of a challenge was both surprising and unsettling.

Their conversation was interrupted as Riya needed to leave to prepare lunch for my anticipated visit. Aditya seized the opportunity to ask if he could join for lunch to update me on his startup's progress. Riya responded warmly and welcomingly, insisting that Aditya should join them without any formality and even stay for lunch.

With Riya's departure, a mix of emotions stirred within Aditya—a blend of anticipation for the reunion and a newfound determination to treat the lunch as a platform for an earnest dialogue with me, rather than just seeking answers as he had in the past.

Upon arriving at Riya's home for lunch, I was greeted warmly by Riya and her parents. It had been quite some time since our last meeting due to my numerous commitments, and it was genuinely refreshing to see them.

Roy expressed his pleasure at seeing me, and I reciprocated, acknowledging the long gap since our last interaction. The conversation took a light-hearted turn when Mrs. Roy mentioned the absence of Riya and Aditya's usual barrage of questions, as she set out wine and glasses for us to enjoy before lunch.

Contrary to her suggestion, I admitted that I had missed their company and the lively discussions their curious minds often provoked. Smiling, I poured wine into the glasses and inquired about Aditya, noting his absence and expressing my interest in his recent endeavors.

Riya informed me that Aditya would be joining us shortly, a decision she had made without consulting me but hoped was acceptable. I reassured her that I was always happy to meet friends, especially when it was fine with her and her parents.

Mrs. Roy chimed in, affirming Aditya's place as family, which naturally extended him an invitation to any gathering. Riya, with a hint of hesitation, then hinted at an underlying reason for Aditya's visit. Mr. Roy, picking up on the nuance, probed for details, but Riya suggested it would be best to let Aditya explain himself upon arrival.

Attempting to ease the slight tension her comment had caused, Riya clarified that Aditya sought guidance over a minor obstacle with his startup. Mr. Roy, ever the optimist, brushed off the concern, considering it part of progress.

Soon after, Aditya arrived, and Mr. Roy welcomed him with the same warmth and interest, eager to catch up and ready to offer any assistance he could.

Aditya's return to Riya's home was met with warmth and a touch of formality, which Riya playfully dismissed, inviting everyone to lunch and hinting at a discussion about Aditya's recent hesitations. Aditya's surprise at Riya's revelation was met with Mrs. Roy's humorous acknowledgment that Riya couldn't have kept silent for long.

The group settled into a congenial lunch, enjoying a reprieve from their busy schedules. This Friday gathering, after a month of disconnect, offered a much-needed chance to unwind and catch up.

After lunch, Aditya shared his concerns with me. I listened intently, reflecting on his situation, pacing the room in thought while all eyes followed, curious about the counsel I might offer.

Breaking my contemplation, I decided to share a story about Ray Kroc, the man behind McDonald's. During a visit to an MBA class, Kroc posed a question about the nature of his business. The room filled with laughter at what seemed an obvious question. When a student confidently answered that Kroc was in the hamburger business, Kroc revealed the unexpected: he considered himself in the real estate business, leaving the students bewildered.

I hoped this story would offer Aditya a new perspective on his current challenge.

Aditya and Riya, momentarily confounded by the anecdote, struggled to grasp the relevance of Kroc's view. The story seemed a divergence from the pressing concerns of Aditya's startup.

With a chuckle at their bemused expressions, I clarified that Kroc's insight at the University of Texas was no fable but a valuable lesson in business strategy. It wasn't about hamburgers; it was about understanding the core asset of one's business. For Kroc, the real value lay in the real estate upon which each franchise stood.

Aditya, still struggling to draw parallels, asked for clarity. Patience was necessary, I insisted, to fully understand the discussion's direction. I explained the distinction between one's profession and business—while Ray Kroc's profession involved selling hamburger franchises, his true business was creating a vast portfolio of income-producing real estate.

This crucial distinction propelled McDonald's to global success. It's not merely about what you sell, but understanding the foundational assets that sustain and grow the business.

As the story settled in, I turned to Aditya, challenging him to define his business, hoping to guide him toward a similar revelation about his own venture. Faced with the weight of Kroc's example, Aditya hesitated, so I encouraged him to express himself freely. I stressed that this moment was for enlightenment, and his thoughts should flow unimpeded. I urged him to speak openly, to delve into the essence of his business, and seek the underlying asset or value just as Kroc had done.

Donning his metaphorical thinking cap alongside Riya, Aditya pondered deeply before articulating his vision. "Well, I'm in the business of Information Technology, aiming to provide a service that enhances people's lives and offers greater convenience," he said.

I turned to Riya for her thoughts. She agreed, supporting the idea that Aditya planned to leverage IT to develop an app addressing a current societal need.

However, I saw an opportunity to deepen their understanding. I acknowledged Aditya's point but suggested he was describing his profession rather than his business. The revelation—that his true business lay in providing solutions, not just IT services—seemed to perplex him at first. Slightly ruffled, Aditya struggled to connect this distinction with overcoming his hesitation.

To ease his frustration, I pointed out his confidence here and encouraged him to carry that assurance into his professional dealings. The real challenge, Aditya explained, was facing the judgment of the outside world—a stark contrast to the safety of non-judgmental spaces like ours.

Riya offered insight, questioning why Aditya would worry about external judgments if he stood firm in his convictions. She reminded him this concern for the outside world was new for him and encouraged him to focus on his vision rather than others' opinions.

Aditya's response was impassioned and fervent. He emphasized how deeply invested he was in his work—not out of vanity, but from a genuine desire to succeed authentically and meaningfully. His 'Game of Thrones' reference underscored his frustration—a humorous yet pointed reminder that the stakes in his entrepreneurial quest were very real, not fantasy.

Sensing the rising tension, I gently steered the conversation back to the heart of the matter. I reiterated my point, shifting focus from the technical IT aspect to the essence of the service—convenience. Aditya agreed, describing how his app would streamline interactions with government offices, sparing users the bureaucratic labyrinth of paperwork and uncertainty.

My understanding of Aditya's vision was clear. He wasn't just creating an app; he was crafting a solution to a widespread problem, easing a pain point for many. This clarity sparked a realization, and I expressed enthusiasm for his ability to identify and articulate the core benefits of his service.

Riya, still trying to piece together the conversation, asked about the difference between making an app and addressing customer needs. I answered simply: "Perception." It was about how one approached their business—whether from the perspective of the customer's needs or merely as a transaction. This distinction was key, not just in strategy but also in overcoming the hesitation Aditya felt. The shift was from focusing on the technical details of the product to the transformative experience it could provide. This was the crux of a successful business mindset—one that could help Aditya move forward with confidence.

The room filled with a sense of epiphany as I emphasized the importance of perception in business. It's not just about the product or service itself but how it's perceived by those you aim to serve. The goal isn't to control or dictate perception but to align with it—to resonate with the collective mindset of your customer base.

To illustrate this, I brought up Riya's recent purchase as an allegory. When Riya explained the concept of dancing shoes—designed with extra cushioning to protect her feet during intense dance routines—Aditya was initially dismissive, likening them to any ordinary pair of shoes.

However, as Riya elaborated on the specific features catering to her needs as a dancer, it became clear that her perception of a "dancing shoe" was shaped by her requirements and the value it provided in her dancing.

I used this moment to drive home the point that the salesman had successfully tapped into Riya's perception, understanding her needs and positioning the shoes as the ideal solution—thus making the sale.

This interaction served as a metaphor for Aditya's situation. Just as the salesman understood the specific needs of a dancer and provided a product to meet them, Aditya's business needed to align with the perceptions of his potential customers—addressing their pain points and offering solutions that resonate.

In essence, I urged Aditya to see beyond the app as merely a technological feat and to focus on it as a means of delivering convenience and solving real problems, aligning his business with the perceptions and needs of those he aims to serve.

The realization that the salesman had effectively catered to Riya's needs helped clarify the concept of perception in business for both Aditya and Riya. It wasn't about manipulation; it was about understanding and fulfilling a customer's unique needs, creating a mutually beneficial situation.

Seizing this moment of clarity, I connected the lesson back to Aditya. "Riya's experience at the shoe store is a perfect example of how businesses can align with their customers' perceptions," I explained. "The salesman listened to her requirements, understood her perspective, and offered a product that met those needs. That's exactly the approach you need for your app, Aditya."

Aditya, still grappling with his hesitation, wondered how this understanding of customer perception would help him overcome his fears. "It's about confidence in the value you're providing," I responded. "When you focus on how your app will solve specific problems and meet your customers' needs, your perspective shifts. You're no longer just an entrepreneur pitching an app; you become a solutions provider addressing genuine needs."

"This shift in perspective is empowering. Your confidence grows when you know you're offering something valuable. It's not just about convincing others; it's about believing in the worth of what you're offering. And when you truly believe in your product's value, your hesitation will fade. You'll be able to communicate more effectively—not because you're trying to sell something, but because you're genuinely helping people by providing solutions to their problems."

The conversation turned from abstract principles to actionable insight. It was about helping Aditya realize that his role wasn't merely to market an app but to provide a service that could significantly improve his customers' lives. This understanding was key to overcoming his hesitance and stepping confidently into the role of a successful entrepreneur.

The atmosphere shifted as Aditya embraced this newfound clarity and confidence. The hesitation that once clouded his mind dissipated, replaced by a sense of purpose and understanding. My words had resonated, transforming his perspective from selling a product to providing a solution—from making sales to making a difference.

Aditya's gratitude was palpable. He now saw his role not just as a business owner but as a provider of solutions, a facilitator of change. This paradigm shift was not about marketing tactics or sales pitches; it was about connecting deeply with the very essence of his business and its impact on people's lives.

As Aditya expressed his renewed resolve and enthusiasm, I felt a sense of accomplishment. Guiding him through this journey of realization and watching him reclaim his confidence was a reminder of the transformative power of perspective. It was a moment of validation—not just for Aditya's business concept but for the mentorship and support that helped steer him back on course.

With Aditya's renewed vigor and strategic approach to addressing customer challenges, the path ahead seemed promising. The lunch gathering, which began with casual conversations and shared meals, had culminated in a significant turning point for Aditya's entrepreneurial journey. As we all basked in the positive energy of the moment, it was clear that Aditya was ready to take his startup to new heights—driven by a powerful blend of innovation, empathy, and a deep understanding of his customers' needs.

The light-hearted banter between Riya and Aditya added a warm, familial touch to the gathering. Riya's playful teasing, calling Aditya "Wonder boy," not only lightened the mood but also acknowledged the potential of his venture to make a meaningful impact.

The discussion about the R.I.C.H.™ framework and its application to Aditya's situation had been insightful. Riya's grasp of the concept and her ability to articulate it impressed everyone, especially Aditya. It was clear that the principle of 'Influence' within the R.I.C.H.™ framework wasn't just about personal sway but about shaping perceptions and inspiring action—a crucial aspect of any successful business.

As the day ended, I mentioned my upcoming commitment—a video call to discuss a Blue Ocean Strategy with a client. Aditya's curiosity was piqued by the unfamiliar term, and his question echoed the room's intrigue.

"Blue Ocean Strategy," I repeated with a smile, sensing the curiosity it sparked. "It's a business strategy, but it's not directly related to your current concerns, Aditya. It's about creating new market spaces, making the competition irrelevant, and focusing on generating and capturing new demand. It's about innovation and opening new frontiers in business. While it's a different concept from what we discussed today, it's another fascinating aspect of strategic thinking."

Aditya's interest in Blue Ocean Strategy signaled his growing engagement with broader aspects of business and strategic thinking. As we prepared to part ways, the day's conversation left an indelible mark—enriching our understanding and binding us together in a shared journey of growth and learning.

Soon after, Aditya's routine jog took an intriguing turn as he noticed a hawker uniquely positioned away from the usual bustling cluster of breakfast vendors. The cart stood out—not just by its location but by its presentation: well-lit, with music playing and a captivating scent filling the air. It was an unusual sight, especially amid the typical morning hustle.

This observation couldn't have been timelier. With the concept of Blue Ocean Strategy fresh in his mind from our conversation the day before, Aditya saw a live example of differentiation in action. The hawker, by setting himself apart both physically and experientially, had created his own 'blue ocean'—a unique market space free from the intense competition of the crowded vendor stretch.

The scene offered Aditya an unexpected moment of clarity. Here was a hawker intuitively applying the principles of Blue Ocean Strategy, crafting a distinct experience that attracted customers. This practical demonstration of carving out a niche deeply resonated with Aditya's own aspirations to establish a unique position in the market with his app.

The hawker's distinct setup, so effectively drawing customers, sparked a surge of inspiration in Aditya. It reinforced our earlier conversation about perception, influence, and the vital importance of differentiating one's offering. As he continued his jog, Aditya's mind buzzed with ideas on how to apply these insights to his pre-launch marketing campaign and beyond.

What had started as a routine morning jog turned into a lesson in innovation and strategy—one that Aditya was sure to reflect on as he prepared to make his mark in the competitive startup world. Armed with the principles of R.I.C.H.™ and a fresh perspective on Blue Ocean Strategy, Aditya felt more equipped than ever to navigate the challenges ahead and steer his venture toward success.

Aditya's chance encounter with the unique Crunchy Munchy Vada (a hot and amazing potato cutlet) cart was more than a simple diversion from his jog; it was a real-time example of the concepts he'd been contemplating. The hawker had not only differentiated his product from the usual street fare but also created an inviting ambiance that made his cart a standout attraction. This experience, embodying the essence of Blue Ocean Strategy, demonstrated how creating a unique value proposition and niche could captivate an audience.

As I came across this delightful scene, watching Aditya fully engrossed, I couldn't resist capturing the moment. I sent the pictures to Riya, highlighting the simplicity and joy found in unexpected discoveries. Drawn by Aditya's evident delight, Riya decided to join us, adding another warm layer to this impromptu gathering.

My teasing remark about Aditya's preference for a morning snack over his jog was light-hearted, yet it underscored the allure of the hawker's setup. Aditya's response, highlighting the cart's unique decoration, confirmed the hawker's success in creating a distinctive and appealing offering.

This encounter wasn't just about enjoying an innovative snack—it was a living illustration of the concepts we'd been discussing. The hawker, likely unaware of business theories like the Blue Ocean Strategy, had intuitively implemented them, differentiating his product and creating an experience that drew people in. For Aditya, it was a moment of inspiration, a tangible example of how applying these principles could lead to a compelling and successful business venture.

The morning's events unfolded into a serendipitous lesson, reinforcing the idea that innovation, attention to detail, and a focus on creating unique customer experiences are key ingredients in the recipe for business success. As we gathered around the hawker's cart, the lessons of R.I.C.H.™ and the Blue Ocean Strategy seemed to come alive, offering a fresh perspective and renewed motivation for Aditya's entrepreneurial journey.

The vibrant atmosphere around the cart became even more lively as Riya joined us, bringing her infectious energy to the impromptu morning gathering. The Roys' invitation for a warm cup of tea later added a comforting layer of anticipation to the day's unfolding events.

Aditya's enthusiastic endorsement of the Crunchy Munchy Vada piqued our interest further. His vivid description of the snack's flavors and the unexpected delight of discovering such a culinary treasure on a street cart was infectious. The snack's quirky name, a mix of humor and novelty, added to its charm and mystique.

Riya's curiosity about the dish's name and Aditya's quick research into its uniqueness reflected the intrigue that distinct, innovative offerings can generate. The hawker's creation wasn't just a treat for the taste buds—it was an experience, a talking point, and a small wonder.

As Riya and I joined Aditya in sampling the Crunchy Munchy Vada, the consensus was unanimous—it was a delightful discovery. The snack's distinct flavors, along with the hawker's clever branding and presentation, exemplified the essence of creating a standout product. It was a testament to the power of innovation, differentiation, and the ability to craft a memorable customer experience.

This unexpected morning adventure, starting with a jog and culminating in the shared enjoyment of a unique street snack, highlighted the day's earlier lessons in a tangible, flavorful way. The hawker's success with his Crunchy Munchy Vada served as a live case study for Aditya, reinforcing the principles of the Blue Ocean Strategy and the importance of distinguishing one's offering in a crowded market.

As we savored the snack and soaked in the morning's experiences, it was clear that the day was about more than just business theories and strategies. It was about the joy of discovery, the thrill of innovation, and the shared moments that make the entrepreneurial journey not just successful but also deeply fulfilling.

As we settled by the riverbank, the serene beauty of the lake and the gentle morning sunlight created the perfect backdrop for a profound discussion. With the sight of the hawker's cart still fresh in our minds, I posed a question to Aditya and Riya, urging them to consider what set the hawker apart beyond his unique snack.

After a moment of contemplation, they pinpointed "location" as a significant differentiator, sparking a realization that aligned perfectly with the concept of the Blue Ocean Strategy. I affirmed their observation with a proud "Bingo!" and pressed on to delve deeper into the significance of the hawker's strategic location choice.

"The hawker's decision to position his cart away from the cluster of other vendors, creating a unique and inviting ambiance, is a classic example of the Blue Ocean Strategy in action," I explained. "He didn't just compete with others on the same stretch; he created a new space for himself—a 'blue ocean'—free from the fierce competition, where he could attract customers looking for a unique experience."

"The Blue Ocean Strategy is about moving beyond competing in existing crowded markets—or 'red oceans'—where businesses fight over a shrinking profit pool. Instead, it's about creating new market spaces—'blue oceans'—that are uncontested and full of fresh opportunities. It's about innovation, differentiation, and creating new demand," I continued.

"The hawker, perhaps without knowing the formal terminology, applied this strategy by offering a distinctive product in a unique setting—effectively creating a 'blue ocean' where he could thrive without the intense competition of the crowded vendor stretch."

"As for how it relates to the R.I.C.H.™ framework, think of it this way: R.I.C.H.™ provides the foundational principles for personal and professional growth—Resources, Influence, Command, and Habits. The Blue Ocean Strategy complements this by offering a roadmap for applying these principles in a way that avoids direct competition and focuses on creating new value for customers."

"It's about channeling your Resources to innovate, using your Influence to shape new markets, building Command in your unique offering, and establishing Habits that focus on creating and capturing new demand. When combined, R.I.C.H.™ and the Blue Ocean Strategy empower you to not just navigate but also create your own market space—much like the hawker did with his Crunchy Munchy Vada."

Aditya and Riya, absorbing these insights against the tranquil backdrop of the lake, began to see the broader application of these concepts—not just in business but in any endeavor aiming to stand out and make a meaningful impact. The peaceful setting of the riverbank, combined with the enlightening conversation, marked a moment of clarity and inspiration, setting the stage for innovative thinking and strategic action in their respective journeys.

Aditya's observation and Riya's agreement highlighted the intuitive grasp they both had of the hawker's strategic decision—a choice that mirrored the Blue Ocean Strategy's core principles.

The hawker's decision to position himself apart from the cluster of vendors was bold, risking foot traffic but setting him apart by creating a unique identity in a market space free from direct competition.

As I delved deeper into explaining the Blue Ocean Strategy, I could see the gears turning in Aditya and Riya's minds. The idea of venturing into an unexplored market space, creating demand rather than fighting over it, was a revolutionary approach that challenged traditional competitive strategies.

"The hawker's unique snack, the Crunchy Munchy Vada, and his distinct setup were not just about offering a new food item; they were about creating an entirely new dining experience on the street. By distinguishing himself from the rest, he didn't just compete—he created his own niche, his own 'blue ocean,' where he was the sole player," I elaborated.

"This is the essence of the Blue Ocean Strategy. It's about making the competition irrelevant by venturing into new market spaces, where the potential for growth is vast and unhampered by existing market constraints. It's about innovation, differentiation, and creating a leap in value for both the business and its customers."

Aditya and Riya, now more engrossed in the discussion, began to grasp the deeper implications of the strategy. It wasn't just about a street hawker selling snacks—it was about a mindset shift, a strategic approach that could be applied to any business, including Aditya's tech startup.

The hawker's approach served as a live case study—an example of how thinking beyond conventional competition could lead to remarkable success. As we continued our conversation by the serene riverbank, the principles of the Blue Ocean Strategy took on real, tangible meaning, offering Aditya and Riya a new lens through which to view their entrepreneurial goals.

Riya's question brought the discussion full circle, connecting their newfound understanding of Blue and Red Ocean strategies back to Aditya's initial concerns about his startup and marketing

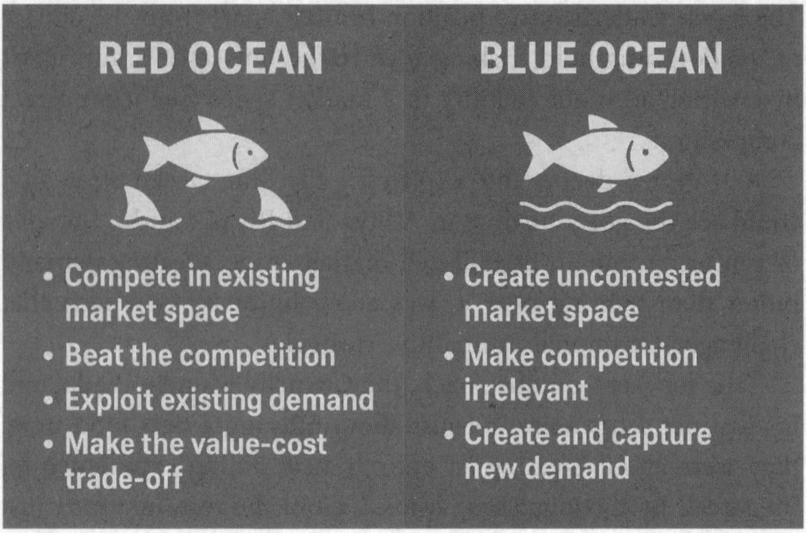

direction. The ocean analogy offered not just a broader view of the business landscape, but also a mirror reflecting Aditya's own position and the strategic choices ahead.

Now equipped with a clearer understanding of these strategic concepts, took a moment to reflect on Riya's question. The insights from the hawker's approach, combined with the strategic frameworks—had given him a fresh way to look at his business.

"I think I'm starting to see the bigger picture," Aditya finally said. "The hawker's strategy—standing out by creating a unique offering and experience—is exactly what I need to think about for my startup. It's not just about building an app; it's about how that app creates new value for customers and solves a problem in a way that hasn't been done before."

Aditya's confidence seemed to have returned, bolstered by the insights and inspiration from the morning's unexpected lessons. "I was worried about leading the marketing campaign because I was viewing it through a 'Red Ocean' lens—seeing only the competition and the challenges. But now, I realize that if I approach it as creating a 'Blue Ocean,' focusing on how we can uniquely solve a problem and create a new market space, the whole perspective shifts."

Riya smiled, pleased to see the positive change in Aditya's demeanor. "That's the spirit, Aditya. It's about carving your own path, not just following the tracks laid by others. Your app has the potential to create its own 'Blue Ocean,' and your marketing strategy should reflect that."

I wanted to also mention to them a case study of how Nintendo, the ace gaming company, used the Blue Ocean Strategy to enhance their product and its visibility.

They applied this strategy to their game console, the Nintendo Wii.

As per Yonder Consulting, who covered the example, the Nintendo Wii launched in 2006 and at its heart was the concept of value innovation—a key principle of Blue Ocean Strategy, which sees low cost and differentiation being pursued simultaneously.

To reduce costs, Nintendo did away with the hard disk and DVD functionality found in most game consoles and reduced the processing quality and graphics. At the same time, they introduced a wireless motion control stick to differentiate themselves from the rest of the market. This allowed them to offer a range of new features and benefits that hadn't been seen in gaming before—such as using the console to get fit or to play in larger social groups.

By pursuing value innovation, Nintendo went beyond competing with the likes of PlayStation and Xbox in a crowded and fiercely competitive Red Ocean. Instead, they opened up an entirely new market. The Nintendo Wii, with its innovative features and affordable price point, appealed to a much broader audience—a Blue Ocean—spanning non-gamers, the elderly, and parents with young children.

Aditya and Riya loved this example. It made even more sense to them now, helping them relate the concept to their own passion projects. As they continued their walk along the riverbank, the conversation shifted from theoretical discussions to practical applications. Aditya, with renewed enthusiasm and clarity, began brainstorming how to apply the Blue Ocean Strategy to his startup.

The serene setting of the riverbank, once a backdrop for quiet contemplation, had become a source of inspiration and creativity.

The journey from confusion and hesitation to understanding and confidence was a testament to the power of strategic thinking and the importance of viewing challenges from different perspectives. Aditya's startup journey was about to begin a new chapter—one marked by innovation, differentiation, and a bold approach to creating value in uncharted market spaces.

Aditya's response reflected a profound shift in how he approached both his startup and marketing strategy. The newfound understanding of the Blue Ocean Strategy, combined with insights from the R.I.C.H.™ framework, had given him a structured path forward—one that emphasized innovation, demand creation, and strategic market positioning.

My summary bridged the gap between theory and practice, highlighting the interplay between creating new demand (Blue Ocean Strategy) and leveraging resources and influence (R.I.C.H.™) to build a successful venture. The emphasis on recognizing the latent need for the product and effectively communicating its value to potential customers resonated deeply with Aditya.

His confidence was now palpable. The shift from uncertainty to clarity, from hesitation to readiness, underscored the transformative power of strategic thinking and mentorship. Realizing that his startup could carve out its own niche—free from the constraints of direct competition—marked a major milestone in his entrepreneurial journey.

Riya's affirmation and my approving smile captured the shared sense of achievement. The embrace they shared was more than just a gesture of camaraderie—it was a celebration of growth, learning, and the momentum they had built together.

As they parted ways, the riverbank—once a space for reflection—had become a launchpad for Aditya's renewed entrepreneurial spirit. The insights gained, strategies embraced, and confidence restored were no longer abstract ideas; they had become tangible forces driving him toward the realization of his dream startup.

The road ahead would surely bring new challenges and opportunities to learn. But with the R.I.C.H.™ framework as his guide and the Blue Ocean Strategy as his compass, Aditya was now better equipped than ever to navigate the entrepreneurial seas, chart his own course, and build a legacy of innovation and success.

My Window of Wisdom

Reflecting on the recent discussions with Aditya and Riya, I felt a profound sense of fulfillment. Guiding them through the intricate landscapes of the Blue Ocean and Red Ocean strategies had been a rewarding journey. It was gratifying to see them grasp these concepts not just theoretically, but as practical, actionable strategies that Aditya could apply to his product and marketing plans. This teaching moment transcended the mere imparting of business knowledge—it was about integrating strategic insights with the holistic principles of the R.I.C.H.™ framework, a philosophy I've long believed in and lived by.

As I pondered the day's progress, the timeless words of Lord Krishna resonated deeply within me: "Happiness is a state of mind that has nothing to do with the external world." This wisdom perfectly encapsulated Aditya's journey from confusion to clarity. His initial sense of despair wasn't a reflection of external business challenges, but rather an internal struggle—an expression of self-doubt and the confusion clouding his mind.

It became increasingly clear to me that, as Krishna suggested, the answers we seek often lie within. It was essential for Aditya to internalize this wisdom—to believe in his ability to find solutions and to harness the power of mindset in shaping a positive, transformative journey. My role as a mentor extended beyond business strategy; it was also about guiding a shift in mindset, helping them recognize how perceptions and beliefs deeply influence one's ability to navigate challenges and life's complexities.

Watching Aditya's transformation, I was reminded of the timeless relevance of true wisdom. Teachings from ancient thinkers like Krishna found a meaningful place in the modern context of entrepreneurship, proving that such principles transcend time and situation. Aditya's experience wasn't just a business success story—it was a powerful narrative of personal growth and self-discovery, a testament to how strategic planning, paired with a resilient and solution-oriented mindset, can lead to not just professional achievement but a life of fulfillment and insight.

As I observed Aditya's renewed confidence and strategic focus, I felt a deep sense of satisfaction and anticipation for what lay ahead. This journey had never been solely about imparting knowledge—it was about inspiring a deeper path of self-awareness and growth. The story that was unfolding wasn't just about external milestones, but about the enduring wisdom that tapping into one's inner resources—mindset, influence, confidence, and habits—is what truly shapes a fulfilling and insightful life.

Therefore, a few key pointers for us to learn here are –

- Understanding and thoughtfully addressing a concern, problem, or issue requires a comprehensive approach that integrates strategic thinking with personal growth. In the context of launching a product in untapped markets, strategies like Blue Ocean can be pivotal. This approach emphasizes creating demand in new, unexplored markets by offering a distinctive value proposition that sets a business apart from the competition.
- When adopting such a strategy, it's crucial to leverage frameworks like R.I.C.H.™ (Resources, Influence, Command, Habits) to enhance its effectiveness. Being resourceful means identifying and utilizing key individuals,

agencies, or stakeholders who can support the venture, turning potential challenges into opportunities. Influence plays a significant role in engaging and rallying these players around the vision, securing their support and collaboration.

- For example, a business may need to engage government agencies, distributors, customers, and other vital stakeholders to establish its market presence. Understanding and mapping the specific requirements and expectations of these stakeholders can provide a clear roadmap for rolling out a marketing plan. With a thorough grasp of product specifications, target audience, and strategic approach, businesses can navigate the complexities of market entry more effectively.
- However, the journey isn't solely about strategic planning and business frameworks. Emotional awareness and resilience are equally important. Confidence levels significantly impact the ability to implement a plan effectively. Nervousness or low confidence can hinder progress, making it essential to be mindful of one's emotional state and actively maintain a positive, solution-oriented mindset.
- Frameworks like R.I.C.H.™ can also serve as valuable tools for personal development, enabling individuals to align their mindset with their strategic goals. By fostering resourcefulness, influence, confidence, and habitual strategic thinking, individuals can better navigate entrepreneurial challenges. It's about transforming apprehensions into well-founded confidence and turning obstacles into steppingstones for success.
- In essence, launching a product or starting a venture is as much about personal growth as it is about strategic planning. It's a continuous learning process that challenges individuals to grow not just professionally but personally, ensuring their mindset and approach are aligned with their strategic objectives.

CHAPTER 9

The Stages of Change

> *"Change is the law of the world. In a moment you become the owner of millions, and in other you become penniless."*
>
> —Lord Krishna

Riya and Aditya, two bright minds, were skillfully guided and mentored by me. They were grateful for our encounter, which played a crucial role in shaping them into the professionals they aspired to become.

We all harbor ambitions; we all nurture dreams. Yet, the stark reality confronts us with how few of us truly delve deep enough to leave our mark. The question looms: are we poised to effect the change necessary to achieve our goals? Often, we find ourselves ensnared by our own thoughts and mindsets, convinced that our perceptions and feelings constitute the sole reality—coloring our approach to life.

However, life is far from simplistic. It teaches us in myriad ways at various junctures, molding our future—provided we are willing to embody change and put in the necessary effort. In the case of Aditya and Riya, whether they transformed or remained unchanged is secondary. The essence lies in their meeting with me, which broadened their perspectives and potentially catalyzed a paradigm shift in their entire approach to life.

Through my R.I.C.H.™ model and its connection to widely recognized frameworks like Ikigai, I aimed to outline a clear approach for Aditya and Riya. Drawing from my personal experiences and learnings, I en deavoured to offer them a fresh perspective. I carefully guided them to embrace the process of change without dictating their thoughts, ensuring they had a reliable process to reference. The R.I.C.H.™ model illuminated the importance of visualizing and delineating their path forward. It underscored the necessity of constructing a vision for their future, fostering a sense of structure and system. This understanding promised a significant shift in their work methods and thought processes.

The challenge lies not in what we know, but in recognizing what we have yet to comprehend or accept: the readiness to enact change. It's crucial to acknowledge that change is not just inevitable but essential for navigating adversity. To thrive amid challenges, embracing change is indispensable.

For Aditya and Riya, possessing the tool, knowledge, and means was only part of the equation; the real transformation lay in converting these resources into wisdom by initiating the necessary changes. It boils down to recognizing the need for change—a realization often obscured by the human brain's tendency to deny it, preferring the comfort of its cocoon. This denial doesn't serve well in the long run, as eventually, a stark awakening comes—often too late—missing the critical window for change. When change fails to occur, it's easy to blame fate or luck, overlooking personal agency in making that change happen. Models like R.I.C.H.™ play a crucial role here, pushing against the inertia of denial and prompting a shift in perspective.

Aditya and Riya were fortunate to have guidance early in their lives, making them aware of the need to evolve and follow a specific path to achieve their goals. However, not everyone is so lucky to have such mentorship. The absence of guidance raises the question: should we succumb to pressures and challenges, or stand strong, overcoming obstacles to enact necessary change? The answer lies in our capacity to rise above circumstances, utilizing whatever resources and insights we have to forge our path and realize our potential.

I was confident in my approach, dedicating myself to nurturing two bright, young talents with the wisdom garnered from my own experiences and achievements. Life had been my greatest teacher, offering lessons that fueled my curiosity and propelled me on a mission. There were moments, indeed, when surrender crossed my mind—when challenges seemed insurmountable. Yet I understood deeply that resilience bears fruit, and I chose to embody the perseverance I always admired.

Having provided Aditya and Riya with the guidance and mentorship they needed, the time had come for me to move on. My work here was largely complete, and other commitments beckoned. With a heavy heart but hopeful spirit, I made the decision to leave, with just fifteen days remaining before my departure. This transition was not merely a change in geography but a testament to the impact we can have on each other's lives—leaving behind a legacy of growth, resilience, and the courage to pursue our missions.

Aditya and Riya had formed a strong bond with me over time, and the thought of my departure distressed them deeply. Similarly, Mr. and Mrs. Roy were saddened by the news, though they recognized the necessity of my return to work.

Riya, particularly disheartened by the idea of my leaving, found it hard to accept. Understanding her feelings, I gently conveyed the importance of my obligations and the unforeseen extension of my stay due to the pandemic crisis, which had stretched far beyond what any of us had initially planned.

The occasion of my farewell was marked by a dinner hosted by Mrs. Roy at their home. It was a moment filled with warmth and reflection, overshadowed by the shared challenges we had all faced due to the pandemic. While preparing for the dinner, Mrs. Roy reflected on the extraordinary circumstances the pandemic had thrust upon us, noting the unprecedented nature of the global lockdown and the collective sense of uncertainty and hardship it imposed.

The evening unfolded as a poignant acknowledgment of the times we had shared, the resilience we had found, and the difficult goodbyes necessitated by the pressing demands of life beyond the pandemic. Despite the absence of direct conversations, the sentiments of hope, concern, and the bittersweet reality of parting were palpably felt, underscoring the depth of our connections and the impact of the global crisis on our lives.

During the farewell dinner, a moment of understanding passed between Aditya and Mrs. Roy, prompting Aditya to ask me how I managed the unexpected extension of my stay due to the pandemic and how I adapted my work schedule to cope with the global crisis, suggesting that, like everyone else, my work must have been affected.

Mr. Roy, witnessing Aditya's flurry of questions, gently intervened, reminding everyone that the evening was meant for farewells and perhaps not for an interrogation, emphasizing the need to give me a break from the year-long attention.

Riya, with a spark of remembrance, brought up a different topic. She excitedly mentioned the promise I had made about rewarding them for their progress and achievements throughout their mentorship period. Amused by her anticipation, I confirmed that the rewards had not been forgotten and were planned as part of the evening's celebrations, specifically as a post-dinner surprise. This revelation shifted the focus of the dinner toward the upcoming surprise, adding a layer of excitement to the already emotionally charged farewell.

Riya's excitement was palpable, and as I caught Mr. Roy's gaze, I encouraged the inquisitiveness of Aditya and Riya, expressing my eagerness to assist them in any way possible. Placing my wine glass on the table, I turned to Aditya to address his concerns. I acknowledged that the pandemic had indeed affected me, as it had many others. My visit to India had been planned with specific goals in mind, and although I did not achieve everything I had hoped for, I held no regrets. The pandemic forced everyone to adapt, and I explained how I utilized my R.I.C.H.™ model to navigate through these times, aiming to make the best of the challenging situation.

Mr. Roy, listening intently, sought clarification on whether this meant embracing significant changes and adopting new ways of working and thinking. I affirmed his understanding, emphasizing that the pandemic necessitated change for everyone, regardless of their initial resistance or acceptance. This period led to a significant shift in how people viewed and conducted their lives.

Riya, intrigued by the mention of a "paradigm shift," asked for a bit more explanation. I took the opportunity to explore the concept further, explaining that a paradigm shift refers to a fundamental change in approach or underlying assumptions. In the context of the pandemic, this meant reevaluating our priorities, the way we work, and even the values we hold dear, prompting a reconfiguration of our personal and professional lives to adapt to the new normal. This discussion opened the door to a richer conversation about adaptability, resilience, and the importance of embracing change in the face of adversity.

I explained to Riya and the Roys that a paradigm shift involves a complete transformation in our thought processes. I illustrated this with an example from my consulting and training experiences, focusing on how the pandemic altered people's entertainment choices—a realm familiar to all of us. Before the pandemic, entertainment typically involved activities like going to malls, watching movies in theaters, shopping, dining out, visiting parks, or spending time with friends. However, pandemic restrictions enforced social distancing and isolated us from these usual social and recreational outlets.

This abrupt halt led us to find alternative forms of entertainment within the confines of our homes. We rediscovered the joy of board games, enjoyed quality family time, and turned to OTT platforms for the latest movies, among other activities. But the shift wasn't limited to entertainment alone; it extended across a broader spectrum of our lives, changing our perceptions and experiences. The pandemic acted as a catalyst for significant change, bringing valuable lessons, positive experiences, and inevitably, some challenges.

Through this explanation, I aimed to convey that the paradigm shift wasn't simply about adopting new hobbies or entertainment methods but represented a deeper change in how we approach life and its many facets in response to unprecedented circumstances.

As Mrs. Roy finished her preparations in the kitchen and brought grilled chicken sausages to the living room table, complementing the wine, the atmosphere filled with warmth and camaraderie. Aditya, savoring the hot sausages, couldn't help but express his delight, to which Mrs. Roy responded affectionately. It was a moment of simple pleasures amid conversations about profound changes.

Mrs. Roy, joining the conversation, agreed with my observations on the pandemic's transformative impact, noting how people have adapted to new ways of living—something she found truly commendable. It was a testament to human resilience and our ability to accept and adjust to change, however unforeseen.

In response, I pondered aloud whether people truly had a choice in adapting to these changes or if it was more a matter of necessity. I questioned whether, without the pandemic, we would have initiated such changes voluntarily. The current levels of happiness and achievement might suggest that, despite the challenges, these forced changes have, in many ways, benefited us—making us better, kinder, and teaching us valuable lessons about ourselves and our capabilities. Yet the irony remains that without being pushed to our limits, many of us might never choose to embrace change, highlighting a fundamental aspect of human nature and the sometimes-necessary role of external pressures in catalyzing personal and collective growth.

Mr. Roy's acknowledgment of the difficulty in accepting change resonated with the conversation's theme, underscoring a common reluctance to embrace new circumstances that could potentially improve our lives. This reluctance, as I noted, often stems from a perpetual state of denial, with many individuals remaining in this state until the end of their lives—missing opportunities for growth and improvement that early acceptance of change could have offered.

Riya, intrigued by the discussion and sipping her wine, asked why, if change is so crucial, it wasn't explicitly addressed in the R.I.C.H.™ model and why there is generally such an aversion to change. I explained that some concepts, including the significance of change, are embedded within the broader principles of models like R.I.C.H.™, much like how Ikigai emphasizes finding one's purpose in life by provoking critical self-reflection. These models encompass various aspects of life, including the necessity for change, within their frameworks. By adopting the R.I.C.H.™ model, individuals inherently learn to adapt to change, as I experienced myself when relocating to the USA—undergoing a significant shift in mindset, working diligently, and reestablishing myself in a new environment.

Thus, models like Ikigai and R.I.C.H.™ serve as comprehensive approaches to life that encourage adaptability and growth. They are not mere theories but practical tools for crafting a fulfilling life, urging us to embrace change as an integral part of our journey toward self-improvement and success.

Riya and Aditya quickly acknowledged these insights, with Aditya relating the concept of embracing change to his own experiences with his tech startup. His initial skepticism transformed into a deeper understanding and appreciation of the changes he implemented, underscoring the practical value of such models in fostering personal and professional growth.

Riya's question about denial mode and how to navigate it sparked a further discussion on the nature of change and our responses to it. I emphasized that many of us might not even recognize when we are resisting change and that change itself is an unavoidable part of life. I likened change to water, which adapts to the shape of its container, illustrating that our willingness to embrace change allows us to shape its impact on our lives positively. Conversely, resistance or denial can lead to stagnation, distancing us from our life's purpose—much like stale water that becomes useless over time.

This analogy seemed to resonate with Aditya and Riya, prompting them to reflect on the importance of being proactive about change. I shared a quote that had significantly shaped my perspective: "Yesterday I was clever, so I wanted to change the world. Today I am wise, so I am changing myself." This statement captured the essence of our discussion, highlighting the wisdom in focusing on self-improvement as a way to contribute meaningfully to the world.

Riya responded with aspiration, expressing a desire to embrace change in a way that would deepen her understanding and effectiveness in her endeavors. This exchange underscored the transformative power of self-awareness and the courage to adapt—principles central to both personal fulfillment and professional success.

Reflecting on the mixture of surprise and curiosity that had crossed Riya's face, I felt the need to clarify my involvement with the Criminal Justice System of California. Contrary to what one might imagine, my role was far from the action-packed pursuits often associated with criminals. Instead, it focused on leveraging technology to foster positive change within the system—aiming for greater efficiency, transparency, and fairness.

I found the six stages of change to be a perfect framework to explain my approach. Initially, the system was in a state of Precontemplation—unaware of the potential benefits that technological advancements could bring. This phase mirrored the early stages of my project when the need for change hadn't yet been recognized.

The journey from Contemplation to Preparation involved raising awareness about the system's gaps and how technology could address them. This phase marked the shift from mere awareness to a decision to act, setting the stage for detailed planning, securing funding, and assembling a team.

Action was when tangible changes were made. Developing and implementing new software tools for case management and data analysis revolutionized how cases were processed and tracked, embodying the core of this phase.

Maintenance followed as a crucial step to sustain these changes. It emphasized ongoing training, support, and adjustments to ensure the technologies continued to meet the system's evolving needs.

Termination, though ideally signifying full integration of change, remained more of an ongoing journey for us. Despite significant progress, the nature of our project meant continuous improvement was necessary, with each stage of change offering a structured approach that clarified and simplified our efforts.

This structured framework not only kept my team and me focused and organized but also broke down the daunting task of transforming a segment of the criminal justice system into achievable milestones. It was a journey of continuous improvement, where each stage of change guided our efforts, making the process more manageable and impactful.

Riya's candid admission and my acknowledgment of her surprise gently reminded me how often the nature of my work evoked strong reactions. The assignment I led spanned 15 counties across roughly 500 miles in California and centered around the Behavior Change Plan (BCP). As a training consultant, my responsibility was to ensure adherence to the BCP, training case managers and counselors in psychological counseling to effectively implement the plan within a six-month window for each inmate. The BCP's success depended on facilitating inmates' progression through the six stages of change, using counseling and other interventions to foster their development.

Aditya's curiosity about why inmates were considered for such a program reflected a common question. I explained that in the USA, the government enables parolees to seek assistance from companies like ours to support their reintegration into society with dignity and respect. This approach aims to help with education, health, family ties, and employment, all designed to prevent recidivism. My contractor, collaborating with several sub-contractors across different domains, created an ecosystem to assist these individuals in their transition back into society.

Riya's realization of the scope and significance of our work highlighted the innovative approach we took to rehabilitation. My role was pivotal in ensuring that case managers and sub-contractors effectively utilized the BCP, tracking inmates' progress through the six stages of change to achieve positive outcomes within the designated timeframe. While I had other responsibilities, the core objective remained facilitating inmates' advancement through each stage, encouraging the adoption and maintenance of new, positive habits as part of their rehabilitation.

Mr. Roy's acknowledgment of the program's significance and the commendable efforts by federal and state governments brought a sense of fulfillment. It was indeed a noble cause, but as I shared, the journey was far from straightforward. The program incorporated a variety of tools and exercises, underscoring that change, while challenging, was achievable with the right mindset.

Aditya's request for clarification on the six stages of change offered a perfect segue to delve deeper into the conceptual framework underpinning our approach. I outlined the stages as follows:

- **Pre-contemplation**: At this stage, individuals are often in denial, not recognizing the need for change. It is particularly challenging because of their lack of awareness or readiness to acknowledge that change is necessary.
- **Contemplation**: Here, there is a growing realization that change is needed. Individuals begin to think about making a change, gradually moving toward readiness as they become more aware of the need for action.
- **Preparation**: In this critical phase, individuals start to formally prepare for change—not just mentally but also by gathering necessary resources. However, it remains a delicate stage, with the risk of reverting to old habits, highlighting the complexity of the process.
- **Action**: This stage marks the actual implementation of change. With confidence and determination, individuals take the steps needed to enact change, moving positively toward their goals.
- **Maintenance**: Having initiated change, the focus shifts to sustaining it. Maintaining new habits is crucial to ensure lasting transformation, emphasizing the importance of this phase.
- **Termination**: The final stage signifies that individuals are confident their old habits are gone for good. Reaching this stage requires perseverance through the earlier phases and marks a complete and enduring shift in behavior.

By explaining these stages, I aimed to illustrate not just the theoretical aspects of the Behavior Change Plan but also the practical challenges and triumphs involved in guiding individuals through this transformative journey. It was about more than implementing a program; it was about fostering genuine, lasting change, equipping individuals with the tools and mindset needed to reintegrate into society and lead positive, productive lives.

Prochaska's Six Stages of Change

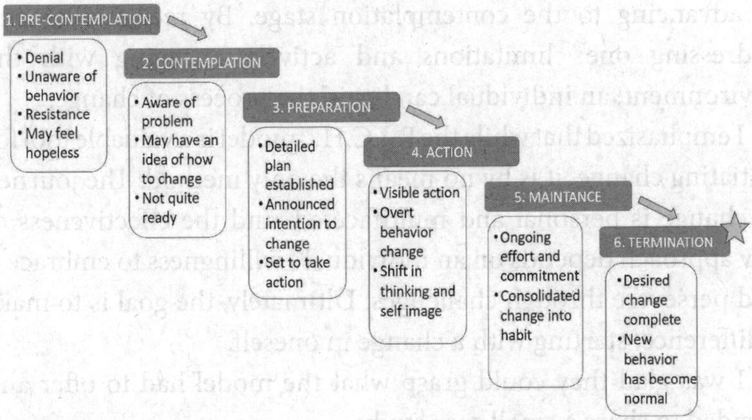

Aditya's summary captured the essence of our discussion, illustrating the journey from recognizing the need for change to effectively implementing and sustaining new behaviors until the old ones can be terminated. My introduction of the R.I.C.H.™ model as a pathway to change sparked further exploration into the mindset that often hampers progress—denial.

Riya's interjection, questioning the validity of relying solely on luck, contacts, and groundbreaking ideas, provided an opportunity to delve deeper into the barriers that prevent individuals from reaching their full potential. I explained that while external factors do play a role, the core issue often lies in an individual's reluctance to engage in critical self-reflection and root cause analysis. This reluctance leads to a superficial understanding of challenges, hindering meaningful progress.

The concept of "see-say," as I described it, is akin to "hear-say" but involves observing situations without deep analysis or a willingness to effect change. This mindset results in passive acceptance of circumstances as they are, rather than seeking ways to improve them.

Aditya's insight on overcoming the pre-contemplation stage—characterized by denial—highlighted the importance of observation, critical thinking, and the R.I.C.H.™ approach to advancing to the contemplation stage. By recognizing and addressing one's limitations and actively engaging with the environment, an individual can begin the process of change.

I emphasized that while the R.I.C.H.™ model is a valuable tool for initiating change, it is by no means the only method. The journey of change is personal and multifaceted, and the effectiveness of any approach depends on an individual's willingness to embrace it and persevere through challenges. Ultimately, the goal is to make a difference, starting with a change in oneself.

I was glad they could grasp what the model had to offer and decided to share a small case study.

In presenting the case study of Ashish and Anand to Riya and Aditya, I aimed to explore the nuances of motivation, satisfaction, and ambition—and how these factors influence our responses to opportunities.

Ashish, who enjoys the comfort and convenience of working from home with a decent salary, represents those who value work-life balance and contentment over career advancement. His satisfaction with his current situation, despite not meeting his initial career goals, suggests that a sudden opportunity to earn a substantial sum, like Rupees 100 crores, might not drastically change his approach to life. For Ashish, the decision to pursue such an opportunity would likely depend on the effort required. Given his preference for maintaining a hassle-free life, he might be reluctant to disrupt his comfortable routine unless the opportunity aligned seamlessly with his current lifestyle.

Conversely, Anand's situation offers a stark contrast. His ambition and dissatisfaction with his achievements, despite considerable success, reveal a profound desire for more—a hallmark of individuals who are never fully satisfied and are always striving for the next milestone. However, Anand's reluctance to go the extra mile, despite his aspirations, suggests a gap between his ambitions and his willingness to put in the necessary effort to fulfill them. Should an opportunity to earn Rupees 100 crores arise, Anand might initially be more motivated than Ashish to seize it, driven by his desire for greater achievements. Yet, his history of not fully committing to the work required to reach his goals indicates potential challenges. To truly capitalize on such an opportunity, Anand would need to overcome his hesitation to step outside his comfort zone and invest the time, energy, and resources necessary to turn this new dream into reality.

By asking Riya to consider the outcomes for Ashish and Anand, I encouraged a deeper understanding of how personal values, satisfaction with one's current state, and the drive for more influence our actions and reactions to life-changing opportunities. This discussion served as a reflection on the complex interplay between contentment, aspiration, and the pursuit of success, highlighting the diverse ways individuals may respond to the same opportunity based on their unique perspectives and circumstances.

Riya and Aditya's reflections on Ashish and Anand's hypothetical opportunity to earn Rupees 100 crores provided a rich tapestry of insights into ambition, comfort zones, and willingness to change. Their analysis not only captured the essence of potential responses to such a life-altering chance but also underscored the importance of readiness to adapt and grow beyond current limitations.

Riya rightly pointed out Ashish's contentment with his current lifestyle and his lack of a compelling goal that might drive him to change his life for the Rupees 100 crores opportunity. This highlighted a crucial aspect of human behavior—contentment can be a double-edged sword, offering peace and satisfaction on one hand while potentially limiting growth and opportunity on the other.

Conversely, Anand's ambition, as noted by both Riya and Aditya, sets him apart as someone more likely to be stirred by the opportunity. However, his lack of focus and unwillingness to step out of his comfort zone present significant barriers. Aditya's insight that Anand needs to leverage and build upon his R.I.C.H.™—encompassing resources, initiative, contacts, and handling of situations—speaks to the multifaceted approach required to transform ambition into achievement.

My response to their analyses aimed to reinforce these insights, emphasizing that possessing aspirations and goals is merely the starting point. The journey toward achieving them requires comprehensive development of one's R.I.C.H.™, involving communication skills, strategic thinking, mindset shifts, and other personal attributes. This multifaceted development is essential not only for seizing opportunities but also for creating them, marking the difference between those who lead and those who follow.

The conversation about Ashish and Anand, framed through Riya and Aditya's perspectives, served as a microcosm of the broader challenges and decisions individuals face in their personal and professional lives. It highlighted the critical role of self-awareness, adaptability, and the relentless pursuit of growth in achieving success—however one chooses to define it.

The hypothetical scenario of Ashish and Anand facing a crisis, such as losing their jobs, offered a deeper exploration of the resilience and preparedness the R.I.C.H.™ model can provide individuals in times of adversity. Aditya's analysis highlighted Ashish's potential vulnerabilities due to his limited engagement in networking and personal development—both crucial for bouncing back during challenging times. This perspective underscored the importance of building a robust personal and professional network, as well as cultivating diverse skills and attributes to navigate through hardships.

Riya's question about the necessity of ambition and aspiration touched on a fundamental aspect of personal fulfillment and contentment. It brought to light that while ambition drives some, others find satisfaction in their current state. My response aimed to bridge these perspectives by emphasizing that the R.I.C.H.™ model isn't solely about ambition in the traditional sense but about developing a prepared, adaptable approach to life's uncertainties. It's about building resilience, relationships, and resources that support individuals through unforeseen challenges, regardless of their level of ambition or contentment.

The emotional moment that followed—when Aditya and Riya expressed their appreciation for the learning and patience I had shared—was unexpected. It served as a poignant reminder of the impact of mentorship and the bonds formed through shared growth and understanding. Their acknowledgment that my impending departure was significant for them was touching, highlighting the deep connections that can develop through genuine engagement and exchange of ideas.

Their reaction reinforced that beyond theories and models, the human elements of empathy, understanding, and connection truly enrich our interactions and learning experiences. While we may discuss strategies like R.I.C.H.™ for navigating practical challenges, the emotional and relational aspects of our journeys are equally vital. Aditya and Riya's response was a testament to the value they placed not just on the knowledge gained but on the shared moments of insight and understanding.

Their heartfelt thanks and recognition of the R.I.C.H.™ model's impact on their lives was a profound moment for me. Their gratitude and realization of how much they valued our time learning and growing together were deeply rewarding—a reminder of the transformative power of mentorship and the exchange of knowledge and experiences.

Their reaction to the concept of winners and points further reflected their understanding that the true value of our sessions lay not in competition but in personal growth and mutual support. Aditya's insight that they were both winners captured the essence of what I had hoped to convey: the journey matters as much as the destination, and growth is a shared achievement.

Presenting Aditya and Riya with gifts was a small gesture to commemorate our time together and equip them with tools to support their continued growth. Aditya's smartwatch, symbolizing how modern technology can enhance life and track progress, was chosen to encourage him to integrate technology wisely into his personal development journey.

For Riya, I selected Steal Like an Artist by Austin Kleon to nurture her creative spirit and remind her that creativity is a process shaped by the world around us. The book's message about embracing influences and the iterative nature of creativity was meant to empower her to explore her potential and discover her unique voice.

Their reactions—surprise, joy, and appreciation—were a fitting close to our time together, underscoring the bond we had formed, rooted in mutual respect, learning, and the shared joy of discovery.

Reflecting on our journey, I felt deep pride in their growth and gratitude for the opportunity to play a part in their lives. Our lessons extended beyond the R.I.C.H.™ model, touching on humility, openness to learning, and the recognition that we are all lifelong students in life's vast classroom. As they expressed thanks and excitement, I knew our paths might diverge, but the impact of our time together would continue to resonate in their lives—and in mine.

As I bid farewell to the Roy family and Aditya, my emotions were a complex blend of gratitude, hope, and a silent promise to return. My stay had unfolded into a series of moments that were enlightening and enriching for all of us. Through shared experiences, deep conversations, and mutual exchange of wisdom, we embarked on a collective journey of growth and discovery that transcended mere knowledge.

The essence of our time together was captured by the R.I.C.H.™ model—an inspiring framework for personal development that encouraged a more conscious and purposeful approach to life's challenges. Yet, the impact of my presence went beyond these teachings, fostering a heightened awareness and a more intentional stance toward crafting a meaningful, goal-oriented life.

Though I took on the role of mentor, I remained mindful of my own ongoing journey. I shared with them the value of remaining open to learning and growth—not as a sign of inadequacy, but as a testament to the continuous nature of personal evolution and the joy found in lifelong curiosity.

Leaving the Roy family and Aditya, I felt a profound sense of accomplishment—not just for what I had imparted, but for what we had built together. The seeds of transformation we planted promised to flourish long after my departure. The assurance of my return kept the flame of this collective journey alive, offering a beacon of continuity in our pursuit of knowledge and self-betterment.

As I stepped away from their home, the impact of our time together lingered in the air, a reminder of the deep connections forged and the shared path towards a richer, more purposeful life. The experience, a vivid chapter in my own story of growth, underscored the enduring power of meaningful relationships and the collective quest for understanding and improvement.

My Window of Wisdom

Throughout my time with the Roy family and Aditya, I emphasized that no theory, model, or behavioral tool offers a panacea. These frameworks, including the principles I shared, serve as mere guidelines, not absolute truths. What has been crucial for me, and what I endeavored to impart, is the guideline of staying a step ahead—not just in pursuit of goals but also in preemptively managing potential crises.

This approach has guided me through various challenges and opportunities, reinforcing the belief that while we may not control every aspect of our lives, we can certainly influence our trajectory through deliberate action and preparedness. The lessons shared, rooted in this philosophy, aim to equip those I leave behind with tools to navigate their paths with intention and resilience, embracing the inevitabilities of life with readiness and a forward-looking perspective.

Drawing from the insights shared through examples, including the contrasting approaches of Ashish and Anand towards life and careers, several key pointers emerge to guide us toward a more fulfilling and successful path. These pointers serve as a blueprint for personal and professional development, emphasizing the importance of proactive engagement with our goals and aspirations.

Avoid assumptions and casual attitudes: Life's unpredictability requires vigilance rather than casualness. The stories of Ashish and Anand illustrate how a lack of preparedness for crises can impact one's ability to navigate challenges effectively.

Clarity of goal: Having a clear, well-defined goal is paramount. If clarity is lacking, seek it actively. Setting SMART (Specific, Measurable, Achievable, Relevant, Time-bound) goals ensures a structured path forward.

Build your R.I.C.H.™: Cultivating Resources, Initiative, Contacts, and Hard work lays the foundation for personal growth and achievement. Small daily changes can cumulatively lead to significant progress toward long-term aspirations.

Pursue happiness and contentment: While striving for success, maintaining happiness and contentment is essential. Being sincere, hardworking, and dedicated, coupled with a positive outlook, can overcome obstacles in pursuit of goals.

Be a relatable force: Strive to be someone others look up to and want to associate with. Your influence can inspire and motivate those around you, creating a positive impact within your community and beyond.

Wishes for a happy and healthy life: As an internationally published author, speaker, trainer, and writer, I extend my best wishes to you and your family for a life filled with happiness, health, and success. May you always find the strength and determination to achieve your goals, and here's to a journey filled with R.I.C.H.™ experiences.

These pointers are not just guidelines but principles to live by, encouraging us to lead lives marked by growth, resilience, and fulfillment.

Remember, the journey towards achieving our goals is as enriching as the destination itself.

Happy R.I.C.H.™ing!

CHAPTER 10

Assess your R.I.C.H.™ Competencies

Competency is the skill required by an individual to perform a specific task effectively. For any activity we undertake, it is crucial to execute the task with the technique and precision that is most appropriate. For example, a welder's competency in welding will determine the success of the job. Similarly, when a carpenter is asked to construct furniture, their skill and competency enable them to create the correct piece with the required specifications.

In the same vein, to become R.I.C.H.™ enabled, one must develop certain essential competencies. In this discussion, we will outline those necessary competencies that will help build your R.I.C.H.™ quotient.

Additionally, you can evaluate where you stand in terms of these competencies. Based on your self-assessment, you can better understand the development plan needed for your R.I.C.H.™ enablement, which in turn will enhance your ability to perform tasks effectively.

This simple exercise will assist you in becoming a more proficient professional and in shaping your approach to personal and professional challenges.

The R.I.C.H.™ model requires the development of certain competencies to become more effective and progressive in one's approach. Please assess yourself on a scale of 0 to 5, where 0 is the lowest and 5 is the highest. Using this evaluation, you can also identify a development plan to enhance that competency.

1. Managing Ambiguity

Description: *Can effectively cope with and manage change, decide and act without having the entire picture, and is comfortable handling uncertainty. Proactively adapts to new risks.*

Unskilled:

- **Not comfortable with change or Ambiguity**

  This is the kind of person who does not own change and cannot work in ambiguity. Therefore, he is low on his R and his I. Since he is low on his R and I, his C and H also get hampered.

- **Less efficient and productive under Ambiguity**

  This leads the person to being less resourceful and less effective on his influencing skills. That means the person's R and I is low and needs to build the same.

- **May not do well on problems with no clear solution.**

  The person lacks solution finding skill because the skills of R, I and C are low. The person is unable to fathom of how to find the right solution to the problem.

- **May hurriedly want to finish everything.**

  This person is not confident because the person has formed wrong H and in order to build the right H, the person will need to put in extra effort to analyze the problem and come to a concrete solution.

- **May like to do things same way time after time.**

  The person has formed a habit of solving the problem through a standard format and whenever such person confronts any challenge, the person tries to solve it with same approach which may not always be effective and needs to sometime be creative/innovative.

Skilled:

- **Anticipates impact of change and modifies behavior of self to smoothly tide over it-**

  This person is in control of the situation and prefers to command the Situation. The person strives to build on his R and I so that his C is in place.

- **Thrives on situation involving risk & uncertainty.**

  This person is excellent on R and I and therefore master's the C and thrives on it

- **Remains calm and focused during time of ambiguity.**

  This person has made his H strong by building on his R, I and C and hence can remain calm.

- **Is not upset when things are out of control.**

  This person has made his H strong by building on his R, I and C and hence is confident that he will get back the control.

- **Is comfortable to act even if total picture is not available.** The person is confident that his R and I will work for him and hence the comfort level is positive.

Assess yourself

- This is a generic development plan for each competency we have created. Based on your score, you may need to be more intense with your development plan if you rate yourself between 0 and 2. That means you will need more hands-on experience with the respective competency. For instance, if you need to develop your skill in that competency, you should seek situations that help you practice the development plan to get your mind accustomed to that competency.
- For readers who score between 3 and 4, you should follow the same development plan but can be a little more experimental in your approach to scale up and score 5 the next time on that competency.

Self –Evaluation Sheet

On a scale of 1 to 5, rate yourself on this competency 'Managing Ambiguity.'

0	1	2	3	4	5

Development Plan Suggestions:

1. **Read book 'Who moved my cheese' by Spencer Johnson.** This book helps you learn about managing ambiguity better, as the story of two mice takes you through a journey of managing change.

2. **Learn and use Pareto Analysis**

   Pareto Analysis is the science of managing your tasks better. It talks about a situation where one could face 10 problems and, in retrospect, how you could respond to it. This tool helps you to identify the top 20% of problems that are affecting 80% of your life and solve those identified 20% problems.

3. **Notice and challenge negative thoughts around uncertainty.**

   As a R.I.C.H.™-enabled individual, one needs to work on the ability to question situations around them. It gives you the strength to break down the situation and work on the challenge piece by piece. Therefore, going further, one needs to make sure that they challenge and break down the situation and tackle it step by step thus building this competency.

4. **Identify and talk to people who can guide you.**

   This helps you to brainstorm ideas and get more clarity on various aspects. That means he needs to build on his R and I to have him talk to people.

2. Strategic Mindset

Description: *Strategic Mindset is the ability to anticipate and prepare for various outcomes as you execute your strategy.*

Unskilled:

- **Comfortable with tactical plans**

  This person lacks the ability to gather resources, and he is also unable to make good habits thereby falling into the trap of tactical plans. That means this person's R and H are low.

- **Difficulty to create vision of future**

  Lacks good habits because the person has not been able to manage their R and C effectively.

- **Finds it challenging to create strategic plan**

  Because he is not in the habit of making good plans the person lacks R and C

- **Has difficulty putting together different elements into a single strategy**

  This person lacks R and I because he is unable to connect the dots, thereby failing to build a single strategy that will help him achieve his goal.

- **May reject the importance of strategic planning**

  Owing to his bad habits, this person has not been able to understand the importance of effective planning. To make a good plan, this person will need to work on their R and I, followed by C.

- **Has narrow perspective-**

  This person is not broad-minded, and he thinks short-term, thereby jeopardizing his chances of creating value through strategy. This makes his R and C low, as he is not able to command and make use of his resources to broaden his horizon.

Skilled:

- **Can diagnose and analyze information to anticipate future consequences accurately.**

This person is good at building resources and has the capability to influence situations. So, his R and I are strong.

- **Can read the environment and acts in advance of the obstacles.**

  This person has the power to command, and has a strong R and I. Hence is in complete control of the situation.

- **Has broad knowledge and perspective.**

  This person has adequate resources and therefore his R and C are strong thereby enabling him to control the situation.

- **Has orientation of Future.**

  This person has a good R and C as he can anticipate and orient his future as per the vision, which shows that this person can build a good strategic plan.

Self –Evaluation Sheet

On a scale of 1 to 5, rate yourself on this competency 'Strategic Mindset'

0	1	2	3	4	5

Development Suggestions:

1. **Develop analytical skills.**

   To develop this competency, one needs to read books, newspaper and other related business articles which help one know beyond what is written and develop skills to trigger an inquisitive mindset. This will develop skills which will help to build your next strategic plan.

2. **Learn and use SWOT analysis.**

   This person should practice and implement SWOT which

helps you make the right moves to build the right strategic mindset.

3. **Read the book 'The Godfather.'**

   This book is about an underworld don and the challenges he faces. He is a successful person but there are others who are striving to dethrone him. This book will help a person to learn and develop how one can strategically face challenges and overcome them with effective planning.

4. **Watch the movies 'The Big Short inside the doomsday machine' and 'A Bridge Too Far.'**

   The first movie is a thriller and based on financial disasters and will give an insight into the way analysis should be done. The second movie will help you learn how they managed to achieve a difficult goal with their able skills of analyzing the situation pertaining to the events related to 2nd world war. This will help you to see of how a strategic mind works and things can be implemented.

3. Decision Quality

Description: *Makes sound decisions that consider objectives, risks and implications. This also determines action to be taken and alternatives to be dismissed.*

Unskilled:

1. **Before analyzing, goes with the first solution available**

   This kind of person is not gathering enough resources to help build his decision. Other than abusing his resources, he is also weak on his command over the situation as he is not driving results.

2. **Does not take help or approaches 'Subject Matter Expert' before taking Decision.**

   This person loses control on being able to influence his circle of influence a.k.a. his orbit of network. This dissuades him to assess and validate his decision. This person needs to work on his 'I' and 'R' as he will then be able to make validated and suggestive decisions.

3. **Makes decision emotionally and sometimes therefore loses control of situation.**

   This person may get pacified at times because of emotions and therefore he needs to work on better command of situation and only use emotions to better his decisions.

4. **Problem definition is not done before taking decision and fails to assess the root cause.**

   This implies that this person does not get to the bottom of things and hence succumbs to what is there in his purview deflecting him from the purpose of decision making.

5. **In front of complex problem, may find trouble to make decisions.**

   This implies that this person loses his stream of control and does not approach the right people thereby losing on his factor of Influence as well. This person needs to build his power of Influence and learn to command the situation to be able to reach out to right people to seek solutions.

Skilled:

- **Makes good decisions after thoroughly analyzing the situation.**

This person uses his skills of appropriate resources around him and also has a good C to control the situation and ensure his decision is well validated.

- **Whenever a decision is taken, it turns out to be correct.**

  This person has used his R.I.C.H.™ appropriately apart from other various qualities of decision making which enabled him to assess and use the power of each element effectively to ensure proper correction and sustenance.

- **Other people approach him / her for solutions.**

  This person has developed an aptitude for correcting the approach of others and aligning them with R.I.C.H.™ thereby ensuring a strong outlook of others as well for solving problems. Therefore, this person is liked as he helps others build their ability.

- **Is not biased and emotional while taking decisions.**

  This person is practical and has an element of rationality involved which is one of the key foundations of R.I.C.H.™ This enables the person to be more practical and result driven.

Self –Evaluation Sheet

On a scale of 1 to 5, rate yourself on this competency 'Decision Quality'

0	1	2	3	4	5

Development Suggestions:

- **Watch the movie '12 Angry Men'!**

  This needs to be watched as this movie shows you how a

group of men come to a decision after great twists and turns and how they learn and unlearn many important things in life to be able to take that important decision.

- **Understand and use '7 thinking Hats' model.**

  This model helps you understand the various possibilities and areas that you could consider assessing the situation completely thereby enabling effective decision making. This will help you build your approach for quality decisions.

4. Drive for Results

Description: Persists to complete tasks and responsibilities, even when there are difficulties! The person is optimistic and firm all through. He/she is motivated by success and passionate about achieving higher results.

Unskilled:

- **Is not able to deliver on time and consistently.**

  This person may not have the ability to either unitize is resources efficiently or lacks resources and moreover, he is also poor with his skill of commanding the situation. He needs to build his C and R

- **Does not push things.**

  This person does not take the effort of commanding the situation and does not therefore build his I and R. He needs to primarily build his C for him to be able to build his R and I.

- **Procrastinates**

  This person has developed wrong habits that entail him to poor performance. He needs to build good habits by building his R, I and C.

- **Does not give 100% to complete the activities.**

  This person lacks ownership and accountability thereby making him lack majorly on his C.

- **Always ready with an excuse for not doing task.**

  This person is not serious and as per above point 4, he lacks ownership. This makes him a poor task master and hence lacks on H, poor habits and therefore needs to work on his R, I and C to develop the right H.

Skilled:

- **Can be depended upon to deliver results-**

  He is a result-oriented person who believes in ensuring desired outcomes. This therefore makes him a high on R and high on I since he uses his skills of resourcefulness and his ability to influence to drive results.

- **Pushes self and others to achieve results.**

  This person is good at controlling/commanding the situation. This means, doing all that he can to influence people and situation that create an environment positive to the outcome desired. Therefore, his I and C are strong.

- **Is creative and innovative to get the things done.**

  This person has a strong source of resourcefulness since he has built it by being creative and innovative with the way he does things.

- **Can set priorities-**

  This person has a strong knack of controlling/commanding the situation since he knows how to build his priorities. He also works on his R which is to use his resources to the optimum to plan and prioritize.

- **Deals effectively with stress-**

  This person knows how to control his emotions. That means he can command/control himself and the situation around him. Effectively he also can help collaborate with others to minimize his stress. Therefore, his I and C are high here.

Development Suggestions:

- **Read book 'Managing for the Future' and 'Managing for Results' by Peter Drucker**

  These books will help you build your 'Drive for results' as these books talks about goals and the way to accomplish those goals. These books will help build the right attitude that is the right habits which will entail the building of R, I and C as well.

- **Watch the movie 'In pursuit of Happiness'.**

  This will showcase how a salesman invests everything and faces several challenges. Yet he has an inner voice driving him to accomplish his mission.

Self –Evaluation Sheet

On a scale of 1 to 5, rate yourself on this competency 'Drive for Results'

0	1	2	3	4	5

5. Interpersonal Savvy

Description: Relating well with all kinds of people, building rapport, being diplomatic and able to defuse high tension situations.

Unskilled:

- **Finds challenging to build Relationships.**

  This person lacks massively in I. He needs to build his I by following the given development suggestions below.

- **Has difficulty to relate smoothly with different thinking people.**

  This is the same as above where he too lacks I and must constantly work on ensuring he builds his intellect.

- **Does not invest time to build rapport.**

  This correlates to point 1 and 2 above, this person finds it challenging to build rapport with another person and this impacts his I which leads to impacting his R as well.

- **Is not able to handle / manage conflict with Others.**

  This person is low on primarily his C which makes him have a poor I and both together make it challenging for him to manage conflicts.

- **Feels shy or not confident in front of others.**

  This person lacks I and C and his I is the primary low point and because he is unable to project himself confidently, he lacks the skill of C as well.

Skilled:

- **Is comfortable to relate to all kinds of people.**

  This person has a good I and hence he can strike a conversation instantly.

- **Develops appropriate rapport.**

This person builds on his R and I since both are needed for effective rapport building.

- **While dealing with people, is tactful.**

  This person has a strong I and hence is able to use his R appropriately to get the desired outcomes.

- **Manages various conflicts comfortably.**

  This person is very good with his I and C and hence is able to manage conflicts since he knows of how to do the process.

- **Is open and Approachable.**

  This person owing to his high I, takes things in his stride. He is positive and always wants to give the other person or situation and opportunity to be heard.

- **Is comfortable to deal with people when he / she does not like them.**

  This person is also good with I as per the above point. Therefore, he can pace himself accordingly to get the desired outcome.

Development Suggestions:

- **Understand 'Rapport Building' concept from NLP (Neurolinguistic Programming)**

  This concept helps you build your rapport building and helps you to also build your I and R and hence it is necessary to learn this skill.

- **Read the book 'Influence: The Psychology of Persuasion' by Robert B Cialdini**

There are 7 principles of INFLUENCING which are important to build your I and this book teaches you about it and how you could get your I in place.

- **Watch the movie 'Chak De India.'**

  In this movie, it shows how a coach influences players from different states to play as a single team for their country. This showcases the power of I and C which enables them to claim victory over all odds.

Self –Evaluation Sheet

On a scale of 1 to 5, rate yourself on this competency 'Interpersonal Savvy'

0	1	2	3	4	5

6. Situational Adaptability

Description: Ability to having adapting approach and attitude in 'here and now' to match the shifting demands of different situations.

Unskilled:

- **Is unable to adjust or fine tune his /her behavior in real time while interacting with different people in different situations.**

  This person has a low I and C because he fails to command the situation and manage people. He needs to build on these.

- **Is not flexible to meet the needs of the moment.**

  This person fails to command the situation since he is low

on C. He needs to build his C, work on his R and I and thereby form a good H to build his flexibility.

- **Does not continuously gauge the impact of his / her behaviors.**

  This person is completely unaware of what and how they do. This person needs to develop a good H by fixing his R, I and C to be able to have proper judgment on his/her behavior.

- **Is not alerted to make adjustment to his / her attitude in real time.**

  This person has a poor H owing to which he/she fails to build on their attitude. This person needs to work on his/her R, I and C to gain a good H.

Skilled:

- **Is flexible and can act differently in different situations.**

  This person could command the situation and hence he can adapt different situations and is flexible as well.

- **Picks up situational cues and modifies his / her behavior Accordingly.**

  This person has a good C and hence he can modify his behavior to suit the situation. This gives him a control over the situation which helps him.

- **Is comfortable to adopt personal and interpersonal behavior.**

  This person is good with his I and he therefore is successful in building strong relationships. This gives him an upper hand when it comes to managing interpersonal behavior.

- **He / She understands that different situations call for different approaches.**

  Based on the previous 2 points, this person is able to command the situation. And this therefore gives him the opportunity to distinguish each situation from the other and act accordingly.

Development Suggestions:

- **Watch the movie 'Cast Away.'**

  In this movie the situation is such that he needs to get adapted or he dies. This movie shows on how the protagonist commanded the situation, built his resources out of nowhere and became a resilient force. In life too, we need to have a strong habit formed to build our strength of situational adaptability.

- **TED Talk: The Strength of Adaptability: Achieving the impossible by Laura Penhaul**

  This short video talks about the control one needs to have that means building the C. This is important to be adaptable and manage situations.

Self –Evaluation Sheet

On a scale of 1 to 5, rate yourself on this competency 'Situational Adaptability'

0	1	2	3	4	5

7. Resilient

- **Description**: Ability to successfully engage with the challenges and opportunities that life brings and bounce back from an adversity.

Unskilled:

- **Blames others for all the wrong things in life.**

  This person has not framed the right mindset and hence is quick to blame others. He needs to work on his R.I.C. so that he forms good H.

- **To come out of stress, addicts' self to bad health Habits**

  This person needs to work on good H thereby negating the bad habits.

- **Engages in negative self-talk.**

  This person is a self-destructive person. When a person faces failure or adversity, he/she criticizes self and talks negative. To overcome this, he must work on his C so that he can develop the mindset of overcoming negativity and challenges to emerge a winner.

- **Has unrealistic self-Expectations**

  This person needs to build his C and then gauge of what R and I will he will need and where he lacks so that he can build on it and form more of realistic expectations.

- **Is stressed out and tired.**

  This person has unrealistic expectations and failure to achieve results causes him stress. Therefore, he needs to build realistic self-expectation and work on R, I and C to achieve the desired outcome. This will lead to low stress and fatigue.

- **Having a sense of hopelessness**

  This person is very low on self-esteem. He/she needs to build his R to gain his self-esteem. For instance, he can befriend quality people who could guide/mentor him to build his life and get him a sense of purpose.

- **"Finds Difficult" to Continue**

  This person is low on C and hence fails to command and continue his life. He needs to strongly build on his C.

Skilled:

- **Have realistic awareness of self.**

  For anybody to lead and build on a new path to accomplish goals needs to be self-aware and this would certainly be a beginning to your goals! This means, your R.I.C.H.™ are in sync.

- **Can see many valuable alternatives.**

  This person has good R and I which in turn helps him to identify different approaches to a particular situation/ problem.

- **Knows where to turn for help.**

  This person has a high R and I and when they face a challenge, he knows the right buttons to press.

- **Views setbacks as impermanent**

  This person is an outcome of a strong R.I.C.H.™ mindset which is an accumulation of your R.I.C.H.™ practice.

- **Can see harmonious side of things.**

  This person's I and R is high which helps him to look at harmonious side of things even in a challenging situation.

Development Suggestions:

- **Do exercise / yoga.**

  The mental strength needs to improve to enhance your self-awareness and your resilience. Therefore, this will aid in building that up.

- **Make time for solitude.**

  Here, as per the above point, this person needs to improve the situation by thinking over it and for this, he needs solitude so that he can clear his mind.

- **Have a good cry.**

  When you let your emotions flow, you feel light, and you feel refreshed. Keeping the same inside you will one day erupt like a volcano and hence letting them out is a good option to think clearer. For this one can use solitude time or meet someone close to you.

- **Think of someone who exudes resiliency and model his / her Behavior.**

  It is a good idea to get inspired by someone and learn from him/her. This gives a whole new perspective and inspires modeled behavior.

- **Read the book: The Happiest Man on Earth: The Beautiful Life of an Auschwitz Survivor by Eddie Jaku**

  It is a book about the holocaust survivor and how he came out alive based on his resilience and is a story worth learning from.

Self –Evaluation Sheet

On a scale of 1 to 5, rate yourself on this competency 'Resilient'

0	1	2	3	4	5

8. Self-Awareness

Description: Ability to recognize & reflect on one's values, feelings, interests, abilities, and multiple facets of identity in shaping one's thoughts, behavior, and action.

Unskilled:

- **Limits exploration of personal beliefs, values, strengths, and challenges**

  This person is poor in R and C and hence he limits his exploration of personal beliefs and other attributes.

- **Rarely shares own views.**

  This person is not confident because may lack I and R and hence hesitant or reserved to speak.

- **Indecisive in face of uncertainty or pressure**

  This person is unable to control/command the situation and hence the C is weak. He needs to build on his C

- **Finds difficulty to recognize own feeling and those of others.**

  This person is low on I and therefore is not empathetic because lacks basic mind programming and needs to open his mind to build the same.

- **Finds difficulty to monitor and regulate own emotions and reaction.**

  This person is low on R and I since he is unable to monitor self. His R is weak because he is not armed properly to face his own emotions and lacks the first orbit of compassionate people to hear him.

Skilled:

- **Understands feelings of self and others**

  This person is good with I since he has worked on building his R.I.C.H.™ to carve out the right direction for him!

- **Consistently and intentionally explores one's own beliefs, values, strengths, and challenges.**

  This person knows that he needs to be open minded. That is building his C so that he could command and work on his R and I to get a good H.

- **Knows when to self-advocate and has confidence to do so**

  This person has a good C as an outcome of building his I and R.

- **Is aware of own potential and that of others.**

  This person has a strong I and R since he knows the power of resources of self and others.

- **Demonstrates self-reflection, looks back at failures and identifies learning from it and applies the learning.**

  This person has formed a Habit to analyze things as an outcome of proper R.I.C.H.™ mindset.

Development Suggestions:

- **Read the book "Emotional Intelligence" by David Goleman**

  This book helps you to know many facets about self-awareness which in turn helps you to build your R.I.C.H.™ quotient.

- **Take self-feedback from others.**

  This will allow you to have a perspective and engage yourself with better actions going forward.

Self –Evaluation Sheet

On a scale of 1 to 5, rate yourself on this competency 'Self-Awareness'

0	1	2	3	4	5

9. Collaboration

Description: Collaborates with other people from formal and informal groups to achieve a common goal.

Unskilled:

- **Is not aware about keeping networks active.**

  This person has a low I and he needs to build on it so that he can make good use of I and build his R.

- **Finds challenging to share information with his / her network.**

  This person has a weak R; hence he is not able to identify the correct resource to share the right information. Apart from this, he also has a low I which could lead this person to be reserved. Therefore, he needs to build his I and R in order to be able to share information.

- **Is unable to handle / manage conflict effectively.**

  This person has a low I and therefore he could be non-assertive and has a low R making him low on cooperativeness too.

- **Finds difficulty in leveraging strength from his / her network.**

  This person has a low R and I and therefore he finds it challenging to identify and build his network.

- **Does not give credit to other's contribution and achievements.**

  This person is selfish and jeopardizes his R and I who causes him challenges.

Skilled:

- **Engages in development of Relationships.**

  This person believes in the power of I and R and hence invests efforts in the same.

- **Resolves conflicts by advocating for and engaging in assertive communication & compromises wherever required.**

  This person is good at I and can influence a situation well. Therefore, he also demonstrates the ability of C where he commands of what and how things need to be done.

- **Uses technology effectively to foster communication and teamwork.**

  This person knows that technology is a resource and hence his R is being well used to build in his competency.

- **Demonstrates high level of enthusiasm and commitment to set goals under difficult situations and encourages others to respond similarly.**

  This person has a high I which helps him to successfully influence people and over a period it becomes his habit owing to high H.

- **Draws on own & others internal & external networks to achieve a goal.**

  This person has a good R and hence works on doing the needful. His H is also high which allows him to constantly demonstrate this behavior.

- **Initiates giving and receiving information and facilitates communication among the group members.**

  This person uses his R well and in turn uses his I to communicate with people which are essential to build the required genesis.

Development Suggestions:

- **Watch the movie "The Terminal" released in the year 2004.**

  In this movie, a person who arrives in a foreign country and has no place to go except living on the airport and that is where he starts to develop relations and resources to survive is the essence of this movie.

- **Read the book "Emotional Intelligence and working with Emotional Intelligence" by Daniel Goleman**

  This book helps you to know many facets about self-awareness, collaboration, and dynamics of relationships. It will help you build these necessary skills within you which make you R.I.C.H.™ enough for your future.

Self –Evaluation Sheet

On a scale of 1 to 5, rate yourself on this competency 'Collaboration'

0	1	2	3	4	5

10. Directs Work

Description: Ability to provide directions, delegates work and removes obstacles so that the work is done as per requirements.

Unskilled:

- **Provides incomplete and vague Instructions.**

  This person is not good with C and hence messes up things by being ignorant to the facts.

- **Delegates work to people without knowing their competency or skills.**

  This person is low on I and R and hence does not realize the potential of others and loses out on his ability to build his R.

- **Sets low objectives that people are not motivated to achieve it.**

  This person is low on R and hence is unable to fathom of how much his people could achieve.

- **Identifies high profile tasks and saves it for self.**

  This person is low on I and R and therefore he does not wish to collaborate and work and loses out on R and I. In the long run, this person will develop the wrong H and that could severely affect his prospects.

Skilled:

- **Able to match competency of people to assignments.**

  This person is good with R and I and realizes the potential of others to be able to utilize them appropriately.

- **Conveys clear expectations of the required outcome and follows up at required interval.**

  This person is good at C and hence wants to always keep a tab on how and what can be done to make it better.

- **Goals set are stretched which pushes the people to perform at higher levels**

  This person has a good R and I which helps him by keeping a tab on it and inspire/influence people by his high I and R

- **While delegating the work, ensures that the person has ownership.**

  This person is good at I and R and can manage people well, set right expectation which instills the element of R in others as well to make them own the task.

- **Follows up the task without Interfering.**

  This person is good at C and hence can monitor and ensure successful completion of task thereby demonstrating C

Development Suggestions:

- **Read the book "Delegating Work (20 Minute Manager), by Harvard Business Review Press**

  In this, the writer emphasizes on the concept of directing work and appropriately ensuring fine results and instilling accountability.

- **TED Talk: "Confessions of a recovering micromanager" by Chieh Huang**

  Micromanagement is hazardous. It can lead to massive failures because one may tend to miss on deadlines, important outcomes and results. This talk will explain on how you can build your competency of directing for better results.

- **Read the book "Execution: The Discipline of getting things done" by Larry Bossidy, Ram Charan, Charles Burck**

  Same as mentioned in the previous point as it will inspire you to know and develop your skills to build this competency.

Self –Evaluation Sheet

On a scale of 1 to 5, rate yourself on this competency 'Directs work.'

0	1	2	3	4	5

Self-Evaluation of your quotient of R.I.C.H.™ for readers

This below exercise is only to trigger your thoughts and to develop your R.I.C.H.™ enabled thinking

1. **Competencies used – Managing Ambiguity, Collaboration, and Influencing Skills**

An employee Ramesh was terminated from his job. Later, he started to look out for new employment, but he was not able to get any calls for interview. As the time passed, his savings started diminishing and during that time, Covid_19 struck the world resulting in lockdowns. For close to 8 months, due to the lockdown, there were no jobs in the market and after those markets gradually started opening. After a rigorous search and effort put in by Ramesh, he could finally land himself a job after 18 months.

For a minute, consider you are Ramesh. What would you have done had you been in the same situation?

2. **Competencies used – Decision Quality, Drive for results and Situational adaptability.**

Tina and Meena are two best friends. One day Tina who works in a mobile shop as a salesgirl discovers that her boss Preeti has offered incentives to all her colleagues but has missed offering it to her. Tina is unhappy and feels she must discuss this with her boss Preeti. That evening Tina, who is sad, meets up with Meena and shares her story with her. Meena advises her to confront Preeti and ask her of why she did that with her and asks her to threaten her boss that she will leave the job should Preeti not extend the incentive to Tina.

What do you think should be done? Is Meena right with her advice to Tina? If yes, why and if not why?

What according to you should Tina do to use her R.I.C.H.™?

3. **Competencies used- Resilience and Self Awareness**

If we go back to question no. 2, considering you are Tina, what was your emotional status at that time.

(Sadness, Happy, Frustrated, Angry, Disgust, Fear and Surprised) Which of these were you dealing with and how?

4. **Competency used- Strategic Mindset**

If you are an employee of a company, at what designation or position do you think you would want to see yourself 5 years from now? And to achieve this, what kind of strategy you would opt for?

5. **Competencies used- Directs work and Strategic Mindset**

Consider yourself to be a product manager of a leading pharmaceutical company and you are assigned to launch a new medicine for cold and cough. Your primary responsibility is to launch this product in 3 districts and each district has one MR (Medical Representative) who can help you. How will you successfully launch the product? What all means and ways will you employ to achieve the same?

Acknowledgements

To me, they will always take precedence over any superpower: my late parents. I shared an extraordinary bond with my mother, Mrs. Sadhana Darooka. She passed away from cancer in January 2022. To me, she was much more than a mother—she was a friend, a guide, a mentor, and my most trusted confidante. I lost my father in November 2023—a man who embodied the strength every child seeks.

Despite the profound emptiness left by their absence, I am committed to living joyfully and pursuing my dreams, honoring my mother's courage, determination, and resolute spirit. She, alongside my father, would have been overjoyed to see this book come to fruition. I dedicate it to their memory. They continue to be the essence of my life and my greatest inspiration.

My beloved wife, Arpita, has been my steadfast partner through every high and low—just as my sister, Ms. Meha Darooka, has. The support of family is the cornerstone on which we build our dreams, and I am deeply thankful for the unwavering presence of mine at every step of my journey.

This book would not have achieved its success without the invaluable contributions of many individuals. I am profoundly thankful to everyone who contributed a chapter on their approach to R.I.C.H.™ or shared a testimonial, including insights on how it may have supported them—consciously or subconsciously. My heartfelt thanks to:

- The joyful and talented Mr. Mohit Kukreti, former Creative Producer of Horses Stable (a start-up funding show airing on MX Player and JioCinema)
- The incredible Mr. Vineet Malhotra, Prime Time News Anchor, Editor & Senior Journalist
- The splendid Mr. Dipanjay Bhalerao, Academician, Heartfulness Meditation Trainer, Corporate Trainer, and Startup Mentor
- The Shark Tank season 1 contestant and highly competent professional, Mr. Akshay Shah, Founder and CEO of IWeb Technologies
- The gracious Mr. Sushil kumar Warkar, Lead HR at Mahindra and Mahindra Ltd.

I am deeply indebted to these global leaders who graciously contributed:

- My Foreword writer, the magnanimous Mr. Kailash Katkar, Founder, MD, and CEO of Quick Heal Technologies
- My Prologue writer, the spectacular Mr. T. Pradeep Kumar, CEO and Group CTO of a global renewable energy company

A big thank you to the dynamic Suhail Mathur, my literary agent, and his company, The Book Bakers, for giving me this golden opportunity. Thank you, Book Bakers. Kudos!"

A huge thank you to my esteemed publisher, M/s Om Books International, for agreeing to give wings to my dream. Your support means a lot to me, and I shall always cherish our bond.

Last but not least, my former colleague and good friend, Mr. Musrrat Baig, has relentlessly helped me improve this book by contributing his expertise on the exercises, competency framework, and other aspects. I am truly indebted to him for being a sounding board and helping make this book worth your time. Thank you, Musrrat.